Praise for Cesca Major

If I Were You

"The queen of high-concept, heartrending love stories. Phenomenal, delivered with the perfect blending of humor and heartbreak. I loved every minute."

—Sophie Cousens,
New York Times bestselling author

"It made me laugh 'til I cried and cry until I laughed. Brilliantly funny, clever, real, and all too relatable."

—Lucy Vine, author of *Seven Exes*

Maybe Next Time

"Just glorious: moving, thought-provoking, life-affirming. I loved this book!"

—Lucy Foley, *New York Times* bestselling author

"A timeless classic."

—Hazel Gaynor, *New York Times* bestselling author

"Haunting, moody, clever, and affecting."

—Gillian McAllister,
New York Times bestselling author

"Heartwarming and life-affirming—a gorgeous read."
—Louise O'Neill

"Thought-provoking, tear-jerking, and page-turning—an amazing and amusing book that will really make you think about your life."
—Katie Fforde

"Ingenious, intriguing, and so emotional."
—Jill Mansell

"Deeply moving, extremely funny, brilliantly knowing, and fabulously observed. Heartbreaking but simultaneously life-affirming. A total triumph."
—Daisy Buchanan

"Superbly plotted, shockingly breathtaking, heartbreaking, poignant, and beautifully written. A love story like no other."
—Cathy Bramley

If I Were You

If I Were You

A Novel

Cesca Major

wm

WILLIAM MORROW
An Imprint of HarperCollinsPublishers

HarperCollins books may be purchased for educational, business, or sales promotional use. For information, please email the Special Markets Department at SPsales@harpercollins.com.

FIRST US EDITION

Library of Congress Cataloging-in-Publication Data has been applied for.

ISBN 978-0-06-323998-2

24 25 26 27 28 LBC 5 4 3 2 1

To my five-year-old twin daughters, Lexi and Inessa, who think the idea of swapping bodies is absolutely hilarious. May all my readers respond like you.

1

FLYNN

Now

I can barely hear Amy as she shouts at me over the roof of the car. Rain flattens my hair and runs down my collar as I yell back. My body fizzes with frustration.

Her freckled nose scrunches in displeasure; her brown eyes narrow. The sharp look winds me, a sudden memory of the night I first met her, the first time I'd seen her look like that. Only this time the anger is directed solely at me.

As I feel my body lift off the ground, the whole world a flash of bright light, the last thing I ask myself is: how did Amy and I get here after the start we had?

2

FLYNN

Two Years Ago

My weekends are mostly spent at bachelor parties. Wedding planning doesn't appeal to a lot of my mates, but preparation for the bachelor party is undertaken with the precision of a large-scale military strike. The target this time: Bristol City Centre.

I've done a weekend in Ibiza (best man missed his flight home and might still live there), a country house near Bath (we lost our deposit), about sixteen clubs in various cities in southern England (banned from fourteen of them), and gone white water rafting in the Lake District (bachelor knocked out with a paddle).

They're easy and entertaining. Men in groups regress about twenty years and I play my part well.

Tonight we are in a karaoke bar in the center of Bristol, about a mile from my house in Redland. The bachelor passed out a good couple of hours ago and is currently horizontal in a booth dressed inexplicably as a nun, as we drink beers around him. Singing publicly is my hell, but I like drinking, and Eddie bought the whole table shots and is currently in a dark corner with a girl he started flirting with in the queue to get in.

I'm just thinking about heading home—the other bachelors are staying in a hotel on the ring road somewhere—when Eddie returns, wipes his mouth, and suggests a strip club. Someone whoops but I quickly counter-offer with a casino. Strip clubs are the places joy goes to die. There's a flash of anger in Eddie's eyes when two of the guys want to come with me.

And then she walks past.

Flushed cheeks, wide apart eyes, smooth limbs. My mouth gapes and I suddenly couldn't care less about strip clubs, casinos, or my own name.

A dotted headband is lost amongst her curls, and she is wearing a dress that isn't a dress but more like shorts and a top joined up. She looks incredible.

I'm about to reach a hand out to stop her and ask her name when she halts abruptly at our table. She is less than a couple of feet away. My chest judders.

Then she points at the prostrate bachelor in the booth.

"Is he alright?" She has a confident voice, loud even over the music, and an accent I can't immediately place.

My mouth is still open.

"Seriously?" She looks round at us, cocking an eyebrow. The others gape at her in different stages of drunkenness.

3

"Yeah," one of the lads says before slumping backward, one arm draped over the inert body.

"Oh my god, you'll suffocate him."

She has big Hermione Granger Energy and is even hotter now that she's close up. I seem to have lost the ability to do anything other than look at her. My stomach disappears. Can I ask her out? Who's she with? How have I never bumped into her in Bristol before?

Her mouth is still moving and I realize she is directing her words at me. "Seriously, is he OK? Why are you all just drinking around him? Does he need to go to hospital?"

She scoots across me to check on him and I feel simultaneously bad it didn't occur to me to do the same, and also can't help noticing she smells of oranges, which makes my head spin even more.

The bachelor groans as she places a hand on his head and her eyes soften as she asks him if he's alright.

He starts to sit up and, satisfied he isn't a corpse, she steps back and gives the whole table of men a withering look.

"Take better care of him," she says.

I start nodding furiously.

She walks off.

Someone sniggers and Eddie rolls his eyes and mutters, "Nutter."

I don't say "she's not," I don't want to rile him up, and I also feel like I've been whacked in the head. It's not just the five or six beers (and shots) I've drunk. I've never met anyone with such charisma. I wonder what she does for a living. The youngest CEO of a FTSE 500 company, a major in the Army, the Prime Minister? Nothing would surprise me.

I watch her weave her way across the bar and perch on a stool.

Over people's heads I see her settle at a high table. She momentarily stares at a girl on the small stage holding a microphone singing a wobbly rendition of "Man! I Feel like a Woman!" There's a guy with her, neck tattoo and a top with ripped-off sleeves like he's just wrestled a bear or something. I hope for my sake he's her brother, because what I'm about to do next feels brave.

I just know I can't leave this place without trying.

I head straight to the bar to ask for paper and a pen. It seems to take them forever to find one and I curse, craning my neck to check she is still there.

"Thanks for that," I say breathlessly, standing in front of her table.

Her vague smile wobbles as she tries to place me and then a line appears between her eyebrows.

"That was kind of you," I say. "Just now. With our friend. A couple of the guys are taking him back to the hotel."

She nods non-committally and my heart sinks as she returns her attention to the man opposite her. I don't think he's her brother. He looks too annoyed with me to be her brother.

I want to stay, want to know her.

"Do you make a habit of rescuing drunk men or is it a one-off thing?"

"Mate," the man on the date says, twisting in his seat.

"I'm just talking to . . ." I leave a pause for her name, which she doesn't fill, just cocks her head to one side and looks at me.

"You know, you're beautiful," I can't help adding.

"Mate!" The guy with the tattoo sounds more cross, which is fair. I think the mystery woman might be about to smile but she swallows it down.

"I'm with someone," she gestures. The same direct tone, the same steady gaze.

"Yeah." The man crosses his burly arms. He does have extraordinarily large biceps.

"That's true," I say, nodding earnestly. Then I look up, meet her gaze. Is it my imagination or is there something in her eyes, a momentary flash of curiosity? Or is it just the reflection of the disco lights? "But," I add, with a winning smile, "you could be with me."

Internally I am asking what exactly it is that I'm doing. I'm flailing here. And I've seen the biceps. But I can't help it. There's something about her that makes me want to behave in this macho and confident way.

"Want to take this outside?" Her date scrapes back his chair. Of course he's tall. A strange rush of energy courses through me which might be the shots and beers but also the imminent danger.

"I just wanted to give the lady this." I produce a piece of paper with my name, address, email, and phone numbers on it. "I work in events and we're always on the hunt for talent."

"The lady sells houses." Tall tattoo-neck says.

6

"Well, I imagine that takes great skill and we need people who have ... skills," I say.

The mystery woman meets my eye this time, and something shifts, a flicker at the corner of her mouth. It's enough to give me a small boost. Maybe I am not messing this up completely.

"She demonstrated a real flair for handling people just now and, well, that's the kind of person I like on my ... my team," I invent.

"You fancy her," the man says.

"I also do, yes."

I nod solemnly and the mystery woman does smile this time and then hurriedly settles her face back into neutral. She glances at the paper in my hand.

"You've included a fax number."

"I just wanted to be available to you on all platforms." I smile back at her in what I hope to be a winsome way.

The trouble is this prompts the man to slide his seat back, make a fist and punch me in the face. The piece of paper with my details flutters to the floor before I can give it to her.

I hit the deck. Then there's general shouting, bouncers, my mates, the man, and, just as I'm hauled out of the club and steered away by my fellow groomsmen, I see her face in the window, brow wrinkled, a look I can't read as I waggle my fingers back at her in a half-wave.

Later, back in my flat, the guys in their hotel, I'm gutted. There was something about that woman in the bar that stirred some emotion in me. I recognize it as hope. Her forthright manner, her kindness, her ability to

7

stand up to our bullshit. I loved it. I want that kind of person with that kind of passion in my life. Someone who would be a voice for people when they aren't able to do it for themselves. What would it be like to be loved by someone like that?

But I screwed it up, went in all smarmy. I don't blame the guy for hitting me. My temple throbs, my eye swollen as I sit, head back on the sofa, feeling battered.

The buzzer to my flat goes and I frown.

Opening the door I practically do a cartoon double take because, against all odds, standing on the threshold of my house is the woman from the bar. And she is wearing a suspicious expression.

"Are you a serial killer?" she asks.

I quickly shake my head. Which makes my head hurt more. But I'm keen for her to know I am not. "I haven't even killed one person."

Her mouth twitches.

"That was very cocky of you in the bar you know." It's a statement, not a question, and I hold my breath.

"We were on a first date," she adds.

I keep holding my breath and then wonder if this is when I should speak: apologize?

"I met him on Tinder."

She's slightly blurry at the edges but I don't dare tell her I need to sit down in case it scares her away.

"He kept picking stuff out of his teeth."

Tentatively my heart quivers.

"He called me Ames. It's Amy until I give you permission otherwise."

"It's a nice name."

She tilts her chin.

"Do you always hit on women you don't know in bars?"

"No, actually!" Which is the truth. I haven't felt like asking anyone out in three years. That thought rattles me, just as I look down and see something that makes me pause. She is holding a handbag in one hand and something bulky in the other. Wait—am *I* about to be attacked?

As she steps forward I wince at her through one eye. It's a frozen bag of peas.

"Well—invite me in then," she says in the same confident, slightly withering tone she used earlier. "I want to see if you really have a fax machine."

I almost fall down in my effort to get her inside. My whole chest fills with warmth, the pain in my eye and head immediately lessening.

"Do. Come in. It's not plugged in, but I do. And," I turn to her, my eyes widening, "I think I have a pager somewhere I could dig out?"

We head inside together as she laughs—throaty, full. I think it might be the best sound I've ever heard.

3

AMY

Now

This has escalated out of all proportion. The frustrations of the last two weeks, which started as a simmer, have grown and grown until tonight's boiling point. The red-hot fury as we shout at each other to just *listen*.

Then the urge inside me for a change. I *need* him to understand me. I need things to change between us, or I have to end it. I know that. I can't keep ignoring the fact he will never be open with me, that I'll never truly know him.

I can barely make him out in this slanting rain, the ominous rumble of thunder which underlines the angry words we're firing at each other.

Then there's a terrible sound and, as my body lifts off the ground, as my world becomes a strange explosion of white, I wonder how it has gone this badly wrong. Maybe he isn't the right person after all?

4

AMY

Two Years Ago

Today has been a blur. Flynn Waller is unlike the usual men I meet. In fact, he's almost the exact opposite of the man I imagined I'd be with. Yet it just feels right, *he* feels right. I've been lost recently, in a funk I can't escape, and he's reached down and pulled me out of it.

I'm not even sure how this has happened. How I'm showering in a man's surprisingly clean bathroom on a Saturday evening when I only met him last night. How I'm singing in this man's bathroom. What is it about him that makes me feel like singing in the shower again?

"You have the most insane voice," he comments when I step out in a towel, strangely shy as I scurry into his bedroom.

"I don't, I well, I used to . . . thanks," I say, slamming the door so I can change.

"That's the first time I've heard you flustered," he laughs, talking to me through the wood. "Seriously, sing that bit again about the baboon."

Stepping into the over-sized tracksuit and top he's lent me, I fumble a response.

"A balloon. And no," I shout back.

I hear him start to hum a terrible, inaccurate rendition of the tune I'd been singing and can't help grinning.

"Up in my baboon ballllllllooooooon."

"Shut up!" I shout back, unable to stop a snort of laughter.

"My baboooon balllooooooooooon."

Seriously, how did I get here?!

I'd left the bar last night ready to head home and lick my wounds all weekend. The Tinder date had been a disaster and the venue had only made things more painful.

I'd stood on the pavement adjusting my coat, feeling sad and small. Pulling out the scrunched-up napkin of numbers, I thought back to the man from the bar. There had been something behind his over-confident manner, something warm and intriguing that had reached inside me and connected. He seemed fun, impetuous. He seemed to know what he wanted: me.

I didn't direct the cab home; instead, I found myself in a Tesco Express at midnight buying a bag of frozen peas for a cocky, posh boy who'd got thumped.

We stayed up for a couple of hours drinking wine.

Flynn had this air about him that immediately put me at ease. Nothing seemed to ruffle him. There was no boring small talk, or chat about past relationships. We just talked nonsense, listened to music. He was so wide-eyed when I told him about a recent protest I'd been on: he made me feel like it really mattered. And he didn't hit on me, even when, around 2.30 a.m., he leaned over to top up my glass and my whole head filled with the smell of him, his closeness. My breath hitched: I'd really wanted him. But then nothing happened.

He slept on the sofa at an utterly ridiculous angle, his legs dangling off it as he insisted I took his bed. Which smelled of detergent. Another surprise.

So the night turned into Saturday morning and he can't have slept.

Just as I was about to make my excuses and head home for a weekend of nothing, he asked if I wanted to spend the day with him. There was a beat as I looked into his open face, with its purple bruise, and saw a wobble in his normally confident eyes. Intrigued all over again, I agreed, and his clear delight made me immediately glad I had.

What were my Saturday plans anyway? A trip to the supermarket, a phone call to a friend, a magazine, making myself dinner for one? This would be fun, different, and I'd been short on fun for a long time. Flynn was shocking me back to life.

I'd never met anyone who exuded so much energy, like a dog straining on a leash, ready to take off the moment you unclip him. We weaved through Bristol streets, talking aimlessly about nothing. I felt like I'd always walked the streets with him.

It's so comfortable, so easy, and I wonder that this guy is single. Surely women are chucking themselves at him? When I tentatively asked about girlfriends he told me he was dumped a few years back.

"Sucks."

"Yeah."

He didn't offer anything more and I stored the nugget of information away for another time.

I saw different parts of Bristol, a city I've lived in for almost twenty-four years, which suddenly revealed another side of itself. Narrow passageways, uneven stone steps, colorful graffiti. He took me to his favorite café, greeted the owner by name, and ordered us enormous green smoothies, coffees, and the most delicious breakfast.

He seems to know half of Bristol. We had to stop three times on the way back from brunch to greet people. I liked being part of that, relished him introducing me in his relaxed manner to his friends.

"This is Amy," he'd say immediately, including me in all the exchanges. My fingers tingled wanting him to take my hand. We still hadn't kissed.

There aren't many photos in his flat, a wash of neutral colors and blank prints. Nothing for me to guess at. I think of the posters on my walls: what conclusions Flynn might reach. A feminist? An activist? A Quentin Tarantino fan? My walls reflect the parts of my personality I most want to project. What does this neutral space say about Flynn?

If we do stray into more personal territory he always manages to shine the spotlight back on me. He has a mum, stepdad, no siblings. His dad isn't around. I'm not sure what the history is there. His mum travels a lot; I get the sense they are very wealthy; he went to boarding school and loves sports. I know I like him because I bite down my rant about the ethics of private education. He runs an events business, loves dogs, all animals, is frightened of spiders, and can't sing. I still don't know if he wants to kiss me too.

I phone my sister Laura in the bedroom as I get dressed after my shower, whispering into the cell phone as she laughs at me and calls me a dirty night owl.

"I'm not. OK, I am. He's really lush, Laurs. I don't know what to do. Tell me!"

"Amy, you always know what to do. You tell everyone else what to do."

"Not this time," I hiss, genuinely thrown by the butterflies in my stomach, the sheer amount I want this man.

"Go and kiss him!" Laura offers.

"I can't just go and kiss him!"

"Of course you can, Ames, it's the twenty-first century. We're allowed to do that now, we don't get arrested for it. Kiss him! Kiss him!" she chants.

I want to laugh but in a small voice I say: "What if he doesn't like me?"

"What's not to like dickhead? You're hot, you're clever, you're cool! Go!" and she hangs up.

I stare at the phone, unable to process how quickly she chucked me off the call. I need her to hold my hand

and walk me through this. Since Dad, I seem to have lost so much of my confidence, not that Laura would believe that. She still thinks I'm the over-confident little sister with dreams of stardom she left back in Bristol.

When I return to the living room Flynn is sitting on a cushion on the floor, back against the sofa, long legs sticking out, a French press freshly brewed on the low table in front of him.

"Coffee?"

I don't feel hot, clever, or cool. I feel awkward and bumbling and out of my depth. "I should go," I say, tongue too big in my mouth. "I'm going to go." My heart's not in it but the words are forthright, my armor, as ever.

He nods slowly. "Fair enough. I suck at making coffee."

The scent hits me, warm and inviting, and the scene looks so welcoming I want to take my words straight back. But I like this guy and I'm not sure I want to be friend-zoned. He isn't giving me any vibes.

Then he stands up, smoothing his wrinkled T-shirt, and steps over.

My breath catches as he stops in front of me, forcing me to lift my chin to meet his eye. We stare at each other for a long moment and there's a look, something I haven't seen before, a question. And then his face clears and I almost think I imagine it.

"So," the word comes out strangled and I snap my mouth closed again, not wanting him to sense how nervous I am around him. I can't think of anyone who has ever made me feel this way. I want this man, feel my whole body lean toward him, my skin wanting to touch his.

He inches a little closer and I find myself holding my breath now, not wanting to break this moment.

"So," he repeats, a lazy smile moving across his face. "So."

His voice is lower, barely there, "So."

"Are we going to keep saying S—"

He closes the gap between us. The unexpected shock of him, the way his mouth swoops to meet mine, the crush of his arms on me. His hands make my stomach flip over a hundred times. Oh my god. This is electric. This is like nothing I've ever felt. Holy shit.

Not friend-zoned.

He pulls back. "So," he exhales, hair sticking up, cheeks flushed. I raise my own hands to my face, heart leaping in my chest.

We both breathe out. And then go again.

I leave at the end of the weekend and by then Flynn Waller is my boyfriend. Numerous times my boyfriend.

5

FLYNN

Now

There's a startling light and a terrifying whirl of noise. What is happening? Where is Amy? Then, with a sudden jolt, the strange tumbling sensation passes. I'm no longer on my feet. I'm lying, breathless and shocked in the dark.

I open my eyes. I'm staring at the bruised sky: sheets of rain blurring my vision, water running into my mouth. I'm lying on my back, brain exploding with questions. What has happened? And, as I lurch to sit upright, where is Amy?

6

FLYNN

Six Hours Ago

"Mate, honestly! It's fine. We've got it. You go and have a great weekend and stop obsessing."

"I'm not!"

Karim gives me a fleeting look as I pull a ball and tee from my bag. I've known him for two decades and recognize it as disbelief. "Really!" I insist.

We're on the eighteenth hole. Today is a thank you for him covering the logistics of this weekend. He said it was unnecessary, but I want him to feel valued; I want everyone to be happy in the company.

"How's it going with Amy? Last time I saw her she was trying to get me to sign another petition. Does that woman ever stop?"

His diversion to stop me talking about the weekend

events does the trick and I laugh. Amy is never without a cause. It's one of the many awesome things about her. She truly walks the walk. She volunteers in the local food bank, she donates time and money to various causes she believes in, she is always signing some petition or joining a protest. I've never known anyone else to care so much about the state of the world.

"It's going really well, thanks. We're going to move in together."

Is it the thought of Amy that adds a little power behind my drive? Karim swears under his breath as my ball rolls to a stop in the middle of the fairway.

Karim places his own ball down, draws out his biggest driver, jiggles into a wide stance and pulls the club back. He is lifting his head too early, I think, cringing as he smashes the ball. There's an unmistakable crack as it hits the trees to our left.

I wait a beat. "Want me to help you look for it?" I ask.

Karim flicks a glance. "Did we find the last seven?"

I laugh. "Fair point."

Wading in the long grass to our left, we find three balls and a discarded can of Coke. Which in pre-Amy days I'd have ignored. Today I pick it up and put it in my bag to get rid of later: Amy's concern for the environment in my head. It's one of the many small ways I think being with her makes me a slightly nicer human.

"I thought this was meant to be fun?" Karim says, rootling amongst the weeds.

"How are you not having fun?" I grin.

"Well, I hope it's worth it. My own relationship is about to take the hit. Cally will be tackling this weekend solo with both kids for the first time . . ."

I cringe again. "Sorry."

Karim gives up searching for his ball. "I'm kidding. It's Amy's sister—of course you need to be there. Bex and I have got this."

"I shouldn't have let you guys do all three events on your own. But we can't cancel now!" My nerves rise, but I try to remain calm on the outside as I wonder about the logistics. Could I event-manage from the hotel?

Karim looks up, "We are more than prepared, Flynn. You've left instructions that are longer than the Bible and you've just spent seventeen holes of golf walking me through every second you'll be gone."

I try to relax but inside I'm still worrying.

"Mate, seriously, it's all good."

"I could get online on Saturday, try to manage things from . . ."

"You need to trust us, mate," Karim says, cutting me off. Do I detect an edge to his voice?

I nod and force myself to take a breath. My heart is still thrumming beneath my polo shirt. "So, is it all going well at home?" I ask, wanting to get back on track.

Karim puts a hand through his hair. "The jump from one to two has been a lot," he admits, "but, yeah. Fed's almost two now and Ali's five months and already crawling." You can't mistake the pride on his face.

"Got a picture?"

"Of the kids?" Karim asks, his eyebrows lifting.

I nod. There's a short beat.

"Of course." Karim pulls out his cell phone, scrolls, and wordlessly hands it over.

There is a small boy, a mass of black curls, grinning down as his arms encircle his baby sister.

"Oh, that's cute," I say, looking at the tiny faces, the sparkling eyes of the over-awed toddler, the raw love on display. I feel an unexpected lump in my throat and cough to cover it, handing the phone back.

"I guess it is," Karim admits. "We've been so obsessed with surviving it that sometimes I forget that." His face softens as he speaks and I experience a visceral wave of feeling—a yearning to have what has made his face change in that way. I think of Amy again. It's going well, I assure myself.

We wander to the edge of the fairway, the ground dappled with the shadows of the leaves above us. "But you, mate, you're in the fun part. City breaks and late nights and a hangover where a small person isn't leaping on you. Enjoy it."

"Absolutely," I say loudly, knowing that is the manly response, that my desire to settle down, for a family, makes me an outlier among men.

"Although . . ." I can't help my face splitting into a smile. "Look what I'm taking with me . . ."

I pull the small box out of the side compartment of my bag and open it, the solitary diamond glinting in the sunlight.

"Woah, nice, mate," Karim says, clapping me on the back.

I take an extra second to examine the ring, one I'd taken an age to choose, the lab-grown diamond big enough she'd be impressed but not so big she'd worry about looking extravagant, before slipping it back inside my bag. My insides jump around every time I think about presenting it to her. I know it's what I want.

There's no more talk of it, of course not, even though I want to ask Karim how he proposed, what marriage is like, how he feels now he's secure in a stable relationship. I swallow the questions down. It's not that I think Karim wouldn't answer them, but it would be too strange, too far removed from what I'm used to talking about with him.

The facts delivered, Karim drops a second ball and I watch him before his ritual: the roll of his shoulders before he widens his stance, draws the club back. And hits it straight back into the trees.

A flock of birds take flight in unison.

"Think you hit the trees there."

"You distracted me by proposing," he says grumpily.

I laugh and clap him on the back. "Sure, mate, that was it. Sure."

7

AMY

Now

My body is tumbling, my head filled with an all-consuming noise. I squeeze my eyes closed against the shock of light that surrounds me. With a terrible suddenness I'm no longer falling: I've stopped. All the breath leaves my body in a second and I'm lying there, heart hammering and head bursting with a hundred questions inside me.

What's happened? Where am I? I was with Flynn. Where is he? Oh god, where is he?

8

AMY

Six Hours Ago

"Why am I looking at your ceiling, weirdo?"

I've angled my phone screen away from the carnage in my attic flat. Laura's even frecklier face looms on the video call. "I'm just packing and don't want you to freak out," I call.

My blush-pink chiffon bridesmaid dress is hanging on the back of the door, but everything else is scattered on the floor or duvet ready to be packed.

"I'm almost done," I add, randomly dangling a pair of socks over the screen in an attempt to prove it. It doesn't fool her.

"Show me."

Unlike Flynn, my eighteen-month-older sister always sees straight through my white lies. Sulkily I lower the phone and scan the room with it.

She audibly gasps, "God, it's a crime scene."

I lift the screen to my face. "It's not that bad," I say, the furrow between her eyebrows deepening with every word.

"It's like a Before photo on a home improvement show."

"You're exaggerating," I sniff.

"I'm not—that's what you do."

"I don't exaggerate, I just add exciting detail!" I protest.

"Like the time you told Dad Jake Bisley had six months left to live?"

"I really thought he was dying,"

"He had flu, Amy. Dad sent his mum flowers!"

Laura laughs and I grin, before the pain of mentioning Dad stops my smile.

"Anyway," Laura says, catching her breath. Had she felt it too? "I'm ringing because Mum just told me you're freaking out about Flynn, and I don't need more drama over the next two days . . ."

It's my turn to frown. "I'm not freaking out, dickhead!"

"I'm not the dickhead planning to dump my boyfriend on her sister's wedding weekend."

Riled, I don't trust myself to speak, so I just shake my head. Laura and Jay's wedding is not a one-day event, more a massive scheduled extravaganza of moving parts and I've been making plans for weeks. Monogrammed umbrellas in case it rains, something blue, something borrowed, a playlist on my phone for the morning of the wedding—all Laura's favorite tunes. A speech for tonight, despite the fact a speech in front of these grand guests makes my insides flip. A hundred hours practicing for the flashmob.

She shifts in the strained silence. There have been more and more of these in the last five years. We were never awkward with each other before.

"Come on then, let's talk about Flynn," she relents.

"No, it's fine," I say, her previous comments still stinging. "You have stuff going on," I add lamely.

"I have time. I'm hiding from Patty. She's currently seeing someone about close-up magic—"

"Why is s—"

Laura holds her hand up, coral pink nails immaculate. "Don't ask. Apparently none of us are allowed to draw breath this weekend. And I shouldn't complain because she's paying for everything and Jay is so happy, you know how he can't stay still. But enough. So . . . Flynn. I thought it was going well?"

I take a breath. "It is, it was, it's, just, he asked to move in, Laurs. With me. Here."

Laura exhales. "Ames, that's a good thing. You told me he's never serious. This is serious!"

"But I'm not sure," I cut her off.

"He's nice, fun. And without him I'd have never met Jay, so I'm a fan."

"I know. But maybe fun is all he can be? I still feel like I hardly know what makes him tick. And moving in feels like the start of a lifetime together . . ."

"Is that not what you want?"

I pick my nail, trying to put into words what I've been

27

feeling in the last couple of weeks. "I always thought I'd marry someone more . . . well, more like Dad, more salt of the earth."

"Dad wasn't exactly down the mines, Ames."

"I know—but Flynn's rich. He went to boarding school!"

Laura rolls her eyes. "The same one as Jay—and I'm marrying him."

"Yes, but you're . . ." I trail away, feeling like this is moving on to uncertain ground. Laura's expression clouds and I quickly get back on track. "But it's not just that, Laurs. I haven't even met his mum."

"Trust me," Laura says, a quick glance over her shoulder, "that can be overrated."

"I swear he's embarrassed of me or something, Laurs . . ."

Laura's face changes, her mouth turned down. "You don't know that. You always do this, assume the worst. It's like you think the world is an unfair place, with unhappy people so you should be too. You deserve good things, Amy."

Her words are quiet, her expression softening. Tears prick my eyes. I really don't, I think.

"Maybe," I say, wanting to get off the phone, stop her looking at me like that. I don't deserve it.

The secret that makes me ache, that eats me up, nudges at me. If she knew it, I know she'd hate me too.

"Anyway," I smile, shaking off the conversation, "it's fine. I can sort it out after this weekend. Which is all about you."

Laura laughs, "It is all about me."

Someone in the background calls her name and she glances worriedly over her shoulder. "Oh god, I think it's Patty. Last time I saw her she was carrying something called a dovecote."

"Go," I smile, as wide as I can muster.

My stomach jitters for her. Laura's not the only one who is nervous; I don't go to places like this with dovecotes, foyers, and chandeliers. It makes me feel even more removed from my sister.

Flynn set Laura up with Jay, a friend of his from school who also lived in London, just after we met, and their relationship moved quickly. Now Laura's mother-in-law Patty is overseeing their wedding weekend like the general of a small army. It's a whole weekend of events. A mini festival. It's intimidating.

When we were young we always said we'd get married in the Bristol registry office, the reception in the pub with karaoke like Mum and Dad did. Has that Laura disappeared for good?

"Just get down here quickly, OK, weirdo?" Laura says. "I need you!"

"I will, dickhead," I reassure her, glancing at the clock and trying to disguise my surprise as I note the time. "Very soon." I swallow and put on my brightest voice, "It's all going to be amazing."

Laura gives me a grateful smile and blows a kiss. We hang up shouting goodbyes.

The sun streams into the slanted attic bedroom as I scoop up the rest of the assorted items I need and tick them off my list.

The little photo clips for the tables, the lace garter I'd bought Laura as a joke, the photo I have framed of us with Dad. I freeze as I stare at the shot. It could have been any Saturday. Him grinning as he squeezed us tight into the frame, both of us dressed in too-big Bristol Rovers gear because Dad always bought them with "room to grow," the bright red tops clashing with our pink cheeks, our buoyant brown curls merging together. I loved the stamp and bustle of the crowd, the hot pie in a bag at half-time, being with Dad. Laura fancied the goalkeeper Steve Phillips so spent most of the time staring at him.

Dad was a lifelong fan, season ticket holder; he'd be there in any weather, morose if they lost, chanting during the game, singing "We All Follow the City" all the way home if they won. We played it at his funeral; it was the thing that finally made Mum cry. "Oh god!" she exclaimed as she dabbed at her face. "I wish I was telling him to shut up one more time."

Staring at the picture, I rub at a smear on the glass, only just realizing it's my own eyes blurring. Get a grip, Amy, this is exactly what I need to rein in. This weekend is about Laura, and I need to get a handle on things, be her port in a storm: organized, dependable, calm. Not dissolving into tears, drawing eyes to me. The trouble is, since Dad I never know when the tears will come. I place the photo gently into my handbag.

Pulling on my tea dress, I secure my hair into a top knot, curls escaping. Then I look at the clock, chewing on my lip. Where is Flynn?

No doubt he'll sweep in unflustered. Nothing seems

30

to faze him. As if summoning him, the door to downstairs opens. He is here. A strange prickle of irritation
rises up in me again. Stop it, Amy. He's not that late.
And this is not the weekend to worry about your relationship. You can tackle it after your sister gets married.
Anyway, I'm not going to dump him . . . am I?

9

FLYNN

Now

Ignoring my aching body, I blink, still too shocked to work out what has happened. My head spins as I look around from my seated position. I remember now where we were: the lane, the cows, and then that noise, that light.

Only something doesn't make sense at all. I'm not where I should be. This isn't right.

My breath hitches: something huge has happened and I'm suddenly frightened.

10

FLYNN

3 Hours Ago

Karim took my clubs back with him and I got a taxi straight from golf. Amy is sitting on a suitcase in the living room, umbrellas and bags scattered around her, looking stunning in a flowery, frilly dress, her curly dark hair shining under the light. Her full lips are set in a line, her nose twitches, the freckles she is self-conscious about smattered over her nose.

She doesn't greet me, just leaps up. "Where's your stuff? Why aren't you changed?"

She's been increasingly tense the last couple of weeks and I tell myself it's just the wedding. I put both my hands up to shield her attack. "Downstairs and I'll do it when we get there."

"I'll start taking stuff down," Amy says, reaching to

scoop up all the matching umbrellas she bought for the bridesmaids. Secretly she's had them monogrammed L and J, knowing Laura will want a keepsake. Amy is always doing stuff like that. Despite her huffing and hiding behind hard edges, she is thoughtful. Leaving me something to eat if she's out, bringing home prosecco if I've landed a new client. She once had an office chair delivered because I kept saying I had a bad neck.

I pull her toward me, her brown eyes widening as I dip my head to kiss her. "I haven't even said hello properly."

"We don't have time," she mutters, although her body leans into me and we sink into a kiss. Whatever is happening between us, at least this doesn't change. Her hands move up over my chest and around my neck, and her tiny exhalation of breath makes the tight knot in my chest loosen—physically we have always got each other and that should count for a lot.

She stiffens against me. "I'll take the umbrellas," she says, pulling back.

That leaves me with the rest, the suitcase bulging with I have no idea what.

"It's two nights, yes?" I say, straining to pick it up.

"I need it all." Seriously, what do women need that requires this much stuff?

I grunt and drag it to the door. "If there's a body in here I'm not doing time for you, Amy. I WON'T GO BACK THERE!" I shout as I navigate the stairs outside her flat.

It takes a while to cram everything in and Amy is

34

increasingly twitchy, not helped when I chuck the car keys at her.

"For fu— Flynn!" She fails to catch them and has to retrieve them from the road behind her.

I cringe. "Sorry." I seem to be getting everything wrong recently.

I think of the ring inside my bag—a possible solution—and exhale slowly. I've been carrying it around for a week, but it hasn't felt right yet. Squeezing myself into the passenger seat, things crammed into the footwell so my legs are forced to bend to my chest, I pull out my cell phone.

I just need to send Karim and Bex over the list of timings and contact details, and ensure they have everything they need to run the three events we have on this weekend. I feel nervous about not overseeing everything. I want to relax, knowing I have a great team, but my brain can't switch off. Twitchy, I think of the things that could wrong, and how I'm responsible. If my team have a bad weekend, maybe they'll leave me, leave the company?

"Finally," Amy says, starting up her tiny car with a little puff.

I bite down reminding her it took ten minutes for me to load the car with all her bags.

"And you really will change," Amy says, side-eyeing my long diamond golf socks as she starts the car.

I look up from my phone, "Not loving my look, eh?"

She doesn't respond. The prickle of worry I've had in the last couple of weeks tickles my insides. Normally she'd smile, indulge me. Since I've asked her about moving in, I've felt something shift. I flex my neck and force my worries down.

I give her a reassuring grin, "The moment we get there. It's cool."

She looks over her shoulder and starts backing out of the space. "It'll be tight. I started packing last night. I made a list . . ."

I shift in the passenger seat and swallow another retort. The fact I made a list too is not going to help smooth things over. The good thing about Amy is once she lets rip we move on: she doesn't hold a grudge.

"Shall I put on some music?" I offer.

"In a bit. I just need to decompress."

11

AMY

Now

Panting into the ground, my brain is still trying to catch up with what's happened. My chest pounds with fear as I slowly open my eyes, everything spinning in and out of focus as I try to catch my breath.

I was with Flynn and now I'm on my own: that thought hits me with a dreadful certainty. Where is he? What has happened to us?

12

AMY

3 Hours Ago

I should probably let Flynn play some music, but I don't want to relent too soon—I can hold onto a grudge for days. He's twitching like an over-excited Labrador, fiddling with the A/C, now on his phone. A thought strikes me.

"The bow tie finally arrived for Reggie."

Flynn is in charge of one thing this weekend—walking Jay's family dog, the Golden Retriever ring bearer, down the aisle. Another Patty idea. This weekend will be like stepping into an alternate reality.

Flynn chuckles. "I love that dog."

"Me too," I reply weakly.

I wish I felt the same, but the truth is I'm afraid of him. When we were little, we lived next door to an enormous Doberman. He'd go berserk and throw himself at the gate every time I walked past him to school. It's made me scared of most dogs.

My cell phone rings in the bag next to Flynn's feet. Laura's "We Are Family" ringtone is faint but I still almost swerve the car in panic. "Can you get that? Tell her we're on track."

Flynn's scrolling on his phone. I imagine it's a viral video of a duck doing something funny or a basketball shot backward across the whole court.

"Flynn," I repeat. "Can you get that? It's Laura."

He's still tapping, no doubt clicking on the next video. "FLYNN!"

He starts a little, "Sure, sure." Rifling in the footwell for my handbag, he sends a packet of Jelly Babies flying as he scrabbles around for the phone. By the time he reaches it the cell phone is silent. He eats one of the green Jelly Babies.

"Can you phone her back?" I ask, jaw clenched. Why is it that the last two weeks almost everything he's done has set my teeth on edge? Since he asked to move in with me it's like I'm spiraling with doubts, looking for all the reasons we don't work. Flynn had pulled me out of a gray time, a pop of color. But things I'd dismissed in the past, other tiny doubts I've had have blossomed into something more. Now I'm noticing more and more what's wrong with us: not what's right.

Laura rings again and before I ask him, Flynn has answered.

"Hi Laura! Not far . . . no . . . oh, by the way the bow

tie came, Amy just tol— No, not mine . . . yes, I've remembered mine! And my shoes, why would I forget
my . . . never mind . . . I mean the one for Reggie! . . . No,
she can't . . . she's driving . . . yep, all on track . . . yep, she
remembered them . . . it's chill . . . I'll tell her . . . Juggle?
Er . . . two balls maybe? OK . . . see you—oh," Flynn
stares at his cell phone. "I think she hung up."

A truck looms in my rear view as he says, "Why does
your sister think I'd forget my shoes? She said she'll meet
you in the foyer at five p.m."

Biting my lip, I stare at the clock. That's just over two
hours away.

"Oh, and umbrellas! She's worried it might rain tonight
and she wants the umbrellas."

The windshield is already covered in flecks of rain so
I think this is a certainty.

"I've got them."

"I know you have, that's what I told her. And Patty
asked her to ask me if I can juggle."

Are all weddings like this? I wonder. Flynn and I are
nowhere close to getting married but I don't think juggling would be part of it.

I glance across again at Flynn, now eating a yellow
Jelly Baby. I try not to stare at his diamond socks. I think
of what Dad used to say about golfers, scoffing at the
price of membership, the stuffy rules.

"What sport needs a dress code to play?"

Dad had a lot of opinions and I cling to them, to the
small and big things he said. It's the least I can do to
keep him with me.

I'm with someone from a different world and now Laura is marrying into it. It makes my next words harder than I meant.

"We need to help Laura make it perfect or she'll have to answer to her future husband's ridiculous family."

Flynn frowns. "They're not ridiculous. I went to school with Jay: he's great."

"The wedding venue has actual flamingos, Flynn!"

"They're just normal human beings."

"But they're not normal, are they? This wedding's going to cost more than three years of my salary, for a start . . ."

"That's just money. They want to celebrate."

"Look you don't understand because, well, you're one of them."

Flynn doesn't say anything, just goes quiet.

I know I'm being mean. Fear of not fitting in isn't helping. He shifts next to me and I wonder why I don't apologize. A few weeks ago I would have apologized. What's happened to me? As if the sky picks up on the mood in the car, the light dims. Despite the fact it shouldn't be getting dark for hours, I have to turn my headlights on.

At least we've left Bristol now, the city disappearing behind us.

"We might make it on time at this ra—" I stop and squint into the distance. "What's that up ahead?"

And I realize exactly what it is.

13

FLYNN

"Flynn, *look*," Amy hisses as she hits my thigh and I glance up to see what she's worried about.

It takes me a few moments to register the traffic that snakes into the distance.

I know this sight will make her more anxious and want to help. "Oh, well, it's probably just the queue to get past ... um ... Weston-Super-Mare ... It won't be all the way to Devon," I say, the smell of diesel permeating the car.

"Why? Will everyone get off there?"

"Of course they will. There's the pier and ..." I give her a cheerful side-eye, "the Helicopter Museum. Loads of helicopter fans. Oh no," I check the time on my phone, and in a mock shocked voice I say, "T'wirly."

This doesn't even make Amy's mouth twitch and my palms dampen as I think of another way to get this trip back on course.

"Let's play some music to distra— to entertain us!"

Amy's Honda's so old she has a CD player and I rattle through the glove compartment and emerge, delighted, with a CD from over a decade ago.

"Oh my god!"

She's there on the cover, "Amy Norman" in simple cursive scroll—a teen Amy sat on a stool, a spotlight above her. She looks so vulnerable in the intimate space and I can't help touching her face, her expression direct, a hint of fear behind her eyes.

"What is this?" I say, turning it over in my hand. How has she never said she made this? How have I never seen it in the car before?

Her voice makes me tingle even if I catch snippets from the shower, or in the kitchen when she's lost in cooking, her hips swaying gently as she stirs pasta. I feel privileged to be the only person on the earth that knows how talented she is—but the thought makes me both secretly proud and utterly devastated. She hasn't sung in public for years—Laura says she refused after their dad died.

I slip the CD out of the plastic casing and notice Amy glance across, feel the pull as her hands momentarily slip on the wheel. Her eyes widen, her voice shrill, "Don't, Flynn."

I distract her by waggling the empty case at her, "You made an album!"

"One song."

"Still!"

"Seriously—put it back."

I slide it in quickly and cover the eject button with a palm. "We have to," I say, desperate to hear it.

"Don't."

The air fills immediately with the gentle tones of the acoustic guitar and Amy's voice—higher, melancholy, beautiful. It seems to reach to a place I barely acknowledge exists and widens the hole inside me.

"Flynn, turn it off."

I'm lost in the wistful song, sad that Amy has refused to sing for Laura and Jay—hearing her voice over the gentle strumming of the guitar, I know the congregation would be a blubbering mess if she did. She told me to drop it at the time and I knew not to push things—I don't want to upset people.

"Flynn, seriously. TURN IT OFF."

Her voice shocks me into ejecting the disc and there is a terrible silence, only the whirs of the wheels over the rough ground.

She can't be as angry as she sounds. Don't ask her: better to leave it. My familiar anxiety at creating conflict makes my stomach drop. Don't push her away, Flynn.

Her voice is tight and high, "Can you check the map on your phone? The address is on the invitation in my bag . . ."

I scrabble to get the invitation, frowning as I see the photo of Laura and Amy with their dad in a frame, a hint of the Bristol Rovers football strip. I slip it back before she sees, wondering why she has brought it with her. I don't want her to talk about her dad—talking about him leads to questions about mine, and I've spent a lifetime avoiding them. What's the point anyway—talking won't bring either of them back.

Amy thinks I'm from Jay's world because of where I went to school. She has no idea.

For a second I can feel the leather of the car that day I drove there, remember the black hole inside me that scared me so much I crammed it full of anything else: sports, friends, jokes, resentment. I paid the money back to Patrick three months ago. I never told Amy; that would have led to even more questions. Eleven years of boarding school fees almost broke me but I don't owe him anything anymore: he holds nothing over me. That thought at least makes me proud.

"How long is it saying it will be?"

I'm dragged back to the car. "Oh, Wookey Hole is coming up soon!" I say quickly, tilting the phone screen away from her so she can't see the long snake of orange and red that shows the entire M5 is basically at a standstill.

"Flynn, seriously. Tell me. Should we get off?"

I tap some more buttons. "There is a longer way round that shaves twenty minutes or so."

"Should we take it?"

I chomp nervously on another Jelly Baby. This journey is unraveling; my chest feels tighter by the second. I feel frozen with indecision.

"Flynn! Focus!"

I nod quickly, aware I need to give an answer, not just remain internally fretting. "Let's take the scenic route," I say, describing it in a way that makes it sound infinitely more romantic and less stressful than it might be.

45

14

FLYNN

Twenty Years Ago

I'm not sure whether it was the thing that screeched that woke me up or the wet or knowing it is happening today. My stomach swirls and tears prick my eyes in the dark. Sneaking out of bed, I see the outline of the awful "trunk" we're taking on the other side of the room.

I peel off my sticky pajama bottoms and ball them up. I don't want to take off the sheet again because last time Mum was so angry. Maybe it will dry before she notices? I stuff my bottoms in the back of my wardrobe and I lie on top of my duvet with a rug over me, trying to forget what's about to happen.

My skin feels all sticky and the smell makes me feel sick, or is it still the thought of Mum finding out? Will she be angry? Will she say anything at all? I stay there until the edges of my curtain get bright. I hear her foot-steps go past. Mum used to come in. She doesn't anymore. I put my pants on and then the scratchy gray uniform, but I can't do up the tie which makes me want to cry again. I don't want to wear a tie. I don't want to leave my old school.

I don't say anything at breakfast and it's just the scrape of my cutlery and the turning of the newspaper which means I shouldn't say anything because I am seven and nothing I say is important. Behind it, Patrick snorts and says something about Blair's Babes but I don't know what that is and why it's bad. Sometimes I wonder what he would do if I reached across and scrunched up all the papers like I want to, but instead I just watch Mum, who is staring at her coffee cup. I want her to look at me but then, when she does, her face screws up.

"What is that?"

You're not meant to knot a tie. For a second I am pleased because it means she'll touch me and she does, placing a hand on my shoulder as she does up the tie, but so quickly I know I won't remember how to do it on my own. In my normal school, we wore Aertex with two buttons. Dad never wore a tie when he was alive. He was always wearing checked shirts that smelled of BBQs. My stomach starts swirling again when I think about that. I don't want to go and I can't help it, it just comes out.

"I don't want to go."

Her hands freeze on the tie and her eyes look just over my shoulder. I know he's paying, I overheard them a few days ago. I don't want him to pay, I like my school where you don't pay.

Patrick scoffs from behind his newspaper, "You don't know how lucky you are." Mum doesn't reply and now the tears do come and she says "Stop that" and I do.

I sit on the back seat and stare at the back of their heads as they talk. I was sad because I couldn't find Muffin to say goodbye and who will leave her raisins and bury their face in her soft fur? I'll miss her warmth and the quick thud of her heart when I hold her close. The cassette is playing something boring with violins and I can't hear what they're saying over it, but I know it's about the island they're going to that has an infinity pool, which I think is a really long pool.

I wish now Mummy had found my balled-up sheet. Maybe she wouldn't have been cross, maybe she would have swept me up into her arms like she used to when I was really small and Dad was still alive, and stroked my hair and put a kiss on my head and told me it was OK. I used to crawl into bed by her and she'd throw an arm around and over me without saying anything and I'd stay there all night in their bed. I'm not allowed to do that anymore. She told me I'm too big to do that, but I'm not big, I'm seven and I know it's my "new dad's" idea. Like all the stupid ideas are.

I have a memory of another car journey where Mum looked back at me over her shoulder and gave me a smile that showed the gap between her two front teeth, Dad playing the song "Fun, Fun, Fun" and singing badly. I stare at her blonde bob so hard my eyes start watering but she never turns around, despite my praying inside she will.

They don't stay. Patrick shakes my hand in the hallway by the housemaster with the bald patch. His hand is limp and he wipes it on his trousers. He doesn't leave when Mum is meant to say goodbye and I want to cling to her and beg her to take me home, I hate it here already and I'm scared.

The housemaster has put a hand on my shoulder and I shake it off and I can't help it but I start to cry, big sobs and Mum says "ssh" and looks around and the other parents are watching and then she leaves quickly when Patrick tells her to come along because she's making it worse. She isn't making it worse, I need her to hold me, to hug me, to cuddle me. I miss my mum. Dad would never have let her leave. Dad would have hugged me too. But then Old Mum would never have made me come here.

She doesn't look back at the door.

I swipe at my face as other boys arrive and my chest hurts more when I see them being held close by their mummies who are crying and telling them they love them. One boy, fair hair and ice-blue eyes, wriggles out of a grasp, rushes past me. His mummy with the softest cloud of hair is still wanting to say goodbye and for a second, I want to run into her open arms and stay there.

The dorm is a big dusty room with wooden floorboards and smeared glass windows. A row of four beds down one side and a row of four more on the other. At the far end a big circular window looks out over sports fields and trees. This school is in the middle of nowhere.

The fair-haired boy is here already.

"I'm Eddie. You're new. Why didn't you arrive in the first term?"

I can't tell him the real reason, that it was my "new dad's" idea so that he can take Mum to the Caribbean for a six-week honeymoon. He isn't my dad at all, and I'll never call him Dad even if it means she'll never talk to me again.

"I asked to move me here coz I thought it looked cool." The lie slips out easily.

Eddie seems to accept it and I'm relieved he doesn't ask me more. He starts to ask me whether I play cricket and I say yes, only a little, even though I don't.

"I'm Captain." He tilts his chin up.

"That's cool."

Eddie smiles at me and for a second the weight in my chest lifts. I try to think back to the last time Mum smiled at me. The weight gets heavier.

Another boy appears, wire-rimmed glasses and messy hair, and he takes the bed on the other side of Eddie. I think his name is Jay. Eddie throws a textbook at him and tells Jay to duck. The boy gets hit on the nose.

"Don't cry to Matron."

I think Eddie might be in charge of us.

That first term is a blur of new things: faces, teachers, subjects, fields, hobbies, sports. Words like cloisters and prep. I learn how to fit in, how to focus on the day ahead, and not think about the things that make my heart hurt. And I can make the boys laugh. I tell jokes, play the fool, make up games. I'm good at sports and that matters here. It's the most important thing and I practice and practice.

If I have to talk about something real, I pretend. My mum bakes brownies and takes me swimming, my stepdad's nice, he plays table tennis with me, I don't remember my real dad. That last one makes my breath catch.

My lies are boring and normal, and the boys lose interest in their questions quickly. We talk about sports instead; when we get older we talk about sports and girls. I find I can do it, that boys don't probe too much. Sometimes I catch myself wondering which memories are true, convincing myself some might be.

I only cry in secret, in the dark, late. No one knows. The lies still come easily. Happy family times abroad, in-jokes we have; scribbled letters from Mum appear— never too long—always quite vague—that I pretend are from her when the others get their mail. None of the boys suspect anything, no one is looking. No one asks where the envelopes are, why the paper is the same as the paper I have on my desk.

And over the years the tears don't come anymore, I've stopped them, and I don't feel the hole in my chest so much. I'm used to Mum never looking back, I'm used to telling boys about this imaginary mum with her soft hands and warm hugs. I lose the remaining memories I have of Dad. Those precious few I had held close to my chest, I try to hold onto them but his face fades, and when I try really hard I simply see nothing. I feel nothing.

15

AMY

The M4 is jammed and Flynn's more focused on his phone and eating the entire pack of Jelly Babies than sorting it out. Then he tried to play my single, the single I'd made that Dad never even knew about. I bite my lip when I think of that last night and the dark thoughts that always accompany those memories.

We're running about an hour late. Not only have I missed helping Laura as she asked, but it looks like we might not even be on time for the dinner. We're stuck behind a line of cars who have also followed their Google maps into the wilderness, braking round every bend, the air smelling of pig shit and my own nervousness.

Now it's started to rain and the sky is so dark it's almost night despite sunset still being a good few hours away. The rain is so much worse and I'm leaning forward in my seat, the wipers on their fastest speed, praying I won't be hit by a tractor swinging round the next corner. Flynn is still tapping on his phone, barely concentrating as we pass the same bloody places. And just when I think it can't get any worse we come up against a wall of cows all moving from one field to another, one halting to stare at us.

16

FLYNN

We're definitely lost. We've been past that five-bar gate about three times. I keep pretending it's a different five-bar gate but we both know it's not.

I was navigating but then I got sidetracked by an email from the magician for tomorrow's fifth birthday party. He has norovirus. Gulping down the flare of worry, I forward the email to Bex with an appropriately stressed emoji. The kids' party arm of the business is relatively new, set up four years ago and something I really care about.

"Are we going in a circle, Flynn?"

The rain is pouring down in earnest now, the wiper blades moving furiously. I start to scroll to find the map and my screen goes black. I can't stop the noise that emerges from my mouth in time. Amy hears it.

"What's happened?" she asks, already in panic mode. "Has it DIED?"

I freeze, immediately thinking about Bex, the replies, how I can get back online to help.

"Flynn?" The car swerves as she stares at me.

"It's run out of charge, yes."

"This is so typical," Amy says. "I hope the comedy tweets were worth it."

"It was work . . . I need to find a magici— woah . . ."

A corner looms and Amy swings round it abruptly, pressing sharply down on her brakes as we are greeted with an entire wall of cows crossing the road into a field.

She pauses for breath, the engine still idling. The rain is pounding on the roof of the car, the windshield a complete wash of rivulets so that the cows in the road ahead are just a blur of white and black. Another ominous rumble echoes around the surrounding hills.

"Fucking great," she says, throwing up her hands. Then she clutches her head. "Oh my god, I've already missed helping her set up, now we're going to miss the dinner. Laura is going to be so mad, she'll say I've done it deliberately or that I don't care . . ."

"She won't say that," I say, trying to bring up the directions on Amy's phone and not be distracted by the cows, one of which is staring right at us, its enormous eyes unblinking.

"You don't get it."

"I do and you're wrong," I say bluntly, my voice raised over the rain, my own temper fraying.

"I'm not," Amy says, angry tears swimming in her brown eyes as she looks across at me.

I try to calm her. "I'm sure she'll understand. We just need to let these cows pass and then we'll ask someone."

"We're still going to be massively late."

"It'll be cool. Others will be in the same boat."

"That's different: they're not me."

And suddenly she has opened the car door, rain streaking onto the driver's seat as she steps out onto the road. I reach for my door handle, pushing it open, shocked by the extent of the rain, hair flattened, clothes drenched almost immediately. I look across at Amy who is standing glowering at me over the roof of the car, wind whipping her curls back from her face.

"Oh my god, Amy, stop being insane and get back in the car."

"You don't understand."

"I do understand you're ACTING CRAZY," I call out.

"No. We're not all laid-back like you, Flynn."

Heat rises inside me as I think of the things I don't say to keep the peace. "Hey, I get stressed, I just don't harp on about it all the time."

"I don't harp."

I can't help the bark of laughter and that makes her glower at me even more.

Stop this, I think, I want this weekend to be happy, focus on the positives of our relationship. Move things forward. I can't screw up another relationship.

"Don't laugh at me, Flynn! This isn't a joke to me!"

"It's not a joke to me either," I say, practically spitting rainwater out of my mouth.

"You could have fooled me!"

"Get back in the car," I shout over the rain that is worsening by the second.

"You just don't get it. You don't get *me*."

"Well, that makes two of us," I challenge. Sometimes it's like she barely knows me at all. That thought shocks me for a moment. Do I really think that? I think of the ring in my bag. I want this woman to be my wife—don't think like that, Flynn. Things are fine.

"WHY CAN'T YOU UNDERSTAND ME!" The chorus is simultaneous as we screech it at each other.

Another enormous rumble of thunder surrounds us as we glare at each other. The cows peer on and, in a terrible, blinding flash, the sky above us cracks open. My whole body is flung backward through the air, everything spinning, before I come to an abrupt stop in the long grass of the verge.

17

AMY

"WHY CAN'T YOU UNDERSTAND ME?"

As our furious words hang in the air, a thunderous boom reverberates through me, drowning out all other thoughts. Before I can say anything else, there's an explosion of fierce, blazing light and I'm moving slowly backward, away from the car, away from Flynn, my feet lifting off the ground, my whole body lurching before coming to a sudden halt half-buried in a hedge.

18

FLYNN

Everything's topsy-turvy and all my breath has left my body but I think I'm alive.

Lightning. I've been struck by lightning. The rain is still heavy and I'm completely drenched. I'm sitting in the long grass of the verge, body aching. But it doesn't make sense. Then I remember I'd been standing next to the car shouting at Amy to get in.

Fuck, is Amy OK?

I'm immediately rattled. "Amy," I call out. But the sound that comes out of my mouth makes me stop immediately. It's not my voice. And, as I struggle to stand, I instantly feel something is very different. My aching limbs are shivering as I stare down my body checking for breaks. My brain can't quite compute what it is seeing.

It doesn't make any sense.

I register my bare arms, weirdly smooth, my torso squeezed into flowery fabric, and, as I start to form a thought, I hear the most horrific scream. A low, terrible yelp.

As I look across I see . . . myself.

I've left my body.

I'm staring at myself. I'm staring at Ghost Me.

Oh my god, I have died.

I have been hit by lightning and I have died and now, over the road, I am standing up and shaking my head.

Then Ghost Me starts panicked screaming. The screams are embarrassing. Ghost Me has really lost it, both hands up to his face, doing great yelps and squeals. Ghost Me is completely petrified.

Now Ghost Me starts shouting, "Flynn, what the fuck, oh my god, oh my god, what the fuck . . ."

And it's definitely my voice coming out of Ghost Me's mouth, but I can hear something else in the words. Someone else.

This is impossible. Actually impossible.

"Amy?"

And the moment I say it I know it's true.

Ghost Me, Amy, stares up at me, fear making everything stop for a second as we both just look at the other one.

"Flynn?"

And then the hands are back up to her face, my face, and she lets out a frightened howl which makes my whole body prickle.

What is happening?

"Are you alright?" I run across to her—to Ghost Me,

61

to her?—dressed in my golf attire: my navy shorts, polo shirt. This is the most surreal moment of my life—bar none.

I'm still terrified that I'm dead or dreaming, but everything feels so solid and real around me. I feel the body I'm in move, I see the hand with the painted nails reach out, I feel the rain drumming on my hair, so much hair, slithering down my skin, making the tight fabric of this flowery dress stick to me even more.

And I realize whose body I am in. I'm in Amy's body. And she is in mine.

"What is happening?" She is properly freaking out. It's still completely bizarre because I am watching myself have a total panic attack in long diamond golf socks, but it's definitely not me. So it has to be Amy.

"Amy, AMY," I shout, but her now blue eyes are completely round in her head. I look weird with all the whites showing and I can't make her hear me. I can see she is barely listening, is clutching her head, patting at her body, pausing as she reaches down.

"Holy shit," she says, her hand over her new groin. "Holy shit."

She can barely register me, and then I notice the cows are still there and now there is a car in the lane behind us, approaching our car which is still running in the middle of this country lane as we both lose our shit on the side.

The driver presses on his horn but there is no way Amy is responding to anything right now, and I'm also freaking out, but I'm glad I'm not dead at least and this is just very, very trippy and I need to think. The guy behind the wheel is still pressing on his horn so I go to get in the car, walking round to the passenger seat.

"Amy, we have to move the car."

She is basically jabbering. At this point I'm really not sure at all what to do. Do I slap her? Do I bundle her into it? She, I, seems a lot bigger and there is no way I now have the strength to do that, and there is no way she is able to drive this car. The beeping intensifies and I can barely see through the rain.

"We have to get out of the way, Amy, we need to figure this out. OK? OK?" I steer her gently by the arm—it's hairy, my arm, that is—and I encourage her to sit in the passenger's side as I gently shut her in and move around to the driver's door. I'm wobbly, like a new-born foal; my center of gravity is all off and for a second I think I'm going to pass out. This is just too bizarre. I see the hand that reaches for the handle, the coral pink nails, the slim wrists, and I open it up. Ducking inside, my whole body soaked, my teeth chatter and goosebumps appear on my arms, I check that Amy is doing OK. She is not. She is now just staring straight ahead, as if in a catatonic state.

Her face is completely bewildered and I feel bad for noticing that I need a haircut. This is not the time to worry about your appearance, Flynn. I reach across and place a hand on her thigh, my thigh, and see her flinch as she gawps at it. Then she is just staring at me, a horrified expression on her face as she drinks in every detail of my face, which is her face.

"It's going to be OK, we're going to work this out,"
I say. My new voice is high, shaky and it makes the
statement a lot less authoritative.

Taking a breath, I reach and pull on my seatbelt, at-
taching it with fumbling hands—how does Amy do anything with these nails? Once secured, the rain is still
sluicing the windshield, the air still filled with the honk-
ing horn. The guy must be leaning on it by now.

I breathe and look at the car. I reach to take the
handbrake off, and jerk forward. And immediately stall
the car.

Amy moans from next to me. I start up the engine
again, breathe slower—don't make this worse, Flynn.
The cows that have now cleared the road have lined the
field on the other side, some staring and chewing as I
try again, revving the engine way too loudly and jerking
a few meters forward to pull in where they all passed.
I stick the hazard lights on and the driver behind us
roars past with a final blare of his horn.

We both sit in the car in this strange space in total
silence, the storm outside, windows fogging, both of us
completely drenched and terrified.

Amy has completely shut down and I have so many
thoughts going round in my head I can't express anything
either. Another flash of lightning in the distance makes
me jump and return to the car, this moment.

Something bubbles up inside me and I can't stop a
sort of hiccupy laugh emerging.

19

AMY

I'm in Flynn's body. I can see I am. I know I'm me, but I can move his hands. The scar on his left knuckle is as clear as day. The navy-blue cotton shorts I gave him for his birthday are now damp and sticking to my legs. I *feel* like him too, my body heavier, balance peculiar, nothing feeling right. My head swims as I stare down at his thighs with their wiry hairs, the ridiculous long diamond socks.

That's when my breathing gets shallower and my vision blurs and the rain feels louder and the whole scene gets hazy and more bizarre.

And I can hear him laughing now. Well, it's not really a laugh, more a crazed snort of hysteria. And on one level the noise makes sense. He is me. In my favorite flowered tea dress, damp and sticking to him from the rain. He has my curly dark brown hair, wet clumps escaping from the wilting knotted hairband, my freckled nose, my face running with mascara. It's absurd. But this is the very furthest away from funny. I am not sure what it is: I can't organize my thoughts, I can't stay in any one moment.

We're pulled over and every now and again a car passes, loaded with holiday things and people. Life going on as usual: as if this hasn't happened.

How did it happen? I just don't comprehend. One moment I'd stepped out of the car, angry and not wanting to stay in the small space with a person who didn't understand me. The next the sky seemed to split open and there was a blinding light as my whole body lifted off the ground. After that all I remember is slamming to a stop, stunned and confused as I lay in the long, wet grass.

It was only when I stood, dazed and blinking, that I knew something was very wrong, felt something was off kilter. When I lifted strange hands to my face, registered the rough stubble on my chin, the nose broken in the middle. I couldn't stop the scream.

Then that sound, my scream but two registers lower, made me scream harder and clutch my face.

Then to see *myself* walking around my car toward me, arms held out, *my* rain-spattered body approaching me, a concerned expression on *my* face, made me scream harder still.

A nightmare, a terrifying nightmare.

"OK," I say in a shaky voice. "OK." I try desperately to get a handle on something and as I'm trying to do so I hear the ringtone on my phone. "We Are Family." I reach for it on automatic.

"Hey Laurs," I say shakily, shocked again that my voice is not my own.

"Flynn? Is Amy driving?"

"Um . . . um . . . yes, Amy is driving. I am Flynn."

"Has something happened?" Her voice is worried.

Where to begin?

I open my mouth and snap it shut again.

"Flynn?"

"No, no, nothing's happened," I squeak.

Laura can't disguise her huff of frustration. "Well then, where are you guys? I was expecting you half an hour ago. I really need Amy."

This sentence makes me feel even more terrified.

"We're . . . we're not far away," I say slowly, and realize there is no way we can go now. My throat closes as I continue, "But we've . . . stopped."

"Flynn, hold on. No, Jay! Tell your mum not to, they've told me they'll dry the seats . . . Flynn, Flynn?"

"I'm here," I say, listening to my sister fretting at the other end.

"What do you mean, you've stopped? Tell Amy to put her foot down. Oh my god, this rain, it's like the worst thing."

"Not the worst thing," I can't help snapping, looking down at my shorts and thinking about what's inside. Not the worst thing at all.

"Flynn, I've got to go . . . Jay! I told her Geoffrey will row her boat, tell her . . . just you guys get here soon, OK?"

I hold the phone limply in my hand as she disappears.

Flynn looks across at me and I get another wave of

the unreal as I stare into my own face, my brown eyes wide in enquiry, my lips parted: waiting. I can see he is doing the same thing.

"OK, we obviously cannot go to the wedding," I say, shaking my head in the hope I can organize my thoughts.

"What do you mean? We have to go."

"Flynn, look at us! Look. At. Us. This is . . ." I can feel my chest tightening as the thoughts crowd in once more and my breathing comes faster.

A hand circles my back. "It's OK, we can work something out. We don't have to go. Don't worry . . ."

The storm is still raging outside and we are both chattering with cold.

"We need to change back, we have to find a way to change back," I say. The moment this plan forms I get a burst of energy, something real to cling to. I reach for the door handle and push it open. The wind and rain batter the side of the door as I step out.

We cannot go to this weekend like this. I can't just roll up and pretend this catastrophic event hasn't occurred—pretend all is fine for Laura. It's not possible. I need to change back; I have to get back into my body before I can even consider doing anything else.

Another rumble of thunder increases my determination and I move shakily around the car, arms sticking out as I accustom myself to this strange, lumbering body. My feet sink into the mud and the diamond socks are soaked as I stagger through the long grass of the verge to the wooden gate.

"Flynn, come on."

We can un-do this, move on like nothing has happened. Clambering over the gate I jump down into the field, some of the nearby cows turning to watch me curiously as they chew.

"What are you going to do?" Flynn calls, attempting to clamber over the gate behind me. "Oh my god, how do you climb in this?"

I look back to see him stuck on the top bar with my dress up around his thighs, my pink pants on show. I look so small, so inconsequential. I always felt too thick-boned in my body as if I was taking up too much space, but from here I seem fragile, a girl who I would normally run to help.

That thought makes me speed up. This is not going to be permanent; it'll be a quick fix, we can pretend the last few minutes never happened.

I turn back and march away, past a Friesian who stares at me with unblinking eyes as I stumble over the uneven field, slipping in the mud.

Flynn is racing to catch up with me and I look over my shoulder, realizing I'm quicker than him as he picks his way over the grass, arms stuck out wide like he's also struggling to balance. For a second I tip my head to examine what I really look like: it's bizarre. Would anyone else realize it wasn't me? His bird-like walk, fast and uneven. The hair barely restrained by the limp polka dot scarf, my face, arms, and legs the same. But there's something in the slope of my shoulders, the stiff way he walks that gives it away, arms slightly swinging as he attempts to catch up with me.

Shaking my head, I turn back and focus again on where I'm headed. I can see the oak tree in the distance on the crest of the hill and my lungs burn as I make my way there.

"Amy," Flynn calls, "wait up."

As I stagger higher, slanting rain striking my face, the fields around me reveal themselves, rolling away in greens and browns, a dark blue silhouette of hills and trees in the distance, a flash of lightning nearby.

We need to change back.

"Amy, come on, we're soaked," Flynn's new voice is lost to the wind and rain.

I'm panting as I reach the oak tree, its branches stretched out like enormous hands. It must be two hundred years old at least. The perfect spot.

By the time Flynn catches up with me I'm standing, arms wide beneath its branches.

"What. The. Hell." He can barely talk, bending over and clutching his sides as the words are whispered. "God, you're unfit," he adds.

I ignore him, nervously jumping at the rumble of thunder I've been waiting for, water pouring down my neck, underneath the collar of the polo shirt. "This is it," I say, closing my eyes, tipping my palms heavenwards and tilting my neck back. "This is it."

There's a tug on my arm. "We need to get back to the car, work this out," Flynn says.

I open one eye, urgency in my voice, "We need to get hit again," I say, determinedly shutting my eyes once more and shaking him off.

"Absolutely not." He pulls on my arm now. "Amy! You'll get yourself killed. You'll get me killed! Come on . . ."

But he is not robust enough to move me. I stand, relishing this new strength that keeps my feet planted, stance firm, my body strong, resisting his urgent tugs.

"Amy! Come on, I'm serious! You can't do this . . ."

I open my eyes again and look at him, that line I get between my eyebrows deep with worry.

And then the rain starts to ease, the wind dials down and I drop my hands to my side. Behind him I see the fork of lightning above the tree line in the distance. It must be more than a mile away.

"Come on," he says more gently now, "the storm's moved on. Amy . . . we've got to go."

20

AMY

Twenty Years Ago

My dad's hands grip my legs as I join in the chant. I can hear his voice the loudest as he shouts out the words at the blue and white players. I join in some of the lines and when I do he jiggles me up and down and I laugh out loud. Somewhere below me Laura is wobbling on the seat asking who's got the ball. Dad said she was too heavy to go on his shoulders now.

I'm so high up I can see everything. The man in front of us has a small circle of skin right on the top of his head, and the rest of the heads look like different colored pool balls. The ground smells of onions and men and rain and I love it. I want half-time because he'll buy us a pie and a Coke and tell us not to tell Mum because Coke rots our teeth, and he'll put his finger to his lips and wink at Laura and me and we'll love the secret sharing.

My chest hurts when I think of how much I love Dad. He's like a double rainbow.

When the match ends it's great because he's in a good mood and telling everyone we're his girls and we're going to be in the stands with him when he's an old man. And people pat us and call us "loves" and we all sing the one about the only good City fan's the one that's dead and Dad laughs every time and tells us not to tell Mum because she doesn't think it's a nice one, but it's my favorite and everything sounds good in Dad's voice. I want to be a singer like him.

We're full and sleepy but we don't complain because it's brilliant walking back through the streets wrapped up in our stripy scarves and football strips, the pavements full of noisy steps and chants and the tink of beer bottles, and it feels exciting and a little bit dangerous, but Dad keeps us both close and I always feel safe with him. These are the best days.

He's promised tonight we can stay up late, painting signs for him to take on a march tomorrow, but we're not allowed to go on that. Well, not yet. Last night him and Mum argued about it because we're not too young to fight against the system. Dad says that we need to stand up for people who can't stand up for themselves. Mum says we can make the signs, and that is a compromise. Which I think is a thing you do if you can't decide one thing or another thing. Laura cried about it because she is scared to go and doesn't want to go to prison, but we wouldn't go to prison. Prison is for bad people and Dad's not bad. He was so proud when I said I wanted to march too and he called me his Firestarter and ruffled my hair, which made me feel warm inside. Mum and him don't argue much and he always wins, so I think I will go.

He grips my hand as we walk back home, and when Laura says it's too far he tells her it's not long, and when I say it he scoops me up into his arms and I get carried all the way back. I poke my tongue out at Laura over his shoulder and she tells on me. Dad tells her ssh, I'm the youngest, so it's fair because she got lifted up when she was small too.

When he's carrying me, I smell his smell that makes me think of a big oak tree.

"I love you, Daddy."

"I love you too."

I close my eyes and rest against his chest, feeling the big thud, thud, thud of his heart which is so huge it fits lots of people inside. He's the biggest, softest man, like a bear, a friendly bear who gives the squeeziest hugs.

When we get home I'm too tired to paint the signs but he isn't cross, he just puts me straight into bed in my Rovers strip and sings me a song as my eyes close. The last thing I hear is Laura and Mum laughing next door, the last thing I smell is the paint, the last thing I see are the glo stars on our ceiling, the last thing I feel is his kiss on my forehead.

21

FLYNN

We're both completely soaked and freezing by the time we return to the car. I attempt to put an arm around Amy but of course I can't reach so loop one round her waist. It makes me immediately feel diminished, like I can't protect her.

Everything about this is completely insane, and Amy is quiet on the walk down. Defeated, she stands next to the car, puddles glistening around us as the sun makes a weak attempt to appear. A car sprays brown water as it passes, not pausing to stare at the strangest couple in the world.

"Amy," I say, distracted for a moment by the sight of our reflections in the driver's window. Without my body I am less confident, less in command of my thoughts. "Amy, let's get to the place and work out what to do."

It's the same expression I'm used to seeing on her face, this troubled brow, only it's on mine now.

"Amy," I repeat. "We're so close, and we're drenched and we're cold. Let's go."

At this she seems to wake, turning a horrified face to mine. "We can't go there," she says. "There's no way. We can't. Not like this."

"What else can we do?"

She flings her hands up in the air, "Literally anything else. Stay here. See a doctor. Call 999. I don't know, Flynn, but we can't turn up to my sister's wedding weekend, the wedding weekend she's been planning forever, the wedding weekend that I need to go perfectly, like this. 'Oh hi, Laura, sorry we're late but I'm just STUCK IN FLYNN'S BODY RIGHT NOW.' "

She is panting as she finishes the sentence, pacing now, mud splattered up the diamond socks, every muscle clenched. I can see she is going to lose it again, and that thought makes me stressed too. But I take a breath, suppress the feeling as I always do.

"We need to just get there and figure out what to do," I repeat, unable to help clamping my arms around my body to try and stop shivering. "I need a sweater," I say, wanting to at least fix one problem. "And so do you." I might not look like me but I can still be practical, still try to fix things and help Amy. If I don't do something, I feel I might spin out of all control. Focusing on other people has always helped me to forget my own troubles.

I move to the trunk and open it up, unzipping my suitcase and pulling out a bottle-green sweater. "Put this on."

Amy looks at it for a moment and then takes it, peeling the polo shirt away and replacing it with the sweater. I take out my navy sweatshirt and wiggle into it, the sweatshirt coming down to my knees.

Simply being warmer has helped calm me. "We can't stay here," I say, gesturing to the muddy road and fields around us. The air smells of manure and aside from the field of cows there seems to be nothing around for miles.

Amy is quiet, taking long, slow breaths through her nose, her lips pursed together.

I take hold of her hand, which feels so peculiar, the palm coarser and about double the size. "Ames. We need to go. Please."

Her ringtone breaks the silence and fresh panic crosses her face.

"Oh my god, what are we going to do?" she says, head in her hands.

"Maybe this thing, whatever it is, will wear off, maybe, if we just get there, it'll work itself out." I'm grabbing at straws, panic swirling once more.

Her phone is still going and I can see her dithering with indecision.

"Amy, what else can we do? We just need to go somewhere and think. We don't have to say anything yet; the actual wedding's not for another two days. We've got time."

Amy bites her bottom lip. I can see she is relenting.

"Whatever we do," she says, "Laura *cannot* know. It's literally the last thing she needs. She's been so stressed and I know how much she wants things to go well. I cannot be the one to screw that up."

I nod, wanting to get off this road, away from the

buzz of flies and the smell of manure. Moving is best, otherwise we're just trapped here with our thoughts, and that has always scared me.

"Flynn, you cannot say anything," she stresses.

"I won't," I promise. "Maybe we'll wake up tomorrow and it'll just be a bad dream," I add hopefully, really wanting to believe that will be true. "And worst case we can see a doctor or dial 999 or electrocute ourselves on Monday. Deal?"

"OK, but you have to promise me you won't give the game away."

"I won't."

"I'm serious, Flynn."

"I know. You can trust me, you know," I say, feeling a familiar frustration flare up inside me.

"If this is going to work we've got to work together, we've got to listen to each other," Amy says.

Uncertainty nudges at my insides as I nod an agreement. We can work together: we're a couple, a team. Of course we can pull this off. Can't we?

22

AMY

This can't be happening. It's not real. And yet I'm standing, drenched, in a muddy, narrow lane in Devon, watching my boyfriend fiddle with my bra. He's complaining that it's uncomfortable and, even in the midst of this hell, I want to say "welcome to my world" like it's news to me.

I'm too preoccupied to do anything other than spiral. I don't want to keep driving to this wedding weekend; I want to drive to the nearest hospital, to force the doctors to investigate what has happened. But I can see my phone flashing and jumping with messages from Laura; I think of the months of planning, her nerves and her escalating worries, and feel myself split in two. My body aches when I think of letting her down. And if Flynn listens to me, and he's *promised* he will, maybe we can pull this off and get through it without anyone suspecting anything.

Flynn might be right that getting there will give us time and space to work out what exactly is going on, and how it can be fixed. Sometimes his endless optimism and refusal to dwell on anything negative grates, but in this moment I am clinging to it. Maybe a miracle will happen?

Watching Flynn, as me, move around to the driver's door and get in pulls me back to the present.

"What are you doing?"

Flynn turns, "I'm driving. You don't have a license."

"Flynn, you can't drive my car: you can't drive."

"I can drive," he says sniffily, flicking his long brown hair, "I just haven't been formally given my license yet."

I'm too overwhelmed to fight it, watching him settle in the driving seat, dress rucked up his thighs. A humming in my ears when it all gets too much. After he stalls for the third time, though, I'm brought back to earth. "Flynn stop, STOP!"

We lurch forward as he brakes.

"Out!" I say and my new deep voice makes me sound way more imposing than usual.

He drops his head, escaped tendrils falling around his shoulders. "I think there's something wrong with your clutch."

"Yes, you," I say, unclipping my seatbelt. For a second, I glance down and spot the photo of me, Laura and Dad. It makes me catch my breath.

I drive us the rest of the way in silence, large brown signs indicating where we need to go, the mile-long drive a canopy of lush greens, rolling fields sloping away in both directions, the bruised sky highlighting the enormous creamy white main building as we approach.

I can't help swallowing as our car sweeps around the driveway, spitting up pebbles, an enormous stone fountain spouting jets theatrically into the air. The place is absolutely extraordinary. Wide stone steps lead up to a grand gilt doorway, soaring pillars and floor-to-ceiling glass windows either side. Huge stone pots crammed with exotic plants in a riot of complementary colors are dotted along a terrace that wraps itself around the building. The website was grand, but nothing could really have prepared me for this place. My insides knot, imposter syndrome settling in.

Flynn hasn't noticed I've fallen silent, and I want to keep driving around this fountain and back down the driveway, back to my flat with the slanted eaves and the ordinary sized rooms and the normalcy of it all. I'm terrified for Laura—is my sister really getting married here?

As I look up, I notice a group standing outside the main entrance. My words trail away as I notice one figure has broken away from the others. Her arms are wrapped around her body, her head dipped into her chest as her curly brown hair, quite a few shades lighter than my own, blows wildly round her. My sister is one inch taller than me at five foot three, with narrower hips and the most toned arms you'll ever come across. She had no need for the wedding diet she had muttered about starting, burning a million calories a day in her high-powered job running the PR for a corporate finance company.

Right now she doesn't look high-powered and capable: Laura looks lost, a tiny figure in front of this preposterously big building, and my chest tightens as I think of all the conversations we've had over the last few months. As she hugs herself for comfort, I know I have to support her. I can't turn back now. Whatever has happened is bewildering, but for now I know I need to help make Laura feel less alone.

"Let's go," I say, a new confidence in my voice.

Flynn is also staring up at the building. Beneath the running make-up I must tidy up before he steps outside, he is ashen. "Flynn?"

I follow his gaze to the small crowd of people—my future brother-in-law Jay stands in the center of them, shaven head thrown back laughing.

"Flynn?" I frown.

He turns to me slowly, as if dragged back from another place.

"Alright?"

Has he had second thoughts that we can do this? Are we mad for trying to be normal when everything is so topsy-turvy?

He shakes his head, plastering a smile onto his face and making me think perhaps I imagined his worried look. Flynn doesn't worry like I do; nothing seems to make him stressed. I remind myself this is crazy for him too and I should cut him some slack.

"Really?" I ask, reaching across to gently touch his hand.

"Great," he says, quickly clapping my hands together.

I bite my lip, can't help noticing his eyes travel back to the same spot.

A couple look down at our car, and he flinches in his seat as they peer in our direction.

I frown, a prickle of unease creeping up my spine as the woman meets my eye and gives me the strangest look. Or rather gives Flynn the strangest look.

"Let's go," he squeaks from next door to me.

23

FLYNN

Amy is more composed, a determined jaw, the back of one hand banging her other palm as she lays out a plan of action.

"Flynn?"

I can barely hear her, wondering again whether I'm seeing things. How is it possible? The group have moved inside and I want to convince myself it wasn't who I thought. Worry stirs inside me. Jay told me he wasn't coming. That his brother would be best man instead. As if things aren't complicated enough.

"Flynn? Are you paying attention? Did you hear me? We just need to see Laurs, get to our room and work out what is going on. How we can fix things. Or at least talk about how we're going to get through the next few hours . . . Flynn?"

My passenger door is flung open and Laura is staring down at me, her mouth a thin line in her freckly face.

"Amy, why are you just sitting here? Where have you been?"

With a jolt I'm reminded again that I am Amy, not me. And perhaps that is why the expression on her face is new to me.

"Hey, Laura. Sister. My sister."

She blinks and ignores me, bending down to look across me. "Hey Flynn," the tone is sugary sweet, more what I'm accustomed to, "I didn't know you got your license! Can I steal Amy? Do you mind?"

"I do," Amy yelps, reaching across with a meaty arm to pin me back against the seat.

I smile up at Laura awkwardly. "She . . . he's . . ." I correct myself quickly, "he's just . . . keen . . . not to miss out."

"Well, I really need you," Laura says, her grip on my upper arm quite something. "Just a second," she directs back at "Flynn" and I am hauled out of the vehicle. "Oh my god, Amy," she shakes her head. "What do you look like? Is that a man's sweatshirt? You so don't have time to change now. Seriously, I need you, like, NOW. Patty is off the charts already."

"Laura, Laura, breathe."

"I just need a friendly face, someone I can tell this stuff to. You get it. She just lost it because the waiter didn't know what a bellini was and she wants him fired."

"Laura, relax, it's cool."

I'm not sure how I've managed it in one sentence, but Laura has gone from looking frantic to pissed off in a few short seconds. Her brown eyes have narrowed, and her mouth moves into what I can only describe as a snarl.

"It's not cool. You know I'm worried she'll terrify everyone. I need you to help mix with people, make sure Mum and Geoffrey are OK, they look totally lost . . ."

She only tails away because Amy has walked around the car, clumsily throwing an arm over my shoulder. "What are we talking about?" Amy says, her big hand gripping me nervously.

"Flynn, hey, I'm just talking to Amy," Laura says, barely concealing a sigh.

"Yes, Flynn. Laura was telling me about the challenges she is facing and I was telling her it'll be fine."

Amy's grip tightens on me. "And you've told her that you'll do everything to help, haven't you, Amy? You've told her that whatever problem, big or small, you've got it. You are here to be her port in a storm, her rock . . ."

"A rock," I mutter. "I can be a rock."

"Thanks, guys," Laura says, head tipping to one side, the most relaxed she's been in the last five minutes.

My shoulders drop.

"Laura, babe." We're interrupted by Jay who has come jogging down the hotel steps, shaven head and the sunglasses he always wears perched on his head. "Mum says she needs you in the aviary, something about the bird man?"

Laura briefly closes her eyes before slowly rotating to face him. Jay freezes on the spot.

"But, do you know what, I'll go," Jay says, holding up both hands defensively and backing away with a grin, "my best love, my darling, my sweetheart."

He grins when he spots us.

"Flynn, mate, good to see you!"

I watch as he reaches forward and holds out a hand for Amy to shake. She just stares at it stupidly.

I step forward to save her, sticking out my own hand just as Jay moves to greet me. And he turns straight into my outstretched hand.

We all freeze and stare down at Jay's crotch and my hand. Jay steps back abruptly as Laura stifles a laugh.

Laura is the first to speak, "Um . . . Ames, did you just touch my fiancé's special place?"

"No!" I explode, "No! I . . ."

Laura starts laughing, Amy looks at me wide-eyed.

"It's fine, it's cool." Jay is flustered.

He steps toward Amy and in a low voice says, "Flynn mate, I need to have a word with you about something. Later," he says, glancing back at me and then giving a significant look at a bewildered Amy. "Something's come up . . ."

My palms dampen.

Amy is still looking dazed and then seems to come to. "OK, Jay, my mate, my friend!"

Jay laughs. "Good to see you mate." Clapping her on the back he jogs back up the hotel steps.

Before I can think more about his words, an enormous blur of fur and energy comes rushing down the steps of the hotel, swerves me and practically bowls Amy over, two paws in the center of her stomach. It is now I learn what I would sound like if I screamed more.

Amy starts flapping her arms as Reggie jumps up on the green sweater, his large tongue now lolling out, his tail wagging enthusiastically.

Laura shouts, "Reggie! Down! Bad dog!"

Just pet him, I think, just before Amy grabs me and turns me into her tiny woman Human Shield.

"Desist!" she shouts, dancing around in diamond golf socks. "Desist!"

I reach forward and ruffle Reggie, forgetting all the madness for a moment as I relish the comfort of being around such an uncomplicated animal. He licks my face with his rough tongue and I laugh.

Laura calls out, "Down! Come on! Down! Flynn—deal with him. It is your job."

Amy's eyes widen in alarm and my heart goes out to her.

"I . . . I . . ." she is stammering, still backing away from where Reggie is now confusedly turning this way and that between us both, clearly caught in the confusion. Has he sensed what has happened? As Amy steps forward, knees knocking in my navy shorts, he curls his lip, his legs stiff as she approaches, and I'm fairly sure I have my answer.

"Let me take him up," I offer, steering Reggie away from a gaping Laura.

Laura frowns, "Ames, you're scared of dogs."

"I . . . I got hypnotized." I seize Reggie's lead and let him pull me away, slipping in Amy's silver pumps.

"Amy, wait," Laura calls.

"I'll be right back!" I call from over my shoulder. "It's cool!"

I cringe as I speed up the hotel stairs, just catching Laura's gabbled instructions.

"Flynn, can you go and help Jay with whatever he is doing? Amy!"

Laura catches me up in the foyer of the hotel, panting as I stand staring once more at the couple I spotted. The man, Eddie, hasn't noticed me in a dripping dress and sweatshirt to my knees, and I dive behind a marble bust as the woman he's with peers around.

Suddenly fingernails grip my upper arm and I am immediately dragged into a small side room, Reggie following on his lead. "Ames," Laura whispers as she squeezes past me.

I immediately realize, in horror, that it is a small toilet and Laura has just reached past me to lock us both inside.

"OK, seriously, thank god you're here, we need a time out . . ." she says, holding up her hand. "Then I need you to help me control Patty, she wants to release doves, Amy—"

"Patty," I say dazedly, alarm gripping me as Laura suddenly lifts the hem of her skirt and pulls down her pants. Oh my god. My eyes start darting frantically around the room. This is not happening. This cannot be happening. I want to turn and pummel my small fists on the wooden door to be released.

"Hello! Patty who I've been phoning you about every day for the last two months Patty. Mother-in-law. Planning this wedding like she's invading Cornwall. Won't let me do a thing. Has arranged eight thousand tasks before I'm allowed to walk down the aisle. The woman who booked this venue because it had flamingos! That Patty."

"Yes, yes, of course," I squeak, reaching for a pot of potpourri to hide behind. Don't look, Flynn, just look anywhere but at her.

"Current obsession is the shape of the dovecote. Do you even know what a dovecote is? No! Who does? I— Amy? What are you doing?"

I'm cringing behind the bowl of potpourri which I now sniff at pathetically. "Just smelling this. It's nice," I say lamely, eyes now determinedly on the ceiling.

"Amy, seriously, what is with you? Get it together. Oh! Are you ready for your speech?"

I can't help a panicked glance down and then remember what Laura's doing and snap my eyes closed as I repeat, "My speech." Another thing to panic about.

Laura seems to have finished and stands up.

"Yes, your speech."

"All up here," I say, tapping my head with one finger, eyes still squeezed closed in case I see anything.

"Well, come on, weirdo," Laura says, squeezing past me and Reggie.

I pat him on the head, feeling flummoxed.

"OK, you weirdo." My version sounds more aggressive.

This is not a good idea. Amy was right, we should never have come.

24

AMY

This was a terrible idea. We should never have come. The dog, Reggie, has already worked things out and I haven't been able to plan with Flynn, or even get changed into dry clothes. He disappeared with Laura and I just wandered around the intimidating foyer with its chandeliers and gilt mirrors, damp and confused, before drifting back outside.

These diamond socks are sticking to my legs. Flynn looks completely ridiculous in my damp dress and his too-large navy sweatshirt. I should have at least wiped the running eyeliner from his face.

I barely take in my surroundings as I search for Jay around the side of the enormous building and down the wide stone steps to a manicured lawn. The least I can do is follow Laura's instructions and help him. If I can just get through this evening, maybe we can work out how to swap back. It has to be temporary, it has to be.

Just then Geoffrey and my mum appear in front of me, Mum's heels sinking into the wet grass, her eyes big behind her leopard-print glasses. They've been together for the last few years, but it still sometimes shocks me to see Mum with another man. Geoffrey could not be more different from Dad, too, softly spoken, studious. I've never really understood the appeal.

I step forward and fold her into a hug, "Mum."

"Oh." Her little squeak of surprise comes from where she is pressed to my chest. "A hug. How nice, Flynn."

Then I remember Flynn's never really hugged my mum before. He's more formal: a handshake or clap on the back. She pulls back, her glasses squiffy as she corrects them. Geoffrey, creases in clothes that are clearly brand-new, sticks out a hand, a Band-Aid on his thumb, and I simply stare at it. He coughs and drops it to his side. I realize a beat too late what I've done, but I'm too concerned about everything else to care. Geoffrey will cope.

Mum seems flustered. "What have you done with Amy?"

"I'm here, I'm here." Flynn is slipping down the grass in my silver pumps, Laura following shortly behind. I cringe as he scoots to an inelegant stop, startling Geoffrey who turns, just as Flynn sticks out a hand. The hand hits his groin and Geoffrey looks utterly flustered as he slowly shakes it. "Did you? Again with the—" Laura's eyes widen, and I swallow down a bark of shocked laughter. Flynn looks pale and small in my dress. Geoffrey is staring desperately round for something to say. Laura glances up at me and we seem to momentarily share the moment before she breaks my gaze.

"Isn't it pretty!" Mum announces over the awkwardness.

Well-dressed guests mill by the edge, rowing boats lined up neatly in the water behind them. The whole scene is stunning, the post-storm sky a wash of brooding purples and grays. The grass, bright with raindrops, makes the ground look like it's scattered with diamonds. In the shallows of the lake, four flamingos preen their pink-tinged plumage.

I stop, all my anxious thoughts momentarily disappearing, my worries this place is too much replaced by the beauty of this view. "Oh Laura," I say, stopping to place a hand over my mouth, my eyes filling, "It looks incredible."

Laura gives me a strange, lopsided smile and I remember she thinks I'm Flynn. That thought makes me want to cry. I haven't anticipated what it might feel like to be at this weekend, a weekend I know means everything to her, and not be with my sister. It might be absurdly fancy, but I know how much she wants to get married to Jay. "Let's get over to the island," Laura says, herding Mum with one hand.

"An island!" Flynn claps excitedly, making us all stare. "And flamingos! Wow, how exciting, my sister!"

I widen my eyes in the hope he might read my thoughts: tone it down. Could we sneak away and try to swap back while the guests are distracted? We head over to the line of boats on the lake and gingerly step on board.

My mum, Geoffrey and Laura all look expectantly at me as we settle on the hard wood. I'm distracted by Flynn who has sat with his legs wide apart, my pants practically on show. I splutter and cough, hoping he might notice and fold his legs. After a pause I realize everyone is expecting me to row the boat.

"Ah! Right! I love boats!" I say, seizing the oars in my hands, surprised all over again at how things feel in this new body, my hands wrapping easily around the wood, my arms moving assuredly as we lurch away from the side. "Oops! Sorry!"

"You OK there, Flynn?" Flynn says placing one hand over mine. "You need to do them both at the same time."

"Thank you, Amy," I say pointedly. "I had worked that one out all on my own."

"I'm just trying to help." He smiles sweetly. "Because we're a team," he adds.

"We are," I say, gritting my teeth as I lose my rhythm once more.

Insects skitter along the surface of the water as we make our way slowly toward the center of the lake.

I am concentrating so hard on what I'm doing, amazed by the strength in these arms, that I barely hear Laura's voice at first.

"So, is it long? Your speech?" she asks Flynn who is trailing a hand in the water.

I freeze in horror. In all the madness I'd forgotten the crucial fact I was making my speech tonight. Flynn sits up quickly, rubbing at his chin in a way that makes my sister frown.

"Quite short," he says. My eyes widen as we meet each other's gaze; one oar slips. "But really meaningful!" he adds, seeing the severe line of my mouth.

Laura visibly relaxes and I send out a silent thanks to Flynn for averting the first crisis.

My speech.

Oh my goodness.

My insides bubble with acid as panic grips me once more. Shall I turn and row us back?

"So, Geoffrey, how's the boules team getting on? Any direct hits on the cochonnet?" Flynn asks as both Laura and Mum share a look between themselves.

"Not yet, Amy," he chuckles. "Last week I missed it by a whisker."

"You'll get there," Flynn says. "And I imagine you're riding high after Portsmouth's result last week? They're transforming under that new manager. I mean," Flynn suddenly coughs and straightens, noticing my bewildered face perhaps? "I mean, I think they are . . . Flynn was telling me. You know me, *Match of the Day*, whoosh," he says, motioning over his head with his hand. "Match of the huh?" His bark of laughter sounds particularly high-pitched in my mouth, and people in nearby boats crane round.

I focus on rowing, the boat rocking with my nerves. Don't make anything worse, Flynn, I pray.

"Laura . . . you look nice. I like your . . . shoes," he says, giving me a hopeful glance. For a second I soften. He is clearly trying.

"Thanks," Laura says, crossing her feet in the boat.

"They were on sale," she says, glancing quickly at Mum. "Ames, do you need to run through what you're going to say?" she adds.

"Yes, yes I do," Flynn says slowly, not able to meet her eye. "I'll practise it with Flynn. He's heard a lot of it already, obviously . . ."

This seems to satisfy Laura and I'm relieved to feel the gentle bumps of the boat on the small pier of the island. I help them climb out and Laura disappears to say hello to the guests, fairy lights dotted around the tables and chairs.

"OK," I say, dragging him to one side once Mum and Geoffrey have left, my whispers urgent. "The speech."

He nods up at me earnestly. It's still surreal to be talking to myself. Normally I'm obsessed with the two lines between my eyebrows that I'm convinced are already forming grooves, even in my mid-twenties, but now I have to admit I can't even notice them as I look down at my face.

"So . . ." I begin, guests passing behind us as they disembark. I reach and straighten the knotted headband in his hair which has slipped to the side. A girl passing us frowns at this sight.

"I had a whole speech planned," I say. "I could write it down, the CliffsNotes at least, so you can just stick with the script."

"Great," Flynn says, tugging nervously on his dress.

I stare at him, he stares at me and then I widen my eyes. "So . . ." I gesture impatiently at him.

He looks blank.

"Where's my phone?"

Flynn frowns. "Back in the car."

"Why would you leave it there?"

"How is that my fault?"

"You were the one who left it there, Flynn!"

"It's literally your phone, Amy!" His tone matches my own.

"But you were last using it."

"Where would I even put it?" Flynn asks, exasperated, as he pulls on the fabric of my tea dress. "Where are the pockets in this thing?"

"Oh my god," I say, starting to panic again, my chest constricting. "Oh god, oh god."

Flynn looks worried. "I have a great memory, just tell me it," he says as I start to flap my hands at my side. A nearby man glances over as Flynn reaches to calm me. "Amy," he repeats, "come on. We're a team, remember?"

"OK," I say, breathing through my nose, "OK, OK." I try to pull myself back to the present, to focus. "The most important thing is thanking the guests for coming, and thanking Patty because she's footing the bill, but obviously don't say that part . . ."

"Gotcha," Flynn says, blinking rapidly.

"I also wanted to thank Mum because, well, it's Mum . . . and, well, I was going to say something about . . . about Dad."

I pause, Flynn still looking at me earnestly as I swallow. I had wanted to make this speech. I had wanted to say these things. In all my worries about feeling out of place, I knew one thing: that I loved Laura more than anything and wanted to make her proud, make up for things. Breathing out slowly I continue, pushing these thoughts down. "But maybe just talk a bit about Laurs and Jay, how good to see them together, looking so relaxed and hap— Flynn . . ." I say, aware that Flynn is no longer staring at my face but gaping at something over my shoulder.

More guests disembark behind us.

"Flynn?" I hiss, smiling and trying to look relaxed as people amble past.

Flynn doesn't seem to be listening and it makes me bristle. Doesn't he understand how important this is? We need to get this right or risk ruining Laura's night. He is always so infuriatingly laid-back; life doesn't come so easily to the rest of us.

Then I look down and notice his hands are clenched, knuckles whitening. My eyes widen in surprise. The whole stress of this change, the idea of this upcoming speech, is clearly affecting him too. I vow to cut him some slack.

Flynn's gaze has followed two of the guests off a nearby boat. I glance briefly at them both. I recognize the man as Eddie, Jay's best man and someone they went to school with. His Roman nose in profile, a muscular arm around a girl reminds me he only just gave up playing semi-pro rugby.

The girl's familiar but I can't place from where. Blonde and slender, taller than me but still dwarfed by Eddie, she's wrapped up in a gorgeously soft, pale pink pashmina, her mouth in matching lipstick moving as she speaks, her hands animating every word.

Then suddenly she stops as she sees me looking at her. An expression crosses her face, her eyebrows lifting in acknowledgment, as if we've known each other forever. As if Flynn has known her forever. It makes me frown.

As the sun disappears behind another cloud I shiver, wondering what this night will bring.

25

FLYNN

The island looks pretty, and Amy looks incongruous walking around it in my golfing attire. She also keeps making comments about the "vintage" wedding theme, the gold candlesticks on the tables, the parchment place settings, the lace place mats to a bemused Laura.

"The distressed wooden chairs really make it," she gushes, a hand reaching for one. Laura turns and gives me a lopsided "what about this guy, eh?" smile and I just panic and add, "They don't look upset," and then laugh.

Laura frowns and I snap my mouth closed, reaching for my second bellini in as many minutes. I'm not sure what's in one and they're not serving beer.

Amy isn't sitting with me and I watch, terrified, as I see who is sat opposite her at her table. Could this weekend get any more screwed up?

The first course moves by in a haze, Geoffrey trying

to ask me about the Bristol housing market as the island gradually blurs at the edges. I drink and brood about the weekend I had wanted. I think of the ring secreted in my bag. I think of the woman sat opposite Amy: Tanya is here. Tanya is here with Eddie. With Eddie. He would have known. My knuckles whiten as I clutch my glass.

"Would now be a good time to buy, then? Or will interest rates fall, do you think?"

Geoffrey is still talking houses.

"Yes . . . do . . ."

"Buy?"

"Why not!"

Geoffrey nods earnestly.

Suddenly Laura is nudging me and I realize with a cold shock that it's time for me to make "my" speech. As I go to stand, the world tilts. How many drinks have I had? It didn't seem a lot, but then I think of my new petite frame and feel a dread that maybe I have miscalculated.

Clutching the table with two hands, the coral nail polish blurring, I stare round at the small crowd, their faces glowing in the evening light. Even I can see the setting is perfect and for a few sentences I think I'm doing well.

"Isn't this setting perfect," I say, remembering to turn to Laura and smile.

Her own is frozen in place and this makes me more nervous, and I search once more for Amy's face. I get the familiar jolt when I see my own pale face staring back at me, my dark brown hair sticking up. I really should have shaved before we left, and my golf gear makes it look like she's the only guest who has decided to come in fancy dress.

Licking my lips, I try to remember what she had urgently whispered to me when we got off the boat. I'd told her I had a great memory. I do have a great memory, but everything feels sluggish and hazy.

"Patty," I practically shout. "None of this could have been possible without Patty."

Patty swivels, her steel-gray bob stiff in the breeze, and accepts a handful of claps. "She has master-minded so many of the details this weekend and . . . and . . ." Past conversations with Amy suddenly spring into my head, none of them particularly flattering. Patty phoning after midnight to discuss the color palette, Patty insisting on hymns in the non-religious service, Patty sending passive-aggressive emails about the appropriate and proper way to manage a wedding. "She is . . . she has . . . flamingos . . . so much . . . you see . . ." I trail away.

My head starts spinning, mouth dry. Looking around, I can see a lot of mouths gaping, while others wait expectantly. Trish starts nodding encouragement at me, making a "go on" motion with her hands.

"And I need to also thank Trish, well," I correct, "that's how you all know her but to me she's just Mum, plain Mum. Mummy, the Muminator," suddenly doing a strange Terminator expression, "so," I clear my throat, reaching for a glass of water and finding it empty. "To you I say, you're great. Really cool. So . . . thanks . . . thanks for being a good mum. And . . ."

Oh, I know this is important, but somehow everything I say sounds like I'm ridiculing someone. Should I mention Amy's father? This thought feels too big for me in this moment. And last time Amy mentioned her dad it had ended up in a row. She had pushed me for more about my own father, beyond the fishing trips and the sporting anecdotes.

"I also want to raise a glass to absent friends," I say quietly. "I know Robert will be looking down and seeing his two beautiful daughters on this special occasion. I know he'll be thinking how fantastic they both look. Amy," I say, realizing my mistake as I do so, "Amy, he'd say. Amy, I love you."

I pause, my thoughts confused, wondering why Laura has shifted slightly in her chair away from me.

"Right. Well. Thank you," I say, and down my drink, a distinctly uneasy feeling washing over me I sit down to a rather muted set of clapping.

"You just managed to make it a million times worse, Flynn." Amy throws up her hands behind a tree trunk out of sight of most of the party.

"I'm shorry, I panic-hic-ed." I cover my mouth with a hand, the coral nails blurring in front of me. My stomach churns. I feel a terrible pang as I see my stubbled face fill with unfamiliar unshed tears.

"You managed to make the speech all about me and not Laura. She'll think I've stolen the focus. Again."

"I'm really shorry," I say, hearing the words on a delay and trying to blink away my drunkenness. I want to lie down now. I used to tease Amy for being a lightweight, but this doesn't feel at all funny. I think I was this drunk once when I was about fourteen and had no clue how much alcohol made me feel out of control. I feel sheepish as I stumble to the boat, leaning heavily on Amy, ashamed I'd been rude to her in the past about this and finding it peculiar that she is the one having to shepherd me.

She half props me, half drags me there, the silver pumps even more slippery. Why don't women's shoes have sturdier soles?

"It came out wrong," I mumble. "Also I think I told Geoffrey to buy a house."

"What?"

"I was being you."

"God, we need to get back," she hisses and steps inside an idling boat. "We have to swap back." She turns to offer a hand. I'm not used to her helping me and I ignore it and step into the boat, which rocks. Huffing, she sits down and, in slow motion, that movement is enough to throw my balance off more.

Slowly I tip backward, watching the horrified faces of the guests as my arms windmill helplessly. Feeling the shock of the icy water as I land with a splash. Reeds cling to every part of me as I emerge pedaling furiously to get out of the lake. Something slimy brushes against my bare leg, dress floating up to the surface.

"EEL!" I scream. "EEL!"

I realize, for the millionth time, that we should never have come.

26

FLYNN

Ten Years Ago

I found out later Eddie had put it on Facebook. That was how strangers found out about it. It was meant to have been a low key party, just the touring cricket team, the night before we were flying to Barbados. But then unfamiliar people started wandering in through the open door, and trashed the place. Wine and beer stains, ruined sofa cushions, smashed vases, photo frames, and, finally, Dad's urn.

It's at that point that someone says gross and someone talks about their granny and after that they leave. Jay gets rid of them. I've never seen him get so angry at Eddie. He almost punches him on the nose.

Mum gets back late. She steps inside, stops short, and takes it all in. Almost every carpet or surface is stained or ruined. She doesn't get angry or make me clean up. She doesn't rail about thoughtless teenagers. She doesn't look at me. She wordlessly packs a small bag and leaves for the Gloucestershire house, messaging Pauletta to work extra hours to fix it the next day.

I stay up through the night. I clean everywhere, I get through trash bag after trash bag, I sweep up broken crockery, I vacuum. Always my eyes move to the ash. I can't clean in there.

I stay and scrub every corner as the day dawns, as Pauletta arrives and tries to make me eat. I scrub and clean until my train to Heathrow. Pauletta pats me on the back as I go.

"You good boy."

I don't cry, don't reach out to envelop her in a hug. Those feelings no longer come. I do what I always do. I poke my tongue out and pretend to be a dog. "Good boy."

Dad's urn.

Pauletta smiles sadly at me and that makes me feel worse, so I turn and leave.

I get the train to Heathrow and meet the other cricketers at the airport. Jay is there, his mum kissing him on the cheek, his dad rolled in in his wheelchair, his hands trembling as Jay leans down to shake his hand goodbye.

"How did your mum react?" Jay asks, pushing his glasses up with one finger.

I think back to Mum's blank face as she took in the devastation.

"She was cool about it," I say, seeing the familiar

expression of Jay relaxing. "Do you think we're going to get smashed around the field this week?"

Jay smiles easily, "I am! You, not so much."

I laugh in response, relieved as ever that my diversion has worked yet again. I swallow down the desire to tell Jay everything. That even destroying our house didn't move my mother to any kind of reaction. That I don't know what to do to get her to care. For a second the urge is so strong that my stomach twists in pain.

"You OK, mate?" Jay notices.

"Hungover," I say quickly.

Jay slaps me on the back.

So easy.

Everyone is waving, the boys a mixture of embarrassed awkwardness and pleasure. I see Eddie's mum in a cashmere coat blowing him a kiss. And I get a yearning for a face in the small crowd to focus on me, to have someone hold me close and tell me they'll miss me, they love me, that they want me to message the moment we land.

I stare down at my phone, scroll to my mum's name. There is nothing. Something freezes over in my chest as the letters blur.

The tour goes well. I'm awarded Player of the Tour and the lads remember my birthday. We drink beers and Jay throws up behind the hotel. Eddie gets off with half of a touring netball team from an all-girls' school. Eddie's a bit pissed at me; the coach has hinted I'm going to be made captain in our last year.

Every solitary moment though, in the shower or in the room when the others have gone down for a meal,

I can't help thinking back to Mum's face when she took in the ransacked house. What did she feel? Surely, she'd felt something. I know how I'd felt when I saw the mess, debris, and, worse, so much worse, the urn. I broke something sacred; I feel so broken inside. Surely, she wanted to scream, to hurl abuse at me, do something. Or am I truly that small, that invisible? I torture myself with these questions in every quiet moment. My anxiety returns, feeling acid in my stomach, chewing on my inside cheek until the pain makes my eyes water.

Everyone's picked up from the airport and I hurry past them quickly, following the signs to the underground.

Jay looks at me thoughtfully. His mum is telling him to come along.

"You want a lift, mate?"

For a worried second I think he sees right through me.

"Mum's just messaged me from the drop point; she's waiting in the car." I wave my phone and quickly move away.

Jay keeps his eyes on me. Does he know? He's never said anything over the years, but sometimes he gets that look. Like he's going to say something serious. I get into an elevator to the drop point and, as it descends the two flights, the emotion that builds in me seems unable to be contained in the small steel space. I want him to ask. I want someone to work it out. I can't keep this in anymore. I can't do it.

Blinking, I stumble out of the elevator, my vision tunneling, my breaths quicker. I have to sit on a concrete divider just outside, watch people wheeling suitcases, shouldering bags, calling to loved ones, slow my thrumming chest. So many units, families, frustration, love. An airport shuttle bus approaches. If I stepped into its path, how many days would it take my mum to notice I hadn't returned?

The travel home makes me feel bone tired. I let myself into the London house, restored by Pauletta so you'd never know what had happened. Glossed over like everything in this family.

Mum is in the kitchen and, when I appear with my cricket bag over my shoulder, my suitcase behind, she looks surprised. I realize she didn't know when I was coming back.

And that fact makes everything I've been feeling in the last few days, since the party, over the last few years, come spilling out in an ugly, messy, snot-filled roar. I step toward her, arms out, pleading with her to listen.

"I'm sorry. I'm sorry about the party. About Dad's, Dad's ashes."

She flinches then the mask is replaced, and that strange blankness descends. "Stop this. Pauletta tidied."

"You should be angry. You should shout at me. Why won't you shout at me?"

She starts to look around her as I approach. A strange moment, all gangly six foot two of me, my mother no longer a woman I stare up at. I still want her to hold me, to bundle me into her arms, to love me.

I cry, years of tears that have been stoppered up inside me. Her eyes widen in alarm.

"Don't, Flynn. You're tired. Go up, sleep."

"I don't want to sleep. I need us to talk. I need you."

I will her to break down too. Where is the woman of my memory? The one who bundled me into her lap when I was small, who whispered love into my hair? She died when Dad died. It's like I'm not here either. I need her to see me now, to remember that she loved me. Fiercely. That she shouted at Rory's mum when Rory hit me, when she ran with me into the hospital with my fractured arm, when she held me next to Dad's bed as I said goodbye. I need that woman, that mother.

"Don't, Flynn. Stop this. Don't. You're being spoiled and awful. The world doesn't revolve around you and your feelings. I've given you everything. You are lucky. Your father would be embarrassed."

That stops my tears. Stops her words. I can't breathe in the silence that follows. Would he have been embarrassed of me?

"I can't remember him. I make up stories about him. I can't remember Dad," I admit, my face wet.

"Of course you can," she says, her mouth twisting. "How dare you."

I shake my head, "I can't. It's just a nothing. A man from a photo, a mix of clothes. I can't remember him, Mum."

"Stop this." She is finally angry. "For fuck's sake—be a man."

Despite me telling Eddie and Jay stories of him whenever they talk about their dads. Their families. They think I'm lucky—no curfew, no overbearing parents, and a dad who I've made out to be a legend. All the stories fabricated by me; all I have is a blurred image, old photos, and a feeling that I was loved. The rest is a strange blank where memories used to be.

Be a man.

She leaves me there in the kitchen panting, tears soaking the collar of my top. She leaves me in there, my chest wide open as I sink to my knees, entirely spent.

Be a man.

I hear the front door shut as she leaves the house.

Be a man.

From that moment to now we haven't spoken about anything real.

27

AMY

Not only did Flynn not listen to my instructions but he managed to make things worse. He made me out to be this self-obsessed, drunk narcissist. Then falling into the lake ensured anyone who didn't think the evening had been hijacked by me, definitely would now.

The sun is setting as I row him back in furious silence. Mum and Geoffrey are flanked either side saying things like "Well, that went well," "I did like the salmon." I can't contribute a word, too upset despite Flynn's teeth chattering comically in my soaked flowered dress. The sky is darkening, large clouds banking on the horizon, the sun lost beneath the silhouette of the hills, and I wish for the millionth time this thing hadn't happened to us.

He looks miserable but all I can see are the glances of the rest of the wedding party. I just need to get him far away so he can't do any more damage.

The moment we get to the other side of the lake, Laura hauls him off and all I see are her arms flailing and his head dangling, dripping curls, headband squiffy, a forlorn expression on his face. I can't face intervening; he deserves the telling-off and he wilts further as Laura turns on her heel and marches away. My chest aches as I see her hurt expression: Laura doesn't deserve this.

"Are you OK?" I ask her as she passes, attempting to assess how bad the damage is.

"Just peachy, Flynn."

I follow her over the lawn and back up to the front of the hotel. "I know Amy feels horrible," I say, talking as I traipse after her. "I think she'd had a lot to drink, she wasn't making any sense. I know how much she'd practiced her speech and that *wasn't* it."

Laura bit her lip, clearly forcibly restraining herself from letting rip. "Leave it, Flynn, OK . . ."

She takes the stone steps to the entrance of the hotel two at a time and I follow her inside. Our bags have been piled up on a nearby porter's trolley. It reminds me of the last few weeks, the things I've put together for this weekend. I've been so intent on being a great bridesmaid, stepping up this weekend to make up for so many other times recently.

"Wait," I say, holding her arm in the foyer, the air filled with the scent of beeswax and flowers.

"I want to give you something, I mean, I know Amy wanted you to have this" I say, moving quickly to my handbag, pulling out the photo of Dad, Laura, and me.

Seeing it makes her inhale sharply as she wordlessly accepts the frame, staring at the photo for an age.

"I love that picture," she says softly, a finger reaching to lightly touch Dad's face. "We lost the negatives, Amy has the only copy."

"I know," I whisper. Why didn't I ever think of giving it to her before now? Why have I assumed her grief over him is any less than mine? My throat closes, the emotion forcing me to clamp my lips together to stop the tears forming as she traces our outlines.

Just then Flynn emerges through the heavy gilt doors. Laura bristles as he makes his way across to us, my tea dress practically see-through, a sad path of wet footprints on the marble floor in his wake.

He is still drunk, his eyes unable to focus as he gives us both a wobbly smile through damp tendrils of hair.

"Flynn was showing me this," Laura says stiffly. "Thank you," she adds, swallowing. "I love it."

Flynn looks lost and I grab at his arm. "Let's get you upstairs and changed," I say loudly, steering him away from Laura before he can say anything and ruin this tentative peace.

"I think I was sick on someone wearing a kilt," he mumbles to me.

Oh for . . .

Dolefully I check us in, feeling guilty about allowing the hotel porter to take our bags. I only have Flynn to manhandle. He leans on me all the way up to our room along the first floor.

"Please don't throw up on the carpet," I say, opening the door on a sea of pristine whites, creams, and grays.

There are sprigs of fresh lavender on the pillows, the

duvet expertly turned down, the softest linen sheets. I steer Flynn into a cream bucket armchair and then move across the room to pull the soft gray curtains closed, the heavy fabric blocking out the night sky now pockmarked with stars. From our window I can make out the silhouette of the island on the lake, the fairy lights still shining from here. I feel like crying once again. I wanted to share in this weekend with Laura, I wanted to create nothing but perfect memories.

If this evening has taught me anything, it's that we must do everything we can to turn back.

"I can't believe you got drunk," I say quietly, looking at Flynn slumped in the armchair.

"It'sh not my fault it takes three drinks and you're gone," he says, standing up, both arms out to the side like he's on a tightrope.

"Three?"

"Amy, the room is spinning,"

I put my head in my hands and pace as he collapses starfished on our bed, dress rucked up, knees wide, my pink pants on display. Just then there's a knock and I leap up to let the porter in, quickly pulling Flynn's dress down as I pass. The porter can't stop a smirk at me as he places our bags down and exits discreetly. I feel a flush of anger at him.

"Oh my god, we have to switch back," I say in a puff of frustration.

"What do you want me to do?" Flynn slurs, arms flung up to the sky from his prone position on the duvet. "Go out in another thunderstorm? Electrocute myself with the hotel hairdryer?"

"I don't know, Flynn, but we can't stay like this."

"Let'sh try and get shome shleep, we can work it out tomorrow," he mumbles, and I know he is already dropping off.

How can he even think of sleeping at this moment? Not that I have another solution. What can we do? Should I just leave? Why has this happened?

"OK, let's try and sleep, and when we wake up this will all be over, we'll have swapped back," I say, my voice steady as if I could fool myself with this confidence.

"And if we don't?" he mumbles.

"Then," I say, sitting down next to him, "Then we'll . . ."

But the next thing I hear is a snore and I know he's already out.

28

AMY

Ten Years Ago

Dad's going to come along. He promised. I tug on my skirt, feeling over-dressed in the small, grimy space, my insides leaping about with the knowledge of what I'm about to do. I want to rush back to the toilet, splash my face for the fourteenth time, consider vomiting, but instead I clutch the sheet of paper and take a breath. Brian has told me to just take my time and go when I'm ready. I want to wait for Dad. I can't imagine doing this without him in the small crowd. I picture the thumbs-up he'll give me, the proud talk to his neighbor. "That's my girl. The songbird."

I crane my neck as the pub door opens and some man arrives in an enormous black cowboy hat. I realize it's Dad and I frown, slow to understand what it means. He

117

reaches me and, as I see what he's holding, the frown deepens. My voice when it comes is suspicious.

"What's with the hat?"

"It's for our bit," he says, smiling at me.

Something lodges in my stomach and my tongue feels too big in my mouth as I say, "We talked about this last night. We're not doing a bit."

He is waving at a couple of regulars like he hasn't heard me and my mind swirls with what to say next. I don't want to hurt his feelings. Dad's always been my number one fan, but he knows how important tonight is, how much I want to forge an identity as a singer/songwriter.

"I thought we could do Jackson. Wearing this for the occasion!"

He is asking me to be the June Carter to his Johnny Cash. Dad loves country music; we've got cassettes and CDs of every living and dead county singer—Tammy Wynette, Hank Williams, John Denver, Billie Joe Spears. His voice is low and gravelly, his natural Bristol twang replaced with a Southern drawl. I love some of the songs too, but it's not the direction I want to go in. I write my own music now. I've already made a single, but for some reason I have yet to show it to Dad. I inwardly squirm at the thought.

I want to write more, make an album. And tonight is part of that. Dad *knows* it and yet here he is. Is the hat just a way of making me feel even more like I can't say no?

"Just the one number. We could do 'Walk the Line' if you like? You love that one."

118

He reaches across and sticks the hat on top of my head and for some reason this triggers something inside me. I feel stupid and small and like everything is spinning out of control. A red-hot anger flares in my chest.

"Dad, don't."

I pull off the hat and it falls to the ground. My breathing is heavier as I see his face shadow. A couple of people glance our way and I smooth my hair self-consciously. He picks the hat up wordlessly.

"I've brought the backing CD. I'll just get on and . . ."

I can't believe he's doing this. I'd psyched myself up for weeks to finally tell him last night. He'd promised me he'd understood. He'd promised.

"Dad. I don't want to sing it."

"It'll be great, Ames, we've always done Wednesdays here together."

We have. I've sung with Dad in this pub since my legs dangled off a stool and the bar manager had to talk to Dad about licenses and underage children. We must have sung 200 covers now—at one point there was talk of putting our photo up behind the bar. I was half appalled by the thought, half gutted when it didn't happen. Dad was always the engine behind our duo—entering us into karaoke contests, buying sheet music for us to practice, CDs to sing along to. I have a part-time job at an estate agency and work on my music—Dad never asks me when I'm going to move out. He wants me close. Mum gets cross, thinks I need to stand on my own two feet, but Dad tells her I'm working on our music and she relents.

119

And it's easy. No rent to pay, these nights with Dad, composing in my bedroom, Laura complaining about her nine to five, saving every penny for her big move to London. "Of course, you only work twenty hours. Of course, Mum is making you a special drink for your throat." A small part of me knows the situation can't go on forever, I can't just put off the real world, I have to be brave. Recently I've been thinking more and more about how that might look, and last night I told Dad I was going to sing something on my own. I was going to sing an original number.

My sweaty palm closes over the scrappy lined paper folded in my pocket, the ink blurring a little with the warmth but the words written on the inside of my brain I've practiced them so much these last few weeks. The melody circling my head when I'm waking and sleeping. Excitement sparks inside me. This will be the first night I can see how an audience might feel. For a second I think I really might vomit. And now Dad is here, not to watch me, not to support me, as he promised, but bringing this absurd hat, clutching CDs in his hand, dragging another stool up onto the tiny wooden platform that Brian grandly likes to call the stage but is in fact a piece of rectangular wood six inches off the ground.

"Dad," I hiss. "Seriously, stop!"

He throws a comment over to the barman and places the stool in place.

I move across to him. "I said I was going to sing one of my own tonight."

"Shall we start with 'Walk the . . .'" He is putting a CD in the system.

My voice rises, "I'm not going to sing with you, Dad!"

A few more faces glance our way and Dad's shoulders go rigid.

"Course you are."

"I don't want to stay singing in shitty pubs with my dad. I told you. I want to be a singer. A *real* singer. I made a single."

"A single—"

I register the surprise, then the hurt in his eyes.

But then I watch him step onto the platform and settle himself on one of the stools. I can't believe he's actually doing this, that he's just ignoring what I want. My head buzzes. He's making me look so stupid. I can see some of the regulars looking at me. I fold my arms and deliberately step back among the other pub-goers, too angry to be really embarrassed.

Does he think I'm just going to give in and join him? We don't fall out, Dad and I—Mum and I scrap a bit, but I'm a daddy's girl. The spitting image of him. He's left the empty stool on his right and the pitiful sight almost makes me follow him up there. But I'm pissed off and need him to understand how important this is to me. He's always encouraged me, but I realize now his hopes for me have limits—he wants me to stay singing in his small corner of Bristol. I want more.

He lifts the microphone to his mouth as the first verse kicks in and the pub fills with the familiar song. His voice doesn't waver, but his eyes lock onto me. I know how much he loves us singing together. He'd always wanted to be a professional, but he told me there was no way his old man was going to let his only son be a singer. He needed a real job, a man's job, something to support a family. So my dad trained as a joiner, and only after his own dad died did he start to sing again.

He taught me from the moment I could talk and took me along to early gigs. I'd watch him up there, listen to his crooning confidence and delight in the applause he received. I was addicted to the places—the yeasty, sweet smell of a pub, the jostling at the bar, the comments chucked back and forth. I started to sing with him and we became infamous in the places we sang. This thought makes me bite my lip. At the same moment his voice falters—can he see how angry and upset this is making me? Does he care?

And then I watch in horror as his eyes widen, as he clutches at his chest, as the mic falls to the floor.

Before my brain can register what is happening a few meters away from me, he is falling sideways, his whole body collapsing, patrons giving shocked gasps as he crumples to the ground. There is total silence for a beat, only the sound of the backing track as it waits for my dad to continue the song. My throat clamps up, my vision wobbles. He will start, any second, any second he'll stand back up and sing the line.

Then a mad rush forward, names being called, an ambulance being summoned. And me standing in the center of the crowd, totally dumbstruck. The lyrics of my song fluttering to the floor as pub-goers stamp around me, as someone's arm draws me away, my shaking hand as someone offers me water. As I start asking for him, shouting for him, eyes swiveling as I search for him. And seeing him, a glimpse, through the gaps of people's legs. His eyes open, staring right at me, unblinking, nothing in them at all. Someone bends over him blocking my view. My dad. My dad.

29

FLYNN

Need water.

Need water.

Ow, doorframe. Who put it there?

Water.

Need light. Not our bathroom. Hotel.

As the bathroom floods into bright light, I step slowly toward the large mirror opposite and notice a number of things. There are spotlights around its edge, bouncing off the gray marble surfaces. There is a row of miniature bottles and some soap wrapped up in fancy paper. There is a figure looking back at me. Disheveled, dry-mouthed, clothes askew. I grip the edge of the sink and lean forward, resting my head against the glass.

I'm still Amy, then.

I close my eyes.

30

AMY

Flynn slept like a baby. Arms splayed wide (how is he still allowed to take up more of the bed even as a woman?), mouth agape, as I twitched next to him for half the night.

Flynn is better at being me than me.

When I wake he is not by my side; my hairy knuckles clutch the covers and I know we haven't swapped back. With a growing horror I feel what's happening beneath the duvet. I lift it up, staring in fascinated disgust at the pyramid.

"Oh my god," I whisper.

Leaping out of the bed, I stare down, pacing as if I can will it back down.

"Oh my god."

I make the mistake of glancing up and see my reflection in the bronze free-standing full-length mirror.

A bleary-eyed Flynn in a muddied top and triangular pants. I can't help but roar. Roar with fear and panic and misery.

Flynn comes running out of the bathroom in just my pale pink pants, "Amy, Amy, what's happened?" His eyes are wide, my dark brown curls flying.

Staring at my boyfriend trapped inside my body, I point manically at him. "THIS. THIS happened, Flynn." I clutch both hands to my head, surprised all over again by what I find. Short, thick hair in my fingers, a different-shaped skull. "I am YOU. I am a man. I am a MAN."

Flynn doesn't reply and this makes me crosser. Why is he so calm? What does ruffle the guy?

"Amy, let's just take it easy, OK . . ."

"Why are you so calm? Why aren't you PANICKING?"

"I *am* panicking. I just—there's no point shouting, is there? It won't help us."

The annoying logic of this statement only makes me want to chuck something at his head, but then I get the strange idea that it would be wrong to strike a woman and that makes me want to laugh and cry and collapse into a ball. I resort to sinking into the armchair in the corner and stare dumbly around the room.

"OK," Flynn says, pacing in front of me in my under-wear. This is beyond surreal. "So, we haven't changed back. So, we need to think about what we're going to do now."

He continues to talk, his feet sinking into the thick, soft cream carpet as he paces in front of the ruffled super king bed with its luxurious velvet headboard. I stare mesmerized at the large piece of modern art on the wall above it, all bold pinks and purples. It's a fluid, beautiful image, the color and lines swirling around each other on the cream canvas. Two figures intertwined so you don't know where one begins and one ends.

"We could bang our heads together? We could go on the internet and look up stuff to do with . . . with lightning . . ."

All the anger subsides as I stare at the figures in the painting, as if it is a dance between two people, who in that moment are becoming one. I remember what we are doing in this hotel room, the plush surroundings bringing home how special this weekend was meant to be.

". . . Or I could ring my Uncle Bernard. He knows so much stuff and he might know about this. He did physics at uni back in the day . . . OR . . . we could . . ."

"We have to tell them," I say in a quiet voice.

Flynn falls silent and stares at me.

"We have to come clean. If this, if this thing is permanent then they'll need to know anyway, right?" My voice is gruff, hesitant. I feel the weight of it all pressing down on my chest. Could this really be permanent?

Flynn has stepped across to me, and he kneels in front of me on the carpet, his hands on my thighs as he meets my eyes. "Amy," he says, his voice soft.

I look up at him, realizing my own are filming with unshed tears.

"Amy, it's not permanent. It's not, OK? We just need to work out what's happened and how we can change it back. You need to keep the faith." He squeezes my thighs and I find myself nodding, wanting desperately to feel his optimism.

Flynn is a glass-half-full person when I have to sometimes remind myself the glass has liquid in it. Sometimes this trait can get on my nerves, his ability to constantly see the positives. Right now, though, it's something for me to cling to. I need to believe him, that this isn't it, this isn't how my life is going to be.

Flynn's energy had drawn me to him; he had this charisma about him, this unchecked energy that meant extravagant hand gestures, big, throaty laughs, spilled drinks, and fun. After Dad I had lost a lot of my spark and being close to Flynn had helped make me feel more alive. I blink, realizing that for the last two weeks I've been convincing myself of all the reasons we shouldn't be together, not the reasons we work.

A rap on the door makes us both stiffen, and then we hear my mother's voice.

Not now, I think.

"Quick," I hiss, throwing half-naked me the throw from the bed. "Be me. Get rid of her." I dive back under the duvet so she is spared Flynn's morning glory.

Flynn pales as he wraps the throw around himself.

"You look like a vampire. Wear it like a towel!"

He doesn't hear, just opens the door to my mother.

"Mum!"

"Amy, honestly, the time! What are you," my mum takes in the throw cloak, "er, are you doing a skit? Do hurry, the minibus is leaving in five minutes . . ."

"Minibus?" I say, sitting up in bed, head spinning, voice gruff. It can't be that time already.

"Not for you, Flynn love," my mum says, "the boys leave in another half an hour. Oh, and do take care of Geoffrey—he is putting on a brave face about it but I think he might be a bit nervous."

This extra information only makes me worry more. What are the men doing today?

"The thing is . . ." I say, casting about for excuses.

"Is this yours, Amy?" Mum says, flinging open my suitcase. "Maybe pop this on?" She holds up a clean, cream summer dress as Flynn continues to stare at her. She shakes it at him. "Come on, Amy, chop, chop! Honestly, what *has* come over you . . ."

Flynn takes the proffered dress in a daze. "Thank you for this," he says stiffly.

I cringe at his robotic tone. Mum doesn't seem to have noticed.

"Oh, we mustn't forget your cozzie!" my mum says while I leap out of bed and drag Flynn into the bathroom as she returns to the suitcase.

"Hold on, Mum . . . Trish," I correct, locking the door behind us both. "Shit, shit, shit, shit, shit," I mutter as I pace.

Flynn has started circling in here again, the cream dress scrunched up in his hand.

"Put it on," I say, helping him step into it. "Where's my bra?" I ask, looking around the bathroom and seeing it abandoned over the towel rail.

There's a knock on the bathroom door. "Why have you locked yourselves in there? Honestly, you two . . ."

"Just going to the loo!" Flynn calls in my voice.

I cringe and he panics at my expression.

"I need a poo!" he adds, which only makes me slap his arm.

"Well, let poor Flynn out, then!" Mum exclaims as I now hit my own head with a hand.

"She was joking," I call back. "I just need her to help me decide what to wear." I shrug. Teamwork was definitely not making the dream work.

I quickly help Flynn into the bra and the dress. As I do I can't help the thought that I am smaller and less lumpy than I often imagined. It must be this strange new perspective, the fact my hand span is bigger, because I've worried about my weight on and off for years. The thought flies out of my head as Flynn continues to fret.

"Flynn, stop fidgeting." My new body means I can easily stop him, and I release his arm when the grip feels too much. A strange frisson seizes me, the awareness that I am physically dominant. It's a foreign feeling, but I can't help viewing Flynn as being more vulnerable as I smooth his curly hair back, my hair, tucking it gently behind his ears.

"Are we telling her?" Flynn asks, his voice soft as my mum shouts.

"Amy, come on now! Laura will pitch a fit. We *must* go."

There's another knock and we hear her footsteps, "Oh Laura. It's fine . . . Amy's just coming!"

Both our eyes widen as we hear Laura move inside the room. "Come on, Amy."

"Coming!" Flynn cries out in a strangled voice. "Shall I go?" he whispers urgently.

I close my eyes, the bathroom spinning. "I . . . I . . ." I don't know what to do. I can't think straight. I try to breathe. "OK, it's too late to decide now so let's just get through this morning. So, don't say anything, OK? And try to act like I'd act."

Flynn nods, "OK. How do you act?"

"AMY!" Laura shouts from outside, "Come on!"

"Flynn, you've seen how I act. Just be relaxed, treat Laura like she's your sister, you know, use nicknames, listen to her, just . . . be me."

"Be you," he repeats, his mouth quivering. His worried expression makes me soften.

"AMY!"

I ready myself to unlock the door as I call out to them both. "She's just coming."

I nod at him.

"COMING, DICKHEAD!" he shouts.

I frown.

"I was using a nickname!" he hisses, panicked.

"Well, maybe don't sound like you want to pickle her liver."

"COMING, dickHEAD!"

I cringe then readjust my face. "Maybe no nicknames."

I open the door to see Laura leaving. "I'll see you both down there," she calls.

"Amy, we really do need to go," Mum says.

Flynn nods at me, paler now. He steps out, adjusting the dress self-consciously as my mother says. "Great. Amy—I've got your cozzie!"

Flynn smiles nervously, "Can't wait," he squeaks. "Mum! Mummy!" Then, just before he follows my mother out, he grabs my arm. "Hey. What's a cozzie?"

Oh Christ.

31

FLYNN

I hurry alongside Trish down the red-carpeted corridor of the hotel, chandeliers twinkling. Amy and I need more time, to work out what to do. She tells me to act like her but I'm not sure I can—what does that mean? I think of all the things I know about houses and music and wonder if that will be enough.

I also realize I've left my cell phone behind—women's clothes never seem to have pockets, which is so annoying. I really need to check in with Karim and Bex about today's events—I shouldn't leave them to deal with magician disasters and angry clients on their own, even if my own world is in freefall.

"Amy, love, is all well with you and Flynn? You both seem a bit tense?"

Clenching my jaw, I wonder how to reply. Swapping bodies does tend to up the tension.

"Flynn's such a lovely boy, you laugh like I laughed with your dad. He's good for you."

I can't help but be a little cheered by this statement, back straighter. "That's a nice thing to say, Trish."

She gives me a strange look. "That's quite alright, Amy," she stresses my name. "I'm just glad," Trish adds. "I'm glad you've got him in case you—" She trails away, her face suddenly more serious, "Well, I'm just glad."

Trish doesn't seem like herself as she seizes my arm and links it through hers, squeezing me close.

"I love you, Amy."

I stiffen in her arms, my tongue too big in my mouth as I try to respond naturally. Why do I find being hugged by her so hard? "Thank you," I say stiffly.

Fortunately Trish doesn't react, "Let's go and get thoroughly spoiled!"

I nod and smile, relieved, and enjoy feeling her comforting figure in lockstep with mine. It's not something I'm used to, this intimate, conspiratorial way of walking, and I like it. We continue down the corridor to the wide landing and a shining staircase that separates in two sweeping curves to the ground floor.

Laura's anxious face looks up as we descend, as does a collection of other women Amy would no doubt recognize. A little apart from them is the woman I do know, the woman who should not be anywhere near this place.

Our eyes meet as I stumble down the stairs, glad Trish is holding onto me. She's tied her blonde hair up in a ponytail, light bouncing off her smooth skin. She gives me a strange half-smile and I don't return it, worry churning in me. I can't face any of that today.

"Here she is!" Trish trills.

Laura glances at me. "Kia, tell the minibus driver we are *finally* here."

I vaguely remember Amy telling me Kia was a second cousin. She gives me a rather frosty look as she darts out.

"Hi bridesmaids!" I say cheerily. Just stay upbeat, Flynn, be fun, be part of the gang! What did Amy ask? Be relaxed! Use nicknames! No, don't use nicknames!

"Let's go you, my sister, Laura!" I say to Laura, who gives me a strange look.

My head throbs, everything in the foyer sparkling back at me. Behind me, through large open oak doors, I can make out the groomsmen still lounging in the breakfast bar, the table rammed with half-full French presses, plates of croissants, pastries, and fresh fruit. The scent of coffee and warm dough clashes pleasingly in the air and my stomach growls.

"Can I grab something from the breakfast bar before we head out?" I ask brightly, turning to the doors.

Laura folds her arms. "If you'd been down when I asked, Amy . . ."

I glance back at the table longingly; Jay meets my eye and gives me a wink. The wink wrongfoots me. Jay and I don't wink at each other—we shake hands, we do the silent nod. I frown at him, feeling a headache coming on. Of course, the wink isn't for me. It's for Amy. I blink both eyes and he frowns. This is going to be a long day.

The minibus idles on the driveway as the gaggle of women carrying big woven bags head through the sliding door. Tanya is loitering, tying a shoelace that looks tied to me, and I avert my eyes as she brushes past me inside. Squeezing into a corner seat, glad that Trish followed me, I get the distinct feeling Tanya is trying to catch my eye.

There is heat in my belly. Leave Amy alone, I think furiously.

Closing my eyes, wanting the dull throb in my head to ease, I lean against the minibus window, the fountain in the center of the driveway still throwing its jets into the sky which is now cornflower blue, yesterday's storm forgotten, a bright day ahead.

"Off we go!" Trish says, squeezing my thigh under the cream dress and making me sit bolt upright in my seat. Trish has never squeezed my thigh before.

This is going to be weird, isn't it?

With no way of communicating with Amy, I'll have to think before I speak, stay alert, on guard. Act like her. Find out what a cozzie is before we get to the mystery destination.

I can do this. Whatever this is. I need to.

32

AMY

I need to pee and I've put it off for as long as possible. Sitting down quickly I try to pretend everything is normal and attempt to hum a song. Just don't look, Amy, you don't need to see it.

I know I can't hide in this room forever, but it's tempting to try. The claw-footed bath with its curved sides would be an excellent place to try and drown myself. I've never been that comfortable in water. Flynn tried to take me surfing last summer, which was not a success. Every time a wave appeared he'd disappear merrily over it and I'd get a mouthful of seawater, the surfboard smacking me in the nose.

Thinking of that day reminds me of other weekends with Flynn. Time away always seems to bond us. Idling along beaches, sharing chips in steamy newspaper, lounging on rugs listening to music from his speakers while he constantly stops me reading. He makes me laugh like no one else, and his childish pleasure in the everyday, his obsession with living in the moment can be a gift on those weekends. And yet I know I can't live in a bubble like that with someone for the rest of my life—it's not real. It's just for weekends. The grooms- men are still in the dining room when I appear in fresh clothes.

"Flynn," Jay waves from his chair. "Saved you a bacon roll. We're just leaving."

"Did Amy enjoy her midnight swim?" Eddie drawls, his ice-blue eyes mocking.

Guffaws of laughter make my skin bristle. Even Jay has joined in, which rankles.

"She was fine, thank you," I say snippily.

"Amy seems like a good-time girl," Eddie says, nodding like he knows me intimately. Which he doesn't.

"I'm not a . . . I mean," I clear my throat, "I'm not sure Amy would describe herself like that," I say, primly smoothing at my khaki T-shirt.

"Oh, you've tamed her." Eddie winks at me, making me grimace. "When did you become such a ladies' man, Flynny?"

Despite the teasing his eyes seem cold and I wonder whether Flynn ever really liked him at school, or if this is just the "banter" that men use as an excuse to hide behind.

"Hey, Eddie. Amy's cool," Jay says, and I feel a rush of surprised gratitude for him. Does Jay really think that? I take in his polished appearance, his expensive watch, his branded sunglasses. I've always held back trusting him completely, with good reason too, but this makes me reassess if I've got him right.

There is sudden barking and suddenly Reggie is making a beeline for me, leash dangling, my stepdad Geoffrey blinking at his empty hand in the doorway.

"My shoulder might never be the same again." Geoffrey steps forward, wiping his brow with one of the abandoned linen napkins from breakfast. A croissant flake remains on his forehead.

Reggie leaps onto me, forcing me to emit a squeak of alarm. Then, in seconds, he rears backward, lowers his body, stares up at me and bares his teeth, a long growl in my direction.

I can't help myself; I scoot backward, knocking into the breakfast table, both hands up and emitting another high squeak. The men around me fall silent and turn to watch me and Reggie, who has lowered his body to the floor as if he's about to pounce on me.

"Jay, stop him, do something," I squeal. "Down, doggie! Dowwwwn!"

Eddie is laughing as he does an impression of me. "Dowwwwwn!"

Jay reaches forward, "Alright boy, alright," taking the dog's collar and frowning. "Rafe isn't coming—he needs to be in reach of the City—so he can take on Reggie." A guy staring at a cell phone barely reacts as Jay steers the dog in front of him. "Not sure even this dog will enjoy where we're headed," Jay laughs, transferring the lead to a bewildered Rafe, still on the phone. My shoulders drop an inch that I'm off this particular hook.

I realize I never asked Laura what the groomsmen would be doing while we'd be enjoying our morning of relaxation. I don't really know any of Jay's friends, but I do know I'll have little in common with any of them. They probably all earn squillions, own yachts and have three homes.

"Where are we going again?" I ask, traipsing behind Jay as we all head across the foyer and down the stone steps of the hotel.

"Well, I assume the coast if the name's anything to go by," Eddie sneers, pulling back the minibus door.

My nose wrinkles. "Name?"

"Coasteering," he says enunciating every letter.

A vague memory of what this might mean flickers.

"The instructor's meeting us there," Jay says, pushing his sunglasses down on his nose and following Eddie inside.

A flicker of apprehension as I repeat, "Instructor?"

"For the cliff jumping! Don't want to do that without someone there. I want to be able to walk down the aisle at my wedding."

"Cliff . . ." My foot freezes on the step to the minibus. "You know," I say, glancing back over my shoulder to the hotel, "I think I'll, um . . ." My voice is faint.

"Come on, Flynn." Jay is holding the minibus door back. I swallow, knowing I can't give the game away.

"You scared, Flynny?" Eddie clicks his seatbelt.

If I Were You

I step into the minibus feeling my throat constrict.

"You alright, mate?" asks Jay, punching my arm as I take the seat next to him.

"Ow! I'm, I'm um . . ." I manage to say in a tiny voice. "Not quite feeling myself."

33

FLYNN

We're deposited outside a large wooden building with enormous glass windows. Wind chimes sound as we approach the steps to the porch where a blonde, bare-footed lady dressed in a plain black tunic stands, palms joined together in greeting.

"Welcome to Moreton Hall Spa. We cannot wait to host you for your Sensory Spa Experience." She bows and her long plait falls forward.

A spa. The last time I was in a spa Amy told me I was making her more stressed. I didn't know I'd been tapping the armrests in an annoying way, but I like to do things, not sit around reading or resting back thinking.

We follow the bare-footed lady inside and I try to look like I'm as excited as the rest of the group; there's a lot of gasping over the branded gold flip flops they are doling out. I'm given an enormous pile of plush towels, the robe as soft and thick as a cloud, and am herded along with the rest of the group. Laura looks delighted over her pile of towels, which is great; I must remember what Amy would want me to do, ensure Laura has a wonderful time.

"Let's get our spa on!" I smile widely.

In the corner Trish seems to be spending about twice as long as everyone else on the form we all had to fill in. When I approach I wonder if I'm imagining things as she quickly folds it in two.

The changing room smells of vanilla, those glass pots with sticks poking out on every surface, and discreet speakers play pan pipes.

I loiter outside the female changing room for an age before Trish appears behind me. "Come on, darling. You alright?"

"Am I!" I say, swallowing down my panic as I follow her inside. "You betcha!"

Tanya is, of course, the first to be dressed in a bikini. She is pulling a bottle of prosecco from her bag like an evil magician. "What happens with the hens stay with the hens!"

This prompts a bit of high-pitched giggling from the group as the rest start removing clothing.

I'm frozen, staring up at the ceiling, the discreet spotlights, the top lockers, the fire alarm—as they all undress around me.

I step across to a cubicle in the corner and hold up the cozzie which appears to be a complicated lot of fabric and string. "Are you ready, Amy?" Trish calls from outside.

"Oh, yes I am, me and my breasts!" I give a strange bark of laughter and close my eyes.

Cool it, Flynn, act normal.

I emerge self-consciously, alarmed to feel straps and fabric in every crevice of this body. I tug on the bottom part as I secure the towel around my neck like a cloak, earning myself a look from Laura. She has knotted her towel around her chest and I realize that's how I'm meant to do it.

"I'm so excited!" she says.

"Me too!" I squeak, following her through the changing room. "Girl power!"

Come on, Flynn. It's fine. You're Amy. You can do this. It's just a few women having a relaxing time together. Don't be a drip.

I emerge into the outside space hunched over and awkward. No one glances my way as I stare around the space with its wood-fired hot tubs, outdoor showers, and enormous tubs of herbs.

Everyone looks like they're having fun: complimenting each other on their toenail colors and tattoos, and exploding into fits of laughter. If I wasn't feeling so out of place I could see the appeal. No one calls anyone Fatty or slaps them on the arse with a towel or takes the piss out of their shit tattoo.

The air smells of lavender and chlorine as the blonde woman shows us the features of the garden.

"You will finish here, at the fire pit, your bare feet lowered in a warm copper tub, where you can focus on your body and its renewed connection to the earth, and reflect as we wrap you in blankets and bring you our herbal tea, centering you in the moment."

Six tree stumps surround what looks like a large satellite dish filled with coal. It glows orange, filling the air with the scent of charcoal. For a moment the smell reminds me of Bonfire Night and, embarrassingly, I feel a sudden sadness wash over me. October has been harder in the last few years. *Stop it, Flynn, don't go there.* I can't help glancing across at Tanya, who has tipped her head to the side like she's about to ace the Outdoor Spa Experience Test.

It's a shock to see her here, and not just because she's practically naked. I had thought I'd never see her again and time seems to unravel and blur. It's like a lifetime ago, and all my memories of us crowd in.

She looks up at me then and I flinch as she gives me a soft smile. I can't return it. I turn in my gold flip flops and walk away.

34

FLYNN

Five Years Ago

Tanya is sitting in the hallway of her house when I knock. It's strange because I can see her there, legs stuck out, back against the wall, but she doesn't respond when I ring the bell. I phone her and I see her silhouette move, lift something, stare at it, and place it back down. I phone again. She repeats, only this time she presses something and I am sent straight to voicemail. Frowning, I bend down, lift the mailbox, and say her name.

She says "Shit!" and scrambles up.

My frown deepens. What has happened? This is not at all how I imagined this would go. She doesn't even know I'm coming over this evening.

It takes her ages to open the door and the suspense is making my nerves jangle more. I know I need to get in and out and make a clean break of it. It's better for everyone if I do this quickly, succinctly, and promise to stay friends. It's been almost a year; I don't want an anniversary to remind me why I know I need to end things. We're not right together.

She's been crying.

This is not good news, because I was fairly sure what I was psyching myself up to say all the way over here was going to make her cry. So, I will be making a crying person cry more, which makes me feel even worse than I already do.

She must know it's coming, though. We have barely spoken in the last few weeks. She has ghosted most of my messages, she has avoided phone calls, she canceled this evening at the last moment with the most absurd excuse (she hurt her foot in the gym earlier).

I feel like she wants me to do it.

And as much as I want a relationship, as much as I hate the idea of being on my own again, I know this isn't it. That she isn't the person I've been waiting my whole life to meet. My memories of that kind of love are fleeting, but the feeling I get when I picture Dad, the way he held Mum and me, the way he looked at her, those feelings are intense and real and my whole body craves the person that will make me feel like that. I know it's rare. Mum never had it with Patrick despite the big showy pretense: the long holidays, the renewal of vows, the gushing speeches at birthday parties. When Dad rested a hand on the small of her back she leaned into him like she couldn't not.

So I know I have to do this: I have to break up with her. She's pretty and my friends think she's fun, she *is* fun. Her insecurity can be touching. I get it, I want reassurance too: I just never ask directly for it. She isn't sure what she stands for, and I'm already half lost. But mostly I don't want to be with someone who will contort themselves into something else for me, or for friends; I can't be with a liar, even if they're small lies, white lies. I can't be with another me. "We're late because of the traffic" (there was no traffic, we were arguing and she had to reapply her make-up), "I told you I went out with him!" (two minutes after telling me she had never met him), "I love action movies" (our first date! She hates action movies). She isn't sure what she stands for, and neither am I. Her truth rests on shifting sands and I feel unstable.

I want someone to stand for something. I want someone who knows who they are. I will know who it is when I find her.

"How's the foot?" Maybe I'm wrong about the foot excuse, and that's why she's crying. I feel a flicker of guilt, "Are you in pain?"

Tanya looks at me as if I have two heads and then clearly remembers what she told me. I chalk it up to another small lie. She'll say it's harmless, better than telling me she just wasn't in the mood to see me, but it solidifies the knowledge of what I want to do.

"I wanted to see you," I say, taking a breath.

She glances at her phone again and I frown, wondering for a moment what has caused the strange expression on her face.

She really does look distressed.

"I—" I stop, realizing I can't do this tonight. That it would be cruel. I might not cry, but I hate to see others hurting like this. I won't ask what's wrong; that isn't my area of expertise. I cast about for something to lighten the mood, distract.

She cuts me off, not meeting my eye, and the words are so quiet I almost miss them.

"I'm pregnant."

"Let's turn that frown ups— what?" My words screech to a halt.

"I'm pregnant."

I blink twice, three times. The door to the house is still open and a gust of cold wind swirls around us; the door bangs shut and I jump.

Holy shit.

Everything I was thinking about on the tube on the way over here disappears in a puff. All the overlapping thoughts in my head are silenced by this one sentence. Barely three words.

They change everything.

Where a few hours ago I was sure of my path, what I was going to do and why I was going to do it, now everything is topsy-turvy.

Tanya is going to have my baby. I won't be listing the many reasons we're not compatible, I won't be seeing myself out. Tanya is pregnant and in that moment everything else melts away. Everything else feels sur-mountable. Because it has to be. Tanya is pregnant and there is no way I am going anywhere.

My shoulders straighten as she starts to sob, her body turning toward me. I shush her and step forward.

"Hey, it's OK. It's OK. That's a good thing, a good thing."

Her chest heaves.

"Hey, come here, come here. Stop, it's OK."

She closes the gap between us.

A baby.

As I glance in the hall mirror and circle her body with mine, I feel a strange jolt. Because for a second I see a flash of my own father looking straight back at me. Then he's gone. And I am left.

And this baby will know their father. This baby will be so loved.

"Ssh. It's a good thing."

35

AMY

I'm standing on a clifftop dressed in neoprene and feel like I might throw up. It's windy and wild, and our instructor, Scott, is telling us what fate has in store for us in his thick Devonian accent. Even the fact his wetsuit is rolled down to the waist to show his eight pack can't distract me right now.

There's plenty of jostling and back-slapping as we prepare to leap into the water. It's so hard to work out what the men are really feeling—surely some of them are scared too? Eddie's wetsuit bulges with his rugby player frame and Jay has removed the sunglasses he seems to wear inside and out. An ashen Geoffrey, squeezed into a too-small wetsuit, a brand-new price tag clearly on show, is pretending to be game. Below us a choppy sea smacks onto the rocks below. He is out of his depth. More at home in a knitted tank top, glasses atop his head as he reads seed catalogs. He's definitely not brave—it took him four years after Dad died to ask Mum out and he'd been working as a part-time teacher at her school all that time. I give him a shaky smile and he nods.

"Well, this is fun," he says, swallowing and craning his neck to see over the ledge.

I tug on my obligatory life vest, not comforted by it because Scott just made me sign something that definitely meant I couldn't sue him if I died.

I step across. "Alright, Geoffrey—nervous too?"

"Yes, Flynn, son, yes—well, no, all fun, isn't it, all a bit of fun." He is growing paler with every passing second.

Is this what men do? Pretend to be OK when they are patently terrified? Do any of them actually want to jump off this cliff or are they just doing it to prove something to someone who doesn't even exist, who they have created in their own mind: the Real Man? I feel Geoffrey could be my ally in this: we could bow out together.

Jay and Eddie jump together with wild whoops and then I watch, in horror, as before I can persuade Geoffrey to quit with me he follows them.

"Got to be a man!" he yells before disappearing into the sea.

My skin prickles as the wind whips around me, nudging me closer to the edge and their splashes and shouts. I would not have put money on Geoffrey flinging himself off a cliff. I wonder momentarily what else I don't know about him.

"I can't do it," I say, shaking my head and wrapping my arms around my chest as Scott approaches me, a wide smile on his absurdly tanned face.

"Sure you can, mate."

"I'm, I'm not that kind of guy," I insist. "*You're* that kind of guy. I mean, I can see from listening to you you're the kind of guy who wears shorts in winter, but I'm more of an indoor kind of guy..."

He interrupts my babbling by placing a hand on my arm. It's a firm grip and I clamp my mouth closed. "It's Flynn, isn't it?"

I nod dumbly, gasping as a gust of wind jostles me again, the long grass tickling the tops of my bare feet.

"Want to do it together, Flynn?" he offers. His eyes crinkle. Even distracted, I can register he is absurdly hot.

"Nope. Nope, I'd rather not do it at all really. Even with you. I mean, it's kind; normally I imagine people are keen to do stuff with you..."

Scott freezes for a second before chucking his head back and laughing. "Alright, mate, I'll tell you what, we'll get this first jump out the way together, then once you're in we'll come up with a plan. Alright?"

"Not really."

He steers my unwilling body closer to the edge, the taste of salt on my lips as the day darkens, a cloud crossing the sky.

"Three, two, one... and..." Scott wrenches me along with him and we are over into nothingness.

I'm tumbling and then there is an almighty shock as I'm submerged in seawater. Whoops and shouts are all muted as I twist and fret in the water, darkness around me. Kicking to the surface, I splutter, gasping for air, swearing and spitting out salty water, blinking in surprise. The cheering, the exalted comments do boost me, and I tread water, looking at the faces of these men with their flushed cheeks and bright eyes. I can't help feeling proud.

Scott's wild hair is flattened as he swims away. "Come on then, lads, let's go."

An hour or so later, my new body aching, we're in a cave: dark, dripping and seaweed coated. We've clambered, we've crawled, we have swum round large boulders in the sea while being smacked in the face by seawater. We have jumped off tall rocks, cliff edges and we are breathless and staring as Scott points to something beneath the surface.

"Don't fight it, Flynn mate," he says, beckoning me.

"I'm fine! I'll stay here. Wait for rescue."

Scott just chucks his beautiful wet head back and laughs.

It's just me and him in the cave and I want to crawl out onto this flat rock and cry among the limpets. I think with fury of Flynn in a luxury spa. Why don't the men want hot tubs and saunas?

Stupid, sexy Scott ends up pulling me through the tunnel to get me out and the other men stare at me as I emerge in his wake holding my nose. Only Geoffrey smiles sympathetically.

Back outside the wooden building we're all wearing

matching hooded towels and sipping hot coffee from branded thermos flasks. The caffeine, the warm liquid, the towel around my wet head and cold ears all help to relax me, along with the knowledge that I didn't die and that I achieved something. Begrudgingly I have to admit it felt good to be brave.

Scott raises his thermos to me. "Flynn mate, you did well, you did well."

I like him a lot more now. I don't even want to sue him a little bit.

"Thanks," I beam, "I couldn't have done it without you. You're a great instructor, so patient and attentive. Thank you s—"

A few of the men are looking at me.

Scott's cheeks flood with color and when he smiles I notice the smallest chip in one of his incisors, "It was all you, mate, all you."

"Alright, let's get back on board before you two kiss . . ." calls Eddie, stepping across to the minibus.

There's general talk as we all troop inside and settle in our seats. Relieved to be resting and returning to Flynn, I click my seatbelt across my body, zoning in and out of the chatter around me.

"How about you, Eddie—long-term? Tanya seems nice," one man says.

"And fit," another guy barks from the row in front.

My body freezes. Tanya. Not the most common name. But it can't be.

Then something slots into place. The girl from last

night, something familiar about her. I'd looked her up on social media in the past—of course I had.

Flynn would have said something, surely? Even with everything, he would have told me.

"Yeah, she's great." Eddie glances across at me as he says it. Then he twists in his seat, a slight smirk on his face, "I hope it's not too weird, Flynn, was going to mention it on the WhatsApp group but figured you wouldn't mind—"

I feel all eyes on me, Geoffrey scuffing a toe on the floor as the silence stretches on.

"No, no," I say. "Not weird."

The engine starts and the whole bus shakes. Nausea swirls within me.

"We always had the same taste in women. Remember Penelope Harkness. Fit," Eddie says, resting his head back and laughing.

I barely hear him, questions bubbling up inside me. Before I can stop, some are spilling out. "That is great. So how are you guys getting on? Is she well? Did she say why she broke up with Fl— phew—broke up with me? Was it serious? I felt it was serious?"

"Want to shine a light in his eye, mate?" Jay laughs, lowering his sunglasses to peer at me over them.

"Ha!" I bark, too loud. The other men all look anywhere but at me. "Sorry, no, I just . . . wow, Tanya, that's a blast, blast from my, from my past. Great. I can't wait to see her, catch up . . ."

"It is fine then," Eddie says, a small smirk. "You're chill about it."

"It's fine..." I swallow, worried the words aren't coming out, "fine...mate," I add. Trying to sound natural, normal. And not like my world is falling in. "Totally chill."

Tanya. THE Tanya.

"Chilled." I force a smile as Eddie twists back in his seat.

Tanya! What the hell is going on?

36

FLYNN

It feels strangely duplicitous being a man in an all-female group and I've spent three quarters of my time in the steam room avoiding everyone. I do have to keep taking breaks and downing water, but the hours are passing and I'm starting to think I might survive this and do Amy proud.

The conversations I've overheard are speedy, excited, overlapping: sickly parents, shit boyfriends, stubborn chin hairs, an arsehole boss who stands too close. Some are deeply personal and yet I'm fascinated to hear the women's reactions. There are no digs or sly comments or bad jokes. In a different world I wonder what I might have shared if I'd had some female friends growing up.

My heart sinks, however, when the next two people to enter are Laura and Tanya, who seem to have really hit it off if the giggling is anything to go by.

"Just off—"

"Ames, I've been looking everywhere for you! Stay!" Laura says. "Tanya was just telling me about launching her new workout app, PushIt . . ."

"Sounds like an STI."

Laura falls silent and I internally smack my own head. Amy asked for one thing and I need to try to do my best.

"I guess it sort of does," Tanya says. "So Amy, is this your first time being a bridesmaid?"

Tanya's eyes are just visible through the steam.

"Yep," I reply absent-mindedly. Even her voice seems to trigger something in me, my skin tingling.

"No, it's not," Laura corrects, waving a hand in my direction. "We've been bridesmaids together twice before."

"Yes. Apart from those two times," I say slowly. I wish I'd left when I had the chance.

"Your speech last night was sweet, about your dad," Tanya says, head tipping to one side. "I'm so sorry, Laura, for your loss," she adds.

"Thanks," Laura says, giving her a grateful smile. "That's kind, isn't it, Amy?" Laura prompts.

I know she wants me to say something nice. I know I should say something nice. If this morning has taught me anything, it is that women in this situation say nice things. I open my mouth and then four years of hurt and rage stops my tongue.

"Very."

Laura gives Tanya a crooked smile.

"Too hot," I say quickly, getting up and pulling on the door to outside, skin beading with sweat. Laura's

159

smile slips and I know I'm not being friendly, but I can't do it; I can't talk to Tanya normally like nothing has happened. I can't pretend.

Any enjoyment at listening to the hens has disappeared, their chats now just annoying, their laughs now too high. Teeth chattering, I stay hidden behind a large ornamental stone pot, waiting for the time to be up. Perhaps if I stay here they might forget about me and, "Gah!"

Someone has crept up and pinched me on the elbow. It's Laura.

"Amy, what are you doing?"

"I'm . . . I'm . . ." I glance about, struggling for words. "Foraging," I finish lamely, plucking something that may or may not be a weed out of the pot I'm hiding behind.

"What is up with you? Please stop being weird and stand-offish and get involved." Her voice softens, "I get that you might be a bit intimidated or . . ."

Intimidated? Is that what Laura thinks Amy would be? Amy is openly snarky about places like this, and the people who frequent them, lecturing on the waste, how monthly spa memberships could more than pay for water for an entire African village.

"But you were just openly rude to Tanya, that was totally embarrassing."

I speak before I think. "She's a cow," I say sullenly, regretting the words almost immediately. Shut up, Flynn.

It's too late, Laura's softness disappears, her face morphing to fury. "You've literally just met her; she is the best man's girlfriend. Why would you say that?"

"She gives off a bad vibe."

160

Laura rolls her eyes, "Oh great, is this going to be one of those things where you've made up your mind about someone because they grew up in a smart house or went to a posh school? You don't know her, Amy."

"I don't do that to people." I think of Amy then, rolling her eyes if I mention anything to do with boarding school, quick to point out she went to a big public school, did everything without any help.

"She just, she just . . . I . . ." How do I get out of this? "She just, she . . . seems like bad news."

Laura takes a deep breath as she looks at me. "Look, Amy, I don't know what is going on with you right now and I'm trying not to be a bitch because I love you. I know you think Jay is posh and his friends are awful, but honestly, if you give people a chance . . ." She takes a breath and rubs her eyes. "I really thought you'd want to make up for last night, but it's like you don't even care."

"I do, I do," I insist, worry coiling around my insides.

"Well, act like it. Please. For me."

Oh god, I don't want to mess this up for Amy. I need to fix it. "I'm sorry," I say, face earnest. "I'm really sorry, I'll do better," I promise.

Laura's mouth purses together and the sad expression on her face lifts a fraction. "OK," she says, nudging me in the ribs. She gives me a small smile. "Hey—you know Mum's talking about getting a tattoo," she adds. "A dove on her collarbone."

"Better than I Heart Geoffrey?" I say and I'm gratified to hear her laugh. This is the Laura I'm used to, Amy's

161

sister with the big loud laugh and the kind eyes. I cannot screw this up.

Back in the steam room I even force a laugh when Tanya makes a joke about it being better than her usual "dishwasher steam."

"... And this suite's meant to stimulate fertility," Trish tinkles with a laugh. "Just saying, Laura."

"Mum, I'm not even married yet!"

"A joke! A joke!"

My muscles clench.

"I better get out quickly then," Tanya says.

My head snaps up, insides twisting with the shock of the statement.

Despite the steam, I feel like Tanya is staring at me as she says it, and I squeeze my eyes closed tighter and wish myself anywhere but here.

It helps fertility.

And for the first time I'm filled with real dread that this weekend is going to change everything.

And I won't be able to do a thing to stop it.

37

AMY

Tanya?

I am not focused on the journey back, the minibus stopping to allow Eddie to pop into an open pub and return with a tray of clear shots. He forces the bus to play the "water game" (everyone chooses a shot from the tray which contains clear spirits or water. Plot twist: none contained water). There's initially some resistance—someone called Pete claims to be a teetotaler—but no one asked him why, or seems concerned, and he is simply told to stop being a pussy and drink it. I watch him as he sips at it slowly, wishing he didn't feel obliged.

I feel one step removed, late to laugh. I've been holding my glass for an age. "I hate Sambuca," I mutter to no one.

Only Geoffrey seems to notice, his bushy gray eyebrows drawn together as he replaces his shot glass on the tray (tequila).

"Here, Flynn," he says quietly, sneaking my shot out of my hand and downing it too. His face twists. "Sambuca," he coughs, handing it back so none of the other men notice.

My eyebrows shoot up as I mouth a thanks. I've never really spent any time with Geoffrey. As much as I want Mum to be happy, I suppose sometimes seeing that Geoffrey makes her happy is still hard for me. I smile back at him, grateful for his small kindness.

My brain is still humming with questions for Eddie, but I know I've been jumpy and strange and need to stop drawing attention to myself. I can understand why Flynn rarely talks about real things if the last couple of hours has shown me anything. Very few conversations stray into personal territory.

Tanya is Flynn's ex. That much I know. But he never talks about her, waves a hand if I ask about her or deflects or tells me he likes to focus on the present. I'm not enormously insecure, I trust Flynn, but there is something about the way his face changes, just for a second, before the benign smile or casual shrug that belies something bigger. She is a huge question mark and one of the reasons I feel frustratingly distant from Flynn. How can he want to move in together if he remains so distant?

The fact she is here floors me. I'd assumed he'd been overwhelmed by the swap last night, staring at that couple. Now I realize he had recognized her. And he hadn't said a word.

I knew he was the one who broke up with her, so I comfort myself with the fact that at least he'd chosen to walk away. But I've never been completely clear on why. Flynn is barely on social media so I'd only ever discovered tiny nuggets: Tanya loves *Strictly*, thinks *Peep Show* is the best TV show ever made, never wears black, loathes public transport. I hate myself for remembering these details, assigning meaning to them. But Flynn has never filled in the blanks.

And now she is here, on this weekend. And Flynn is being secretive. Maybe I can discover more, make more sense of Flynn and his past. Perhaps this is the silver lining to this switch.

Any thoughts I had of leaving evaporate as my curiosity takes flight. If I'm in Flynn's body then of course I can find out more. If he doesn't communicate with me about his past, she might. It's not that I don't trust him, I think hurriedly.

But as we bump around the narrow lanes, past fields dotted with hay bales, sheep, a small voice whispers, why didn't he tell you about her last night? Why didn't he say she was here, introduce you?

It solidifies my desire to find out more. It can't hurt.

38

FLYNN

I need to persuade Amy to leave. Now. Desperate to ensure the fragile peace with Laura continues, I huddle quietly in the corner of the minibus on the way back. I just need to find Amy and persuade her to go. Too much is at stake now and this swap, whatever it is, doesn't show any sign of ending.

I glance at the back of Tanya's head on the minibus: I won't let anything screw us up.

As we circle the gravel driveway back to the front of the hotel, I twitch, ready to race out. Staying feels dangerous. My plan is ruined but I know my relationship could be too if we stay.

I'm the first out of the minibus. "Amy, where are you headed?" calls Laura from behind me.

"I need to see Flynn."

"But I need help with . . ."

But whatever Laura needs help with is lost as I march through the foyer, hair still damp, curls sticking to my neck slick with oil.

Up the staircase and down the corridors. Get me out of here.

The room is empty, Amy is obviously still not back. I have a momentary panic that she might have hurt herself and hope she stayed safe. I curse again at the turn this weekend has taken.

I've always been more comfortable around men, an all-boys' school, male sports teams, no sisters. I didn't really know any girls or women, not ones to form a friendship with, and I was always told women were bitchy, that men were straight talkers. In the spa I got a glimpse of a wide range of conversations, a solidarity among this disparate group of females, and I wonder if that is actually true.

Glancing up in the mirror, I'm reminded again that I'm Amy. A hot rage descends and I lash out with a foot, stubbing my stupid toe—or Amy's stupid toe—on the bedpost.

"For fuck's sake," I swear, zipping open my bag to pack. I find my cell phone, with no charge, and plug it in. It immediately pings with messages. I must check them; I hope Karim and Bex are OK. Work feels a million miles away now, but I feel the familiar panic that I'm responsible for them, that I should look after them, or they might leave.

Then I see the zipped compartment on the side of my bag, can't stop myself pulling out the hard square case nestled inside it.

167

Dolefully I sink onto the foot of the bed and stare at the diamond, glinting at me hopefully. The band was dotted with tiny stones too. It flashes in the light from the windows, making rainbow stripes dance on the cream wall opposite. I'd wanted to throw myself into a marriage, have kids, settle down.

There's a knock at the door and without thinking I get up and cross the room, just remembering to close the box and hide it in my closed fist.

It's Tanya, refreshed, rosy-cheeked, her blonde waves worn down like a mermaid. She's wearing a floaty pale blue dress thing that I remember she bought when we went to Devon for the weekend. Thinking of that robs me of any words.

"Hey Amy, sorry, I know it's a bit weird me appearing like this. The boys aren't back yet so I just wondered if we could have a quick chat?"

She takes my shocked silence as an invitation and steps inside the room. Wordlessly I close the door behind her.

"Oh, great view. We're around the other side overlooking the pavilion. This is gorgeous—isn't that lake divine . . ."

I haven't been in a room with Tanya since that hideous day. When I had thought things were coming together, that the future was bright.

She stands framed in the picture window, playing with a strand of hair, sending me spiraling back in time once more.

"So, this is a bit awkward, but I sort of picked up that maybe you don't like me much and," she holds up a hand, the words fast, "I can *totally* understand that Flynn told you about me, and that's why you don't like me."

Crossing my arms, I tilt my chin in defiance, hackles already raised. "Don't flatter yourself, Tanya," I huff, "Flynn hasn't told me anything."

She cringes and I try to temper my words, think like Amy. It's absurd to think Tanya will catch us in the lie, but I don't need to create more problems.

Just seeing her though is making me feel things I thought I'd buried long ago. My stomach twists as I take in her familiar face, chewing her lower lip in a sure sign she's nervous. I thought I'd never see her again; I thought that part of my life was over. There was no need to open the lid on those memories. If they flare up I make sure I do what I've always done, secure the box a little tighter in my mind, focus on what is in front of me.

Now though, seeing her here, makes me falter. I hate myself but I can't help asking it, desperate to know, yet also wishing she wasn't here reminding me.

"How's Charlie?" I blurt. I don't mean to make my voice so brittle. I want to take it back. I don't want to know, don't want to think of them.

Her eyebrows lift, "Oh, Flynn has told you, then?"

I nod briefly, the hurt momentarily stealing my reply. "Only a little," I whisper, thinking back to the last time I'd seen them together, how I'd felt when I'd learned the truth.

Tanya's face relaxes. "Yeah, really good, thanks. So, before Flynn gets back," she says, business as ever with

Tanya, "I just wanted to be sure he hadn't made me out to be a bitch. Because I didn't mean for any of it to happen, and I thought he was cheating on me!"

"He wasn't," I say stonily, my despair quickly replaced with anger. "Look, Tanya," I say, realizing this situation could actually present me with a solution to this problem. "I'd appreciate it if you don't talk to Flynn this weekend, if that's OK by you? Better to let the past stay in the past—yeah?"

"I guess," Tanya says, fiddling with her hair again.

"OK then," I say firmly, happy that with this sorted she can leave now. I don't want her around me for any longer than necessary. "Well, thanks for coming to talk," I force out, wanting her to leave, wanting her to stop reminding me of the worst moment in my life.

"Of course, um . . . well, thanks for hearing me out. Glad Flynn hasn't soured things. He's a good guy," she says, and those words sting too. If I'd been so good, how had any of this happened?

"No problem," I say tightly, ushering her back across the room. Her familiar perfume as she moves closer makes me want to bundle her up and shove her into the corridor. I blink as the scent fades, opening the door.

"And I hope you're really happy with Flynn," she adds, searching my face as she stands on the threshold with me.

"I am," I say through gritted teeth. "Really happy," I stress.

Tanya moves into the corridor, and my body loosens. There's a noise from my right and I look up.

Amy is standing at the end of the corridor, watching Tanya leave our room.

"Flynn," Tanya says as she passes Amy, a glance back at me.

Amy nods at her, a bemused expression on her face.

Then Amy looks over at me standing in the doorway. I feel the hard edge of the box in my squeezed fist, a physical reminder of everything I stand to lose. I try to smile, to look relaxed, try not to let Tanya back into my thoughts. But I can't help this strange feeling that I now want to chase after Tanya, get her to tell me more. My heart has cracked open again—maybe I wasn't as over things as I thought.

39

AMY

Cream dress disheveled, long hair dripping, Flynn is chucking stuff on the bed when I step inside. My mind is in turmoil, the questions coming thick and fast. Was Tanya here to see me or Flynn? Why was she here?

"What did she want?"

Flynn ignores my question, zipping up his toiletry bag. I know he's heard me.

"Flynn?"

He doesn't meet my eye. "Look, Amy, you said it last night, this is insane. We need to leave."

What is he hiding? I'm used to him deflecting—he's always waved away questions about himself—but I'm not used to not trusting him. "Why was she here?"

"And I need to phone Bex and Karim or get you to and pretend to be me. They've messaged but I want to phone them, check on today's events . . ."

"Flynn, stop changing the subject . . ."

"I'm not . . . it's work."

"Forget work!"

He is measured in his response but I can see his fingers twitching. "Fine for you to say, when it's not your work. I should never have let them do this weekend without me."

I rub my eyes with my fists. "Flynn," I say softly, trying to temper my own voice, "Why was Tanya here?"

He pauses, his eyes almost comically sliding around his face.

"She wanted to borrow . . . borrow something."

"What?"

"A . . . some milk. They've run out."

I throw up my arms. "You're lying."

He doesn't argue with that.

"Why are you lying? Do you want to leave because of her?"

His frantic look confirms this is the case. "No! I just think it would be a good idea to get checked out. We can go to the hospital, get the doctors to look us over. Maybe this has happened before? Maybe there are specialists for this stuff?"

"Flynn, we can't leave. Not now."

The thing is, it isn't just about Laura anymore. I've felt a change, a newfound curiosity. This different body experience was terrifying and crazy, but if I am going to be stuck inside Flynn's body I could at least try to work some things out. "What did she want to talk to me about anyway?" I ask.

173

"Who?" he mumbles, like he doesn't know.

"What do you mean 'who'? Tanya, your ex, the ex you didn't mention was here. Your blonde, thin, stunning ex. Your ex who just left our room."

"She's with Eddie," he says. "And this isn't about her," he adds firmly, chucking his toiletry bag on the pile.

"Of course it—"

"It isn't about her," he shouts.

This makes me blink. Flynn rarely gets angry. I can count the occasions on one hand. When a man shouted at me in the street about our recycling bin and when a bouncer called me a slut. Never at me. Once I broke his laptop spilling tea over the keyboard and he still didn't yell.

He rakes a hand through his hair, something he often does, but gets it tangled in my curls. "Ow. I just think we should get checked out," he says, turning to drag my suitcase over and putting things in it.

My frustration spills over.

"We can't leave," I say loudly, taking the things out the moment he places them in.

"Stop it," he says, returning a hairbrush.

"You stop it," I say, taking the hairbrush back out.

"Amy, stop!"

"You stop!" I step forward and I'm towering over Flynn. He visibly flinches as he stares up at me. The shift unsettles me, the feeling of physical dominance completely foreign. I step back in surprise, breathing heavily.

Laura doesn't knock, or we were arguing so loudly

neither of us hear her. She's suddenly standing there in the middle of our room glaring at both of us.

"What was that before, Amy? Running off and—" She stops then, notices Flynn, as me, packing his bag.

"What are you doing?"

"We need to leave," Flynn says, returning his toiletry bag.

Laura lurches back. "Amy, is that a joke? Because it's really not funny."

"Not a joke," Flynn says, trying to sit on the bursting bag to close it, legs wide in his dress, flashing my white cotton pants.

Panic flares immediately. This is the last thing I need now; Laura is already fed up and now her face is dissolving.

"Ames, is this real? Please. Please don't go ..."

"We're not leaving, Laura," I assure her. "Fly— Amy is just having a ... she is just ..." Why can't I lie easily? What can I say? "We're *not* leaving," I finish. "We wouldn't leave your wedding weekend—would we, Amy?" My voice is a warning.

Flynn is sitting on top of the bag with a glum expression. Laura waits. Then she swipes at her face, angry tears swimming. "Amy, I don't know what your problem is, why you appear to be choosing this weekend to have whatever drama you're having, but I *need* you to stop being a selfish cow. You knew I needed you to be here for me. I just want to get things right, make Jay and his mum happy, so ... so ..."

She is tearing at her hair and a well opens up inside me. I hate seeing Laura like this, so used to her being in control, being composed, giving me stern looks, older sister advice. Now she looks fraught and miserable.

I step forward, a meaty hand on Laura's shoulder. "Hey, it's alright. We're here to help," I say, raising my eyebrows at Flynn.

"Flynn," she shrugs off my hand, her look one of barely concealed disgust, "it's not up to you to fix this situation, this is between me and Amy."

My hand falls to my side.

"Yes, but . . . Amy didn't mean leave, leave, she just meant leave . . . soon for the flashmob practice."

Flynn's head snaps up, eyes round.

Laura's eyes narrow as she stares at him, sniffing. "Amy . . . is that true?"

His face is a mess of emotions, lips quivering before he gives her a brief nod.

"Right, OK," Laura says, turning to leave. "OK. I need you, Ames."

I nod. "She'll be there," I call as she steps out of our room.

Flynn stands up jabbering almost immediately. "I can't do this, Amy. I can't."

His angst is discombobulating. Flynn never gives in like this and the change is alarming. I'm so unused to him asking me for anything, or fretting like this, that, despite my suspicions over the root cause, I find myself feeling sorry for him.

For the first time this weekend I really want to make

this work. I put a pin in my other feelings. "If we can work together, we can pull this off," I reassure him.

The glum expression on Flynn's face, my face, doesn't shift. Is it something to do with being him that is making it easier to channel his enthusiasm and energy? "Come on," I urge him. "We can help each other. I'll teach you the dance and you teach me . . ."

His eyes lift to mine. "Nine years of private tennis lessons."

"Well—we'll think of something for that later. Come on," I say, offering a hand and surprised all over again to pull him up with one hand, the muscles in my arm flexing. "We can pull this off."

"Really?"

I nod decisively. "Absolutely."

The tentative hope on his face makes me aware how rarely he asks for help and how rarely I offer it. I wonder momentarily whether our changing status is to do with our bodies—can I see his vulnerability because he is no longer bigger than me? Taller? Is it that simple?

He inches forward and I make a comical bow, holding out a hand.

"Let's dance," I say and pull him close, laughing at the surprised expression on his face. Normally he is the one instigating fun, he is the one loosening me up. This feels good.

For a wonderful second we're back. Flynn and Amy. Amy and Flynn. The evenings in my Clifton flat, speakers cranked up, the random shuffle of music as Flynn grabs my hand, waltzes me across the carpet, brushing past our sofa as he spins me theatrically round. If I've had an exhausting day—a house sale fall through, a chain collapse, an unpleasant owner or viewing—those moments dissipate under the eaves as I'm reminded why this giant human Labrador of a man is my best friend.

Despite his air of chaos he is thoughtful, always washing up if I've cooked, bringing me tea with the absurd quarter of sugar I like. He seems always to be crackling with energy, bouncing on the heels of his feet when he takes calls. Recently I've been so focused on my worry that there is nothing more than the Fun Time guy, but as I hold his hand now and he smiles, I'm reminded of the wonderful bits of Flynn.

Here in front of me, tongue clamped between his teeth trying desperately to get this dance right, I feel a swell of love for him, my boyfriend trapped inside my body trying to get the moves right.

He looks up at me, mid dreadful attempt at a body pop, appraising him, suddenly strangely self-conscious. "Am I doing it wrong?" His worry is clear, he really is trying.

"You're doing brilliantly," I say, and the way his shoulders drop and his expression relaxes makes my chest swell for him.

He can do this. We can do this.

40

FLYNN

Nerves kick in as I head downstairs in a long green dress with a ruffly bit on the bottom that Amy told me to change into. I can do this, I tell myself. I want to do this. For Amy. Everything feels like it's unraveling this weekend, but this is my life preserver. Something in our room clicked between us, a new way of being together, and I felt a strange relief at her taking control of the weekend. It feels nice not to be carrying the stress about things on my own.

The ballroom is cavernous and female voices bounce off the polished parquet floor as I push open the heavy double doors. Overhead tiered chandeliers flash and floral wallpaper shimmers every time the sun shines through the floor-to-ceiling windows. Heads swivel in my direction as I approach. I straighten, repeating Amy's pep talk as I left our room moments ago.

I can do this.

"Amy," Laura looks up, "you go in the front with me. OK . . ." She claps her hands and picks up her cell phone, scrolling down to select the song.

The hens are waiting in two rows and I go to stand in the middle with Laura. Unbelievably, I discover that Tanya is in the second row. What is she doing here? She met Laura barely two seconds ago and now she is here? My look must have lingered because she smiles and says, "Hey. Laura needed a couple more," as if she's read my mind.

Her presence throws me off and, as Laura scoots to stand next to me, I fail to notice the opening beats of "Don't Stop Believin'." The part Amy taught me. Laura and Amy, opening the flashmob in time with each other.

Laura huffs and quickly runs over to start the song again.

"Sorry," I cringe as she returns. She gives me a tight smile.

This time I'm better, but it's so fast and I can't move with all this material. Rucking the dress layers, like fishing netting, into my pants, I go again. I'm beading with sweat and aware that I can't seem to make this body work the way Amy does. I'm stiff and jerky and Laura keeps side-eyeing me, which only makes me miss more steps. The moves Amy taught me start to muddle the more panicked I become.

"Amy—we can go again," Laura says, blowing her cheeks out.

I clench my tongue between my teeth and nod. I'm sporty—I can do this. It's just dance.

Tanya is, of course, impeccable. It appears effortless and I can't help but twist round and watch her, blood simmering, as she moves her limbs fluidly. I forget the next step.

Laura casts me a confused look as she starts the whole routine again. My arms flail, less a dance move and more a cry for help. I want to show Tanya I can do this too. My movements become wilder as my competitive streak kicks into gear.

Laura sidles over to me. "Ames, what are you doing?" she asks out of the side of her mouth.

"Something new."

"Well, don't. You told me you had it down."

"I do," I protest, thinking of the hours Amy had put in perfecting this routine in her living room.

"Did you even practice?" Laura looks hurt and my cheeks burn as some of the other hens look round.

My shoulders sag. It's impossible.

"And again," Laura calls out. I'm letting Amy down.

I just can't seem to get into a natural rhythm, tripping over nothing, jerking my hips, waving my arms. The body works with the mind, and never has this seemed more obvious than now.

How can I get out of this? I need time. Time to get this right, or time to find a decent enough excuse not to do it.

"Ow." I stop and clutch my side. "Muscle. Pulled," I say, which could be true—some of these moves have definitely stretched this body in ways I'm not confident it can stretch. Laura can't disguise the flash of annoyance as I stumble inauthentically to a cushioned chair lining one of the walls, collapsing in it.

"We can wait," she says.

I wave a hand, "No, please, I can just watch. It's my . . . my groin," I say, hoping that will stop further questions and covering my crotch with one hand. "Groin pull," I add.

Laura nods tightly and starts up the music. How do I navigate this relationship? I don't have siblings and it seems fraught with complications. I'm unused to seeing a complex side to Laura; she and I get on fine. In Amy's body I seem to be walking through a minefield, unaware when and where I'm about to blow it all up.

I don't dare stand up again. I have a new respect for Amy and what she can accomplish in this body. If I'm being honest, I'd always dismissed her dancing as frivolous. Sports are important, our culture places it front and center: it takes skill and effort and fitness. But as I watch these women pull off these moves, I realize it requires no less skill or dedication to do what they're doing. I get a flash of sadness that I can't join in without exposing how much work I have to do. I need help, I need Amy.

Finally the time is up; the tennis tournament will start soon and some of the women are playing doubles.

"Well, thanks everyone," Laura says as people go to leave. "It's so nice to see people have made a real effort to make this a special surprise." Then she turns and faces me, "You all know how important it was for me to do this one thing for Jay."

Tanya gives me a sympathetic grimace which only makes me feel worse.

What am I going to tell Amy when I see her? Can I pretend it all went well or is it another thing I need to keep quiet about?

Swallowing, I stand, walking to the door, only just remembering at the last moment to limp. It's too late—Laura has seen.

"Groin pull all fine now then," she calls.

I close my eyes, wondering just how many secrets I can keep from Amy in one weekend.

41

AMY

Watching him disappear through the ballroom doors makes my heart jitter. I just pray Flynn can hold onto some of the dance moves: his style of dancing could be described as enthusiastic, but lacking finesse.

"Flynn."

At some points he made my body move with carefree abandon—bits I don't like jiggling jiggled—but, rather than worry and judge, I found myself grinning and spurring him on.

"Flynn."

A large hand on my shoulder makes me squeal and spin around.

Eddie snorts with laughter. "Oh my god, mate, what was that noise?"

My heart is hammering as I try to style things out. "Sorry," I say, coughing to hide my discomfort. "Sorry . . . mate. Just, yeah, I was miles away."

"Psyching yourself up for the big tournament? I'm going up to change now. Going to bring my A game, mate," his chest puffs up. "Someone's got to take you down."

"Ha," I say, plucking at my pristine white top. "Yeah. I'm going to get lots of games."

"How's your serve these days?"

"Oh," I say, mind scrambling for the correct response. "Yeah, I serve it all, good."

Eddie frowns and I sense that hasn't landed as I might have liked.

Who organizes a tennis tournament the evening before they get married? This whole weekend is like Gold Duke of Edinburgh. I feel like we should all get badges.

"Where's Tanya?" I ask. This could be a good opportunity to find her, probe Flynn's past with him safely away in the ballroom.

Eddie's eyes roll. "Don't know, some girl thing to do with dancing. Top secret."

I glance over my shoulder. She's in there with Flynn. Eddie's eyes narrow as I turn back around. "Why'd you ask?"

"Just curious," I say quickly, sensing a menace underneath his words.

This is confirmed when he presses his hand back on my shoulder, his grip a little too tight. "Well, leave her alone, yeah, that'd be best for everyone." His smile is cold and I wonder again what has happened in the past. Why would Eddie bring her here? As I assess his flint-like eyes I know I would avoid a man like Eddie with his hard edges and bitchy retorts dressed up as "banter."

185

"She's with me now, mate," he says. The mate part doesn't sound friendly at all.

"I'll see you in a bit." I cross the foyer away from him before reeling backward when Patty, with her stiff gray bobbed hair and pearls, appears through the revolving doors, a cloud of fur by her side.

"Just the man, here he is." She immediately hands me the lead. Reggie looks as reluctant as I do as he growls at me.

"Stop that, Reggie. Flynn, take him. Jay told me you adore him and you've barely seen him this weekend."

"I . . . but . . ." There are no excuses. Flynn had meant to look after Reggie. With a deep breath, I gingerly accept the lead.

"A quick spin."

Miraculously, Reggie allows me to guide him back through the doors, as I'm murmuring, "Please don't bite me, please don't bite me."

Down past the hotel, we take the steps across the lawn, past the bandstand where uniformed men and women are stringing up fairy lights and rearranging flowers, all a reminder of why we've all descended on this stunning place. I can't believe Laura's getting married here. Instead of seeing the extravagance, I see the beauty of the place and feel guilty for being so judgmental. My teasing wasn't friendly, it was couched in my opinions about capitalism and the uneven distribution of wealth and all the things that got me out on protests with Dad and her in the past. I wish desperately I was with her now, preparing for tomorrow, getting excited about things. Why did I have to moan about the expense? The luxury. Sometimes I needed to set my beliefs aside and just enjoy the moment—like Flynn, I realize with a start.

Trembling, I reach and release Reggie from the lead, screwing up my eyes in case he's considering an attack. Instead, he spins on the spot and bounds away, joy personified. I can't help a small, relieved smile as I watch him gambol.

The lake is a balm, the sky perfectly mirrored in its smooth surface, the odd insect or duck causing ripples that make the idling rowing boats rock. Two of the flamingos are standing on the side of the lake, legs bent, necks curved as they preen. Reggie romps and I start to relax as he sniffs his way along the water's edge.

In Flynn's body I'm noticeably fitter, and as I walk I enjoy feeling its strength, my limbs moving powerfully and fluidly. There is still a disconnect, a strange feeling of being at sea when I move a certain way, but I'm starting to master his limbs, enjoy the perspective I get being taller than others, the way it makes me feel capable, powerful. I've neglected fitness in recent years, attending the odd Pilates session when guilt has taken over, but I want to feel like this in my own body, able to run and dance and scale mountains without pausing to catch my breath every second.

We plunge into woods, the canopy of branches making dappled shadows on the ground, and for a moment I enjoy the feeling of being alone, watching this crazy dog spin and bark at fallen trunks and random foliage. His enthusiasm reminds me of Flynn, how a walk is full of small exclamations. And yet, I remind myself sternly, what is all that masking? I still don't know what lies underneath that cheery façade.

Up ahead a bench looks out over the fields, two people still in the center, the woman's head resting against the man's shoulder. It's after a few moments I realize it's Mum and Geoffrey. Something about the scene feels private, his arm around her shoulders. I'm about to call out but something gives me pause and instead I edge nearer to catch what they are saying. They're speaking in low voices.

"You'll have to tell them sometime . . ."

That makes me straighten. Who is them?

"You'll feel better if you tell them."

Tell who? Tell them what? My heart starts to pitter patter. Why does Mum sound so serious?

"Not now, Geoffrey."

"They can take it, Trish, they're all grown up now."

"They're still babies to me."

My stomach lurches with the knowledge that it is "us" she is keeping something from and I step forward, twigs crackling, Reggie crashing into the scene behind me. Geoffrey cranes his neck.

"Ah, hello young Flynn." The words sound false and I feel a flood of anger that Geoffrey appears to be in on a secret I am not privy to. I've known Mum for two decades longer; I'm her daughter: that should count for something.

Is Mum swiping at her eyes before she also turns? My anger dissipates immediately, only confusion remaining.

"Flynn love, everything OK?"

"Everything's great," I say after a beat. "Yeah," I say, my head swimming. What is going on? "Yeah, great."

42

FLYNN

Not normally nervous, I can't help planting myself close to the fence, hands on the wire as I watch Amy wandering around the court, clearly lost.

The two pristine grass tennis courts are thrumming with guests warming up; others are assembled in the sunshine. Amy barely spoke to me when I saw her, dazedly handing me a delighted Reggie on a lead. At the time I was relieved, I didn't want to admit how badly the flashmob had gone, but now I'm concerned something else is going on. Should we have done more to stop her playing, come up with an excuse?

There is no way this isn't going to be a disaster. Even in my six-foot-two-inch frame she seems strangely vulnerable, her shoulders rounded, her gait hesitant, her movements jumpy and uncertain. I can't help my insides clenching in sympathy for her. But there is another part of me, a shameful part, that is concerned about my reputation.

Sports have always been something that has defined me, my name synonymous with sporting success. I'd spent hours as a child throwing, hitting, kicking a ball at the wall of our garage, desperate for a playmate, the inside of the house too cold and sad to want to spend time in, the monotony of practicing emptying my brain of anything else.

It was the thing that gave me confidence, allowed me easy access to a world of men. Other boys at both prep school and senior school admired my natural ability to hit a ball with any number of bats or rackets. It was like a language, and I'd always been fluent in it.

Can I run on and pull Amy away? I don't want her to take this thing away from me.

Then I think of her face back in the bedroom, teaching me to dance, wanting so desperately to try and make this weekend work for her sister. So I send up a silent prayer and cross my fingers.

"Hey," Laura says, offering me her plate with a scone topped with a dollop of clotted cream and jam. She stands next to me.

"Oh, thanks," I say, taking it from her.

I've barely eaten all day and quickly stuff the scone into my mouth, crumbs spilling down the green maxi dress Amy dressed me in. When I look up Laura is grimacing at me.

"You're a savage." Fortunately, she follows it up with a laugh and, uneasily, I join in.

"I'm sorry about the flashmob, I was a bit tense. It will be fine, it's just a bit of fun."

"I'm going to practice later," I say, glad she seems happier now.

"I guess it's about the only thing I've been in charge of this weekend," she admits, "so I wanted it to be great."

"It will be," I say.

"Thanks." She stays next to me looking at the court as people are given their mixed pairings. "So, Jay told me Flynn almost played first pair for Sussex."

"Hampshire."

"Well, somewhere. Honestly, men and sports," she says, puffing out her cheeks. "It's like the only time they feel they can cry."

"That's not true!" I exclaim, causing Laura to look at me oddly. "I mean," I cough, "it's important, isn't it? It's how we, how men, I mean, can come together, to bond, to connect."

Laura listens and then tips her head to one side. "I just wish they'd be as passionate about other things," she says, staring back at the players.

I think of my friends. Many are quick to anger, but I can't recall seeing many of them cry. I'd always thought Jay was quite in touch with his emotions, but even he doesn't really cry. The last time I saw him do so was after a football loss, and he barely got out of bed the day after Chelsea lost the FA cup to Leicester. Should men reserve that kind of emotion for things in their own lives? I shift, realizing there is truth in what Laura is saying.

Things went south at school between Eddie and I over sports. He never forgave me for captaining the cricket team in our last year. Surely that isn't why we lost touch?

Laura breathes out slowly. "Well, I better go and see if Mum's OK ..."

I think of Amy wanting to please Laura, the atmosphere back in the hotel room, the scenes from last night, and I grab Laura's arm as she goes to leave.

"Hey, before you go," I say, "I really am sorry about before and the dancing." I add, "Stuff is going on with me and Flynn right now, I'm a bit distracted."

Laura turns back to face me. "I promised myself I wouldn't do this and just focus on, you know, my wedding. But," she breathes through her nose, "is this all about how you don't want to move in with him like we talked about on the phone yesterday? Or have you actually dumped the guy? Because you told me you wouldn't this weekend." The words tumble out in a rush.

"I ..." My mouth drops open, my brain slow to catch up with what she is saying. What? What did Amy say yesterday? Yesterday.

"Or was it all an exaggeration?"

"An exaggeration," I repeat.

"So it was?" Laura rolls her eyes. "So there isn't a drama? You were just scaring the shit out of me that you were going to dump your boyfriend at my wedding."

"Dump him," I say, panic flaring immediately. "Why would Amy dump m— Flynn?"

Laura narrows her eyes. "Why are you talking about yourself in the third person?"

"I . . ." My brain has gone into overdrive. Was Amy about to dump me? Is Laura serious? I knew that the prospect of me moving in had made her nervous, it's why I knew I had to go bigger, but I had no idea things were so bad. All my worries seem to make the world blur. "I'm just, I . . ."

"Well, if it means anything, I don't get it. Most women would love a man who wants to move in quickly, make a commitment . . ."

I'm starting to feel light-headed, her words jumbling as I try to work out what she is telling me.

"We're not going to break up," I say—a promise to myself? I think of our room, a box nestled in amongst my clothes.

Dump me?

Some of the players are warming up on the court, taking turns to serve. For some reason Amy has chosen to stand in the center of the court and keeps ducking and shielding her head.

"What is he doing?" Laura frowned. "Can he ever be serious?"

The last conversation—and this question—makes my voice hard. "Not everyone needs to show they're stressed all the time." A thought I've often wanted to level at Amy, who doesn't understand just because I'm not always explicitly talking about stress, doesn't mean I don't feel it.

Laura folds her arms. "Is that meant to be a dig at me?"

"What? No," I say.

"Because I'd be a lot less stressed if my maid of honor didn't keep going AWOL."

How is this going wrong again? Laura never talks to me in this tone.

Just then Reggie snuffles into my hand and I bend down to ruffle his head, plunging my face into his soft fur.

Laura is slack-jawed. "I thought you were scared of him."

Looking up at her, my arms still round Reggie, I shake my head. "I sort of got over it."

"Right," Laura says slowly, her brow furrowing. "I feel like I hardly know you at the moment."

I can't meet her eye, pressing my face back into his fur to avoid a response. Over his fur I scan the guests, idly wondering who else is in the tournament. Patty, white socks up to her knees, her gray bob clipped back, is deep in tactical discussion with Amy who appears to just to be nodding dumbly. Jay is standing nearby talking to his partner. Of course, it's Tanya.

This weekend is so messed up.

43

FLYNN

Two Weeks Ago

I often wonder where I'd be if I'd met Amy before Tanya and everything that happened. If I'd met Amy and my dad hadn't died, and the world I inhabited with my mother hadn't imploded. If I had stayed at my public high school in London with my local friends and my parents who loved each other. If I'd turned out to be an entirely different person.

I'm frightened. The signs are all there. Recently she has started to ask more questions, frustrated by the shallow replies or vague details I offer. Some of my small lies contradict other lies or have grown into bigger lies. "I thought your dad got you a set of Russian dolls?" "I thought he taught you how to fish?" "You told me your mother wasn't there, do you not want me to meet her?

196

Are you embarrassed of me?" I feel panicked, everything unraveling. And I can't let her go, I can't mess this one up, because I need Amy. I feel it in my bones, that we will make each other whole, make each other better.

I'm trying to offer more, I know I need to trust her, but thoughts of the past, of the things that have happened when I've opened up, seem to send me back down a familiar path. I know if we live together, if I can show her I'm in this forever, that all that will come. Once I know she isn't going to leave too I can relax.

I've spent a lifetime handling worries, plastering on the brave face. I'm famous for it at work. With a hundred demands on our time, emails and angry exchanges, invoices not paid, performers not showing, clients bailing or suddenly changing their plans. We have to turn on a pin, we have to accommodate everyone, we have to stay upbeat and positive and easy to work with. The job is perfect for me. A mask I wear all the time. Like the mask I've always worn. Sink the worries, swallow down the fear, keep it light, keep it moving, don't push people away moaning. Don't break down.

Be a man.

Keeping Amy is like a challenging work problem to be solved. If she's pushing away, I tell myself she's not. I ask myself how I can fix this. How can I be proactive and turn this situation around? I can't lose her.

We are meant to be together. I know she needs me as much as I need her. I want to be the man that removes the line between her eyebrows, who makes her face break into a smile. I want to be there to see her find her confidence again, boost her to be brave. I want to be with someone who fights for people, who fights for a brighter corner on this earth. She is real and when I'm with her I feel real, tethered.

If I can assure her I'm committed, I can allay her worries about me. Surely she can trust that the rest will come if I show her how ardently I want to be with her?

"I want to move in with you."

I pretend not to notice the surprise that flitters across her face. I need to know that this can work. That I can make it happen with sheer will.

"We should live together," I repeat.

She pleats the duvet with her fingers and a panic churns inside me. Is this not what she wants?

"I'll pay for his 'n" hers sinks if that's your worry?"

The light-hearted comment comes easily and she lets out a small laugh. Is that uncertainty behind the noise? I keep my expression light, hopeful. She can't quite meet my eye.

"Let me think about it," she says.

I assure myself that's a yes, a maybe yes. How can I make things more concrete?

I realize I need to do more to reassure her that I'm serious. It won't be enough to move in; I need to demonstrate that she is the woman I want to be with for the rest of our lives.

I form bigger plans. Laura and Amy are so close, were so close, and I want to show her family, the world that I am in this forever. That I want to build a life together. Laura's wedding is in two weeks. Two weeks is long enough for me to plan a proposal. A clear signal that I am in this for the long haul.

I swallow down the bubbling anxiety as I start to think of the logistics. Like planning an event on a tight deadline. I think of the stunning setting, how everyone she loves will be there.

There'll be people there, witnesses, a crowd. The thought galvanizes me. No one would say no in that setting. Not that she would, I remind myself, she might say it's fast or we should live together first, but I think she'll say yes. Of course she will. I know when things are going well that she loves me too. I know that I can be the man she wants me to be. We have so much fun together.

I'm lost in plans as she finally looks up at me.

"I just need a little more time," she says quietly.

And I nod robotically, already moving on to bigger things in my head.

"Of course," I reassure her and I'm gratified to see her relax, to sink into me as I throw an arm around her.

"I love you, Amy Norman," I say in a too-loud voice.

She whispers something quietly into my shoulder. I think it's I love you. I'm sure it is.

44

AMY

The reality of the situation hits me. I am dressed in whites, and everyone is expecting me to be exceptional at tennis. I'm a good athlete, a legend among the men here. I blink rapidly.

I last hit a tennis racket circa 2009 and that was in an attempt to hit Pauline Michael's shoe over the school roof. It smashed a (first-floor) window.

Flynn's face is a picture through the wire of the fence as he clearly comes to the same conclusion. In two years together I'm not sure I've ever caught a set of keys he's flung at me. His expression only makes me more nervous.

I wish we'd been able to talk more before I was summoned to the court. I wanted him to reassure me that my worries about Mum were in my head.

"Flynn!"

I know I can catastrophize and Flynn is always calm.

As much as I want him to react, sometimes his mellow approach really is what I crave. In this instance I need him to tell me Mum is fine, that I shouldn't be fretting.

"Flynn!"

Someone nudges me and I finally register a woman calling Flynn's name—at me, of course—and turn to see Flynn waggling his fingers through the fence. "You'll be great."

I still feel a shock at seeing myself staring back at me, even if the expression on my face is pure Flynn: wide eyes and smiling. I can't do anything more than nod back.

"Flynn, you're being paired with Patty," Jay calls out. "Eddie, you're with Tanya."

I can't help watching as Tanya walks over to Eddie, in a perfectly cut tennis dress, her swishy blonde pony-tail bouncing as she moves, both of them looking beautifully blonde and glossy. I should feel grateful—here's an opportunity to find out more. An evening of tennis ahead. And yet my stomach churns as Patty jogs onto the court to stand next to me, loudly telling someone I played first pair for Hampshire as a teen.

Gulping, I grip my racket. I should have left with Flynn when I had the chance. I'm completely out of my depth. I barely remember the rules. Something about love? I was brought up on a diet of football. Now sports don't register at all, matches are too hard because they remind me of Dad, and it was never really about the game itself, just the excuse to go together.

Nearby I can hear Patty repeating the fact to Tanya and Eddie.

"A county player!"

Because of course Flynn is a star sportsman.

Tanya replies, saying she knows, and I realize, with a punch to the middle, that Flynn must have once told her that fact too. It makes something simmer within me. How can I know that detail about him but so much of him is so often a blank? I thought our connection did go deeper, but am I just like every other girlfriend he's had?

Eddie rolls his eyes. "We'll see what ten years has done."

As I line up, I think of a way I can engineer a meeting with her. Perhaps she can shine more of a light on the mystery behind their relationship. Flynn doesn't seem at all like the kind of guy to have a deep, dark past. I don't want to be insecure, but there's an underlying niggle, an instinct, the thinnest thread I feel like tugging on.

All these thoughts disappear as Patty starts to discuss our approach, placing me on the backhand side because I'm the stronger player.

"I think that's a mistake. I should be on the forward-hand side," I say as she frowns at me. "The other hand side. I don't want people to be too jealous. I'm quite rusty."

"Don't be modest."

When I wander off, she reminds me which side she means and I nod and walk there, as if I was just joshing around. I make a sort of clown-like face and her lips disappear in a line.

The game begins. Patty soon realizes that I am the

weaker link of our pairing and, when I duck another volley shot, shout as another ace whizzes past me and clash rackets with her as I attempt to hit something that flies down the middle of the court, tensions rise.

By the end of the set, which we have lost dismally, I stagger across to grab a water bottle from the table next to the court.

Patty has stalked off, possibly to lodge a formal complaint with Jay who might have told her Flynn is a sporting legend, and I'm left alone. Tanya has grabbed a bottle from a nearby chair and, taking a breath, I step across to her.

"Hey," I say, as nonchalantly as possible.

"Oh hey," she says, starting a moment, water dribbling on her chin. She frantically wipes at it.

My own heart pitter-patters with nerves. Here she is, the woman I've been wondering about for the last few years, standing in front of me. Close up, her skin is even smoother, her eyes sparklier, and I feel that familiar mix of admiration and envy.

"That was nice of you," she says, indicating the court.

I'm lost.

"Pretending not to be brilliant. I'd forgotten you were never really competitive, not like . . ." she trails away.

"Oh, yeah," I say, nodding earnestly. "Yeah, I thought it was better to try to give other people a chance."

"It's kind of you. You were always kind," she adds.

I don't respond, my brain turning over a hundred questions.

"You know your girlfriend hates me," she says suddenly.

It's the curveball I didn't see coming. "Oh!" I scrabble around for something to say. "Well, that's, that's Amy. She can be jealous. Of exes. Women, right?!" I roll my eyes and shift my weight, letting out a laugh I've never heard Flynn use.

Tanya frowns. "I guess."

"But I'm fine with you being here. Fine. You can tell me anything. Really anything." I give her an intense stare and she glances across the court.

Eddie is standing with Jay and some of the other groomsmen, and in a rush she turns back to me, startling me with the speed of her next sentences, "Look, Flynn, I wanted to catch you, I wanted to say . . . Well, I came here this weekend in part to see you. I still think of that last message you sent me, when you saw me with Charlie, I just . . . I just wanted to say I get how you were feeling. And I'm sorry."

She stops, breathes deeply, shoulders slumping with clear relief.

"Right," I say, attempting to process what she is saying, unscramble the meaning. "Right, well, thank you for saying sorry. That is, that is nice," I finish lamely.

What message? Flynn always told me he broke up with her. In fact, he always gave me the impression that he didn't like Tanya. He's never mentioned anyone called Charlie. Who is he and why would seeing Tanya with him affect Flynn?

"So," she says, tucking a strand of hair behind her ear. "So are we OK?" she asks, words tentative.

"Are we OK?" I repeat slowly, still pondering the things she has thrown out.

Patty waves me over, another game starting. "I have to go."

Are we OK?

45

FLYNN

I feel a visceral longing to be out there, not watching from behind this fence. The thwack of tennis balls, the shouts, the cries all remind me it's my happy place. The back and forth, the rules, the simplicity, the ritual: I know where I stand. It's not shifting, I know who I am out there. Now that I'm not in my body it's like a drug; I'm craving the endorphins sports give me, the release.

It's also harder than I thought to watch Amy lope about, swinging the racket wildly, eyes rolled in panic. Or worse, duck, which she has done a number of times. Patty has started to streak across to her side and cover for her. Every now and again she glances my way, sweat beading, anxiety showing, and I can do nothing but grimace or give a thumbs-up. The thumbs-up is strained and over the top every time I think of Laura's words. Is

Amy really considering breaking up with me? Are my worst fears coming true?

"Flynn's not on his game today," a voice says from behind me.

Geoffrey has found a scone from somewhere, a dollop of cream just next to his lip.

"Hi, Geoffrey. Yeah, he's . . . he's struggling to find his form. A bit."

At that moment Amy ducks and squeals when someone serves at her. Geoffrey's head tips to the side. "Flynn is certainly being a gent, letting others win."

"Yeah, yeah. He did say he might . . . might do that."

"He's a nice guy."

"Thanks, Geoffrey." I give him a wide smile and he frowns.

Trish waves from the other side of the court, two proseccos in hand.

Geoffrey falters, suddenly standing very close, his voice low. "If you want to talk to your mum this weekend about anything, Amy, you should. And if Flynn says anything about seeing us, well, no matter, just make sure you and your mum have some time together, alright?"

He gives a furtive look over his shoulder and I can't help the confused laugh. "You alright there, Geoffrey? What have you and Trish been doing?"

This is all a bit peculiar; I have no idea why Geoffrey's being so cloak and dagger. Normally our conversations revolve around sailing, sports, and global warming. He's never normally cryptic or personal. Perhaps this is how he talks to Amy?

"Nothing, nothing, just wanted to check in, see what had been said, if anything, but clearly he hasn't, not that he should have—"

My confusion deepens as Geoffrey tugs on his collar. "I just think you could talk to her, your mum, that is, she'd like that."

"Right, Geoffrey, OK mate. Well, I'll be sure to check in with her."

It's Geoffrey's turn to look confused as I go to slap him on the back and turn it into a sort of strange rub that I imagine Amy might do. "Thanks."

The dollop of cream is still on his lip as he melts away.

I'm still thinking about the exchange as I make my way to the pavilion, wincing as I knock a hip into a table on the way in. Will I ever get used to this new body? The disconcerting feeling that mind and limbs are not in tandem? It seems so obvious to me that I'm not Amy, and yet Geoffrey just accepted that is who I am.

The walls are lined with huge wooden boards, the names of past captains glittering in gold; the air smells musty like unaired rooms and old socks. It's the smell of PE classes and for a moment I feel an overwhelming longing to be back at school, when life was structured and simple and I understood the rules.

I push open the restroom door to see a man at the urinal.

Eddie turns.

"Oh hey," I say from the doorway, realizing staying would look strange, but leaving meant entering the Ladies, a terrifying place I could only imagine smelled like perfume and sunshine.

He's in his tennis whites, a grass stain on his shorts, an alarmed look on his face. "What the—"

"Sorry," I say, turning to leave. My hand is on the door when, almost as an afterthought, he calls out.

"You need to tell your boyfriend to stay away from my girlfriend."

I freeze before turning slowly back around. Eddie's blonde eyebrows are knitted together, his chest jutting, chin tilted. What is he saying? What has happened?

"He wouldn't want to go near her," I say, unable to stop the disdain dripping from every syllable.

"Well, he has, and he scared her."

"Scared her. What the . . ." Scared? My nerves jangle despite the strange laugh I've just emitted. What's happened?

"Just tell him to leave her alone. He needs to get over it. Typical Flynn, trying to be everyone's favorite boy."

I'm shocked how Eddie is speaking to me, or rather to Amy too, as though he barely likes me.

Favorite boy! Over it! This is unbelievable. I haven't talked about Tanya, and I've barely thought about her, these last few years. If I have, I've forced myself to shift those things, shuffle them to the back along with all the other stuff I've shelved.

"He is over it!" I don't mean to shout that last line and I don't mean Jay to appear in the room at that moment either.

"Amy?"

"I . . . oh, for fuck's sake." I push past him and into the Ladies room, relieved to see at least it's empty. Despite my frustration I also can't help noticing they do smell of perfume.

What the hell was that all about? What has Tanya told Eddie? Why would Eddie say that stuff? I remember all the small moments Eddie has thrown comments my way—is it that? Or is it something more? My stomach drops, a worried glance back outside. Geoffrey's odd behavior, Laura's ominous words and now this. What has happened?

46

AMY

In terrible news it turns out Patty is some kind of tennis demon. Jay has informed me that they have a court at home, of course they do, so we scrape through to the next round of this tournament. Hours have passed; it feels like these matches might never end as the bright afternoon slips into a softer evening. Fortunately, I think others are convinced I am being a gentleman by holding back—only Patty is annoyed by my good manners.

I've started to remember the rules, the sidelines, the boxes you need to serve into, and have spent a large part of each game stepping backward and watching Patty zip all over the place with the energy of a twenty-something. She's a phenomenon: hair held back with a toweling headband, a plentiful supply of energy drinks and bananas, and an off-putting grunt as she strikes each ball.

Lumbering around after her, I have done my best to swipe and swing at the ball but have not covered myself in glory. Patty has stopped telling people I played for Hampshire. Through the fence I can see Flynn watching me in his green maxi dress, his fists curled around the wire and a wistful expression on his face. He'd so desperately want to be doing this, it makes me a little sadder for him.

"Tanya and Jay, you're up."

Patty is beckoning and I realize, with a gulp, that our next match is about to start.

Tanya is jogging on the spot, pausing every now and again to stretch, and Jay is leaning against the netting grinning and chatting to Laura. For a second I watch them, the easy way they are leaning into each other, the way Laura throws back her head and laughs at him. They'd fallen for each other so hard and so quickly I had always held back. I'd been worried it was fleeting and wouldn't last. I had good reasons to mistrust Jay.

From afar they look perfectly suited and I feel a yearning for Flynn and I to be returned. He makes me feel relaxed, he quiets the noise in my head. How has it taken this swap for me to see that? Why am I willing to chuck it all away?

"Flynn."

Patty digs me in the arm, "Come on. It's your serve."

The service has probably been the biggest humiliation of the day so far and I make the mistake of looking at Flynn through the fence as I manage to get my fourth double fault in a row. It is incredibly difficult to work out how to get the ball over the net into that reasonably small square. We are a game down and Patty is barely hiding her displeasure.

It's Tanya's turn to serve and I can't help admiring how she looks in her perfectly cut tennis dress, her long, tanned legs looking longer as she curves her body and slams the ball down into the square. I draw back my racket only to feel the ball whizz past my ear.

"Fifteen love."

The game continues in much the same way and we are looking at utter annihilation. It's five games to none and I can almost smell the scones and cake and feel the bubbles of the prosecco I'm craving. Distracted, I take my place at the net as Patty serves behind me.

I'm not sure how it happened. Tanya receives the serve and dashes to the net the other side of me. The ball is arcing over my head and I believe I can hit it, I want to hit one, I want to try to salvage something. I pull my arm back and I swipe at the ball in the air, squeezing my eyes shut as I do so.

Almost at the same moment I hear a satisfying noise from my racket and watch in delight as the ball is no longer flying over me but is very much flying away from me. This delight morphs rapidly into horror as I realize where the ball is heading and it explodes into Tanya's face.

Her racket clatters to the ground, she grabs at her head, Jay comes rushing over and I am frozen in fright, staring at the weapon in my hand, dread pooling in my stomach.

"Is she dead?" I whisper as Patty stands at my side.

She huffs, "We'll give them the game."

Tanya steps to the side, a perfect red circle blooming on her cheek, and I bite my lip.

They call time on the game and, horrified, I walk like a zombie off the court, still amazed at the strength, the speed and feeling terrible.

From somewhere behind me I hear two women talking but I want to get away from here, escape.

"Is he . . . crying?"

47

FLYNN

I can't find Amy. One moment one of the elderly guests was telling me about his accountancy job while I had half an eye on Amy and her game, and the next Tanya was clutching her head, Jay was checking she was alright, the game had been called off, and Amy had disappeared.

Ignoring everything else, I rush to the steps to the hotel, worry biting at me. What happened? Why has she gone? She isn't in the bar, the billiards room, or the orangery, and the waiters preparing the dining room stare at me as I burst in, hair askew, searching for her. She isn't in our bedroom.

Has she left? Has she walked out? Would she do that to me? What happened with her and Tanya?

I have to fix things. I need to remind Amy that I love her. That we love each other, that none of this stuff should split us up. Panicking, I move around the side of the hotel, gravel crunching underfoot, the sky streaked now with purples and blues.

My eyes scan the lawn, the perfectly mown grass that becomes a motionless lake, the island almost shrouded in darkness. Were we there only last night? It feels like forever ago. Everything is changing, upending. It's in that moment that I spot the solitary figure silhouetted in the bandstand.

She's hunched over, head hanging, and I'm struck again by how mad this is, to be watching myself, staring at my own slumped body. This weekend has spun off its axis. We need to remind ourselves we can do this, together. I think of her bowing at me in our room, laughing at my rigid attempts to copy her dance moves. I think of our hands intertwining in the mirror.

Then I think of Laura's words earlier, the suggestion that Amy might not see a future with me.

The thought hits me straightaway and I race back up to our room, panting as I grab what I need and head back down the stairs. For a second I think I can hear someone call Amy's name but I keep going, knowing what I can do to rescue this situation, to remind Amy that we love each other, that we can get through anything together. I just need time, I think desperately, I have to buy us time.

She is still there, desolate and alone as I approach across the lawn, the lake glinting in the distance, the soft evening light turning the water pink. Crickets make sleepy music and the fairy lights wink at me as I approach her.

"Ames . . ."

She doesn't reply, simply staring out at the lake, lost in thought.

"Amy," I say more gently.

She doesn't even look at me, just closes her eyes, her voice weary, "Don't, Flynn."

I trip up the steps to the dusty wooden floor, the air filled with the scent of the roses that are twisted around the pillars of the bandstand.

"Flynn. I don't want to talk to you."

"We have to talk to each other. We're in this together."

"Is Tanya OK?"

I wave a hand, "Fine. She's fine."

Amy still stares ahead, her whole body drooping, tennis whites crumpled.

There is a pause. In my mind she turns, nodding her head in agreement as she sees me, standing there as her. As she remembers it is *us*. Amy and Flynn. The couple their friends shout at to get a room, the couple who laugh at the same stuff (toddlers who swear in public, the fallout over the new John Lewis Christmas ad, You-Tube videos of people slipping on stuff), the couple who go on last-minute breaks to Paris, North Wales, Norfolk and always have a good time because they only really need each other.

"We're not in anything together anymore," she says simply, and that sentence strikes real fear into me. All the images of us together dissolve in a second, replaced by Amy accusing me of not listening to her, her nerves that it might be too soon to move in, the things she doesn't find funny, her questions I brush off, avoid, Laura's words.

"Amy."

"I thought I knew you," she says suddenly, turning on her seat. "I mean, sometimes I feel like I don't get you, that you misunderstand me, but I knew we hadn't been together that long, that we would work these things out, but I thought I could trust you at least . . ."

"You can trust me," I say, stepping toward her.

She twists round to face me fully, my big body almost making the tiny stool she's perched on buckle. "I can't though, can I? What have you not told me? About Tanya?" She tilts her head to one side.

My voice hardens as I remember Eddie's warning in the restroom. "I don't know what she's said, but there is nothing to tell you about Tanya. The past is in the past and I don't see why it needs to affect us . . ."

"That's the trouble, Flynn, we're different. I want to know, want to share the past with you, to grow closer."

"We're already close!" I insist. The talk of the future, the panic about the past fuels my next move.

"I love you, Amy, so very, very much."

She lets out a tiny sigh. I don't want her slumped over and questioning everything, I need to do something big.

"And . . ." I do it without a second's hesitation; I need her to see, really see, how serious I am about her.

I bend down on a shaky knee in front of her, my pale blue skirt rucked up. She is frozen on the stool above me, her eyes round as she stares at me on the dusty wooden floorboards, looking up at her solemnly.

"Flynn . . ."

"...Amy, I know this is fucked up and we are literally in each other's bodies, but I still want to be with you forever. Even if we can't fix this thing, I need to know you'll stay with me, and we'll face things together."

Amy looks shocked; her whole body stills and her arms drop to her side. She slithers off the stool and then takes a step backward, bumping into the pillar of the bandstand.

I know things haven't exactly been working out as I planned but I thought doing this big gesture would jolt Amy to remember what's important, show her how serious I am. She hasn't said yes, but then her mouth is just working up and down, up and down, so I hope it might be on its way.

She puts both her hands up to her face; I see the scar I got on my left knuckle flash in the light. "I don't believe this," she says.

"I know," I say, my smile widening. "I know it's crazy and unexpected, but I want to marry you, Amy. I love you. I need us to move in, to move forward. It's always felt right with you. I love everything about you. Even when you're...me."

"I literally don't believe this," she repeats, her face pale beneath the stubble.

This isn't the reaction I'd prayed for. The yes is definitely taking longer to come than I'd hoped. Anxiety bites at me. This is my last move, I know this. Since asking to move in I've felt her slipping away. This is the only way I can think of to stop her leaving.

"It's true," I say, holding up the ring a little higher so

she can see the diamond, the flash of platinum studded with tiny stones, know that it is real.

"I can't believe you would choose this moment to do this. After today, after all this," she waves a hand around the place, "you decide *this* is the best thing to do. Oh my god, Flynn." She buries her face in her hands.

I'm still balancing on one knee; my leg has begun to ache, my smile falters.

I've had a lifetime of being told this is all women want. Commitment. I thought this was the only way to rescue things.

"Even if I wasn't ... ACTUALLY YOU, even if the answer might be yes," she stresses, "you really thought, after everything I've told you about this weekend, that this would have been a good weekend to do this?"

"I ... I love you," I say, desperately searching. "I love you and want to marry you, Amy. Start a family. It's always a good time to say that, surely?"

She opens her mouth to say something else and then freezes, her eyes drawn to something behind me. And her mouth opens wider, her eyebrows lifting.

"Oh my god," she says.

And I look around. And I see three slack-jawed faces staring at us from the entrance to the bandstand.

48

AMY

This is completely insane. Why is Flynn doing this now? How can he not understand this is *not* the moment? And marriage? Two weeks ago he wanted to move in and I still haven't agreed to that. This weekend has clouded my thoughts further. One moment I can see how great Flynn is, how hard he tries. Then I hear things that muddy everything I thought I knew about him.

I love being with Flynn, I do. But I sometimes feel that I don't truly know him. He deflects every conversation I've ever started about the difficulties in his past.

I know his dad died when he was young, but he has only ever shared a handful of chocolate-box type memories with me—the Ferris wheel, another where he ruffled his hair after a rugby match which embarrassed him in front of a friend. He won't introduce me to his mother—there's always an excuse, but I know it's because he

221

thinks I'm not good enough, smart enough. And he was with Tanya for longer than me and I know nothing about that relationship.

I need to feel that the person I choose to spend the rest of my life with is able to share, to talk to me in a deeper way. What if we can only just have fun, laugh? This weekend has highlighted how little I know him.

I simply can't understand how he would ever imagine this would be a good idea. Obviously we cannot do anything other than just get through tomorrow and then work out how to undo what's happened to our bodies.

I get another stab of fear that this situation is permanent and swallow it down. I need to deal with this proposal first. Staring at him kneeling on the floorboards, my skirt pooled around him, looking hopeful, I'm reminded again that Flynn is not a bad guy. In the last two weeks I've tried to convince myself otherwise, but it's not true.

Opening my mouth to say something, to explain, I hear a noise from the entrance to the bandstand and glance up to see my sister's horrified face, staring at what she thinks is me on one knee proposing to my boyfriend the night before her wedding. Behind her is Tanya pulling on Eddie's arm, but I dismiss them quickly, only able to see the look on Laura's face: disgust and betrayal.

I want to immediately explain things to my sister—not sure quite how that will go, but I can't let her think this is what is happening. Before I can, however, Eddie has shoved Laura out of the way and is stalking across the bandstand in my direction. His mouth is set in a hard line and his whole body is tense. He stops in front of me. He is massive, everything is coiled.

"What the hell," he starts.

"Stop it, Eddie." Tanya is breathing heavily behind him, not looking at me.

Eddie holds an enormous palm up to her. "I've got this." Then he turns back to face me, our eyes on a level. "I didn't think I'd need to say anything this weekend, but clearly after what you just pulled I do. You need to back off," he says, stressing each word.

"I have," I say, my heart racing as Eddie moves into my space. My back bumps up against the pillar once more, petals tickling my skin as his raging face inches closer.

"You hit her, deliberately," Eddie says slowly, spittle landing on my face as he enunciates every word.

"No, honestly I didn't," I protest.

"I don't think it was deliberate," Tanya tries to add.

"We were all there." Eddie grabs the front of my shirt and my eyes widen. "She warned me about you this weekend, but I didn't think Flynny would cause a problem, never has, too nice . . ." he spits. As if nice is a crime.

"Get off him," a voice says from behind Eddie.

It's Flynn, standing in my green maxi dress, curly hair loose and wild, a dangerous glint in his eye.

Eddie doesn't even look over his shoulder, a woman's attempted intervention clearly water off his back.

I think he might punch me and I cringe and close my eyes in anticipation.

When I open them I realize Flynn has leapt on Eddie's back, all five foot two of him, ruffled skirt hitched up, cry of "Get off him" on repeat.

Eddie has started to shake off the tiny figure like he's back in the scrum and Tanya and Laura are both openly staring at the scene as Eddie, Flynn on his back in my body, moves around the bandstand floor in some twisted dance.

"Oh my god, Amy, get off him." Laura has moved behind and is pulling on Flynn's bare leg, Tanya just gazing at me.

I'm totally at a loss for what to do, body still shaking from the shock of Eddie's threats and completely confused as to why Tanya would think Flynn would present any kind of actual threat to her, that he would want to hurt her. That's not him. Is it? What the hell happened between them?

Flynn has slipped down, arms around Eddie's waist, Laura now pulling on both legs, making it look like the world's most screwed up wheelbarrow race.

Should I intervene? This is absurd. I need to talk to Laura, but of course I look like I'm Flynn and my head is spinning watching this strange scene play out in front of me. I need to think. We should never have come. This has spiraled completely out of control.

"Stop it," I say shakily. "Stop it," I repeat, running across the space.

I don't see his fist before it's too late, but I feel it crashing into my head.

"Fuck," I howl, clutching my face as Eddie snatches

his hand back, rubbing at his knuckles, Tanya shouting "What the . . ." Flynn finally slipping from his waist, landing heavily on the floor, curls mussed up, chest heaving.

Laura has stepped forward now and has started shouting at Flynn, who is adjusting the green dress and looks like he's planning to launch himself back on Eddie for punching me in the face.

"I can't believe you proposed to Flynn at my wedding."

"Eddie, oh my god, you *hit* him."

"Tanya, he hit you in the face. He could have killed you."

"I didn't mean, I didn't wa—" I jabber, nursing my eye. "Fuck."

"Is this your way of getting at me? You just couldn't make this weekend about me, could you?" Laura is still focused entirely on Flynn, who is still in a messy heap on the floor. I hate him making me look so undignified but I'm in too much pain to say anything.

Everyone is yelling now; I'm staring at Flynn, Flynn is looking back at me. The puzzlement crosses his face. He's the only one in the world who also understands what is happening, the disaster.

"I didn't."

"You proposed," Laura interjected, still furiously gazing at Flynn who had barely noticed her there, scrambling to his feet to check on me.

"Are you alright?"

I flinch as he reaches up a hand to touch my face. "We need to get ice on that."

I swipe him away, oblivious to the pain, just wanting

225

to repair things with my sister. "It's not like it looks, Laura."

"Eddie," Tanya looks almost in tears. "Let's go back to the hotel."

"Laura, believe me."

Laura turns. "Flynn," she says wearily, "seriously, leave it. This is nothing to do with you."

I falter—what can I say? I want to tell her the truth but I don't want to make things worse. Our predicament would overshadow everything.

Flynn seems to realize he needs to fix things with Laura for me. I beg him silently with my one eye, get this right, Flynn, please.

"Laura—Flynn's right, it's not how it looks, I..."

"So that's just a pair of earrings, is it?" Laura motions to the box in his hand.

He swallows, closing his fist over it. "Well, you see," he can't help the panicked look in my direction, "I was trying to...I didn't think..."

"No, that's exactly it, Amy, you *didn't* think. I genuinely can't believe you chose this moment to sneak down here and do it. I mean, this is literally where we will be dancing tomorrow night, celebrating my wedding to my *husband*, but of course you needed to make this about you and Flynn. Yesterday you were going to dump him, today you want to marry him. Anything to stay in the center. You couldn't give me one weekend..."

She takes a breath, tears in her eyes, and pushes past Flynn out of the bandstand and down across the lawn.

49

AMY

Ten Years Ago

"You didn't think of maybe skipping this the day of his funeral?"

"It was important to Dad too. They're going to send him home but this *is* his home. He has a wife and kids!"

Laura's hands grip the wheel of the car as we make our way back out through Easton to the city center, past smashed windows and debris in the road from the protest. She picked me up as the police started arresting people.

"I brought you an outfit."

A black dress is draped over the back seat and the sight makes me feel nauseous. A small part of me wishes I had been arrested, that I could skip today completely. Dad wouldn't have minded. He still talks about being dragged off in the St Paul's riot. Talked. He talked. I can't think of Dad in the past tense.

Natural causes.

"Mum didn't need this today."

I fold my arms and pout.

Laura glances over. "I've lost my dad too, Amy, for fuck's sake."

"I know." I meant to spit the words but they come out in the smallest, saddest voice. I love Laura, I loved my dad. This is all so unfair.

The shame of that night has tortured me. As Mum and Laura have pulled together a funeral, I've just been a bitch, lashing out, storming off, unable to tell them what is eating me up from the inside. Dad's slack face staring at me from a dusty pub floor wakes me in a sweat.

Laura was pale as she discussed catering, readings, burial arrangements with Mum. I only poked holes in the plan or criticized whatever they decided.

Mum made excuses for me.

Laura finally broke the night before the funeral. "You're not the only one whose lost your dad, you know?"

It was true, but the pain and guilt of knowing it had been my fault simply made me spit back a swear word and storm off.

It had been my fault, I was sure. If I hadn't told him my plans the night before, if I hadn't been so mean to him before he'd gone up on stage, if I hadn't broken his bloody heart. Natural causes. Bullshit.

I'd lied to Mum; I'd lied to Laura. I hadn't told them

the things I'd said before he went up there. Now all I can do is lash out at anyone who wants to be kind to me. I don't deserve kind.

I want someone to tell me what to do, how to be now that he's gone. He was always giving me direction, his reassuring voice brushing away worries. That night had been one of the few times where I was breaking out of his plans for me. He wanted me to be a singer, but he'd wanted me to stay in Bristol with him. He wanted us to do it together. And I'd broken that dream. And I'd broken him.

The funeral is full of familiar people filled with soft words and sad looks and I move through it on automatic. Everyone telling me he loved me, telling me I looked like him, had his talent, had his fire. Claps on the back from the guys from karaoke nights, the football, our street, his work. Laura nodding on the other side of the room, our eyes meeting. For a second she gives me the smallest smile and blows me a kiss. I want to run over and hold her so damn tight, beg her to stay with me.

She is still leaving for London. She is still going to university, like Dad hasn't just died. She is leaving us too. My head spins with it. How can she? How can she leave me behind?

"Come," she'd urged.

That idea had scared me more. Uproot it all and leave Bristol—the only city I'd ever known.

"I can't leave Mum."

"Mum has her friends, has school, we'll come back loads and visit. Amy, come!"

"My job."

"London has estate agents, Amy."

"My friends."

"You'll make other friends, and we'll be back, it's only a couple of hours on the train."

"I can't afford it."

"You can stay with me until you can."

My breathing quickened. It was so tempting. Laura could make my decisions for me. Laura could tell me what to do. Like Dad had. For a second I wanted to nod, to trust that it would turn out like she said it would. But I couldn't. I was scared. And instead of saying that, instead of admitting I was frightened I wasn't as brave as her, wasn't as clever, I wouldn't know where to begin, afraid to tell her I was writing songs, I did what I often did when I felt uncomfortable and became a bitch.

"You don't get it. I can't leave. How can I leave? Someone has to stay. Someone has to pretend to give a shit."

She'd stepped backward, hurt flooding her face, and hadn't asked me again. Despite me willing her to inside. Ask me, ask me again. I'll come, I'll be as brave as you.

We get through the day. Laura does a eulogy that makes Mum cry but I can't find the tears. I just keep staring at the coffin, frightened of the moment they're going to take it away, that he is finally gone. All I can see is that last look on the floor of the pub, the last person to meet his eye, his daughter who totally disappointed him.

As a tear forms I feel Mum's hand on mine, feel her

squeeze, but can't squeeze back. I know how much she loved him; they'd been together for twenty-four years, married for twenty-two of them. Dad had always joked that Mum getting pregnant had forced them to, but anyone could see how much he adored Mum. I want a man like that, a relationship like that. I want a best friend.

The moment comes and we watch the coffin disappear behind the small curtains. Dad's gone. My knees tremble and I sit down abruptly in the pew and stare at my hands. He's really gone. I'm meant to just go on living without him. I've never felt smaller and less sure of myself. I watch as Laura and Mum move past, then sit and stare at the curtains until the officiant taps me gently on the shoulder and tells me I have to leave.

I need someone to tell me what to do next, which foot to put forward. All the certainty I had, the path I thought I could pursue seems to crumble away. I started all this with my stupid big dreams. I hurt the one person who loved me unconditionally. I'll never forgive myself.

50

FLYNN

I can't believe Eddie hit her, I'm going to jump back on his back and try and bite that asshole. I miss my six-foot-two-inch frame, my strength. My smaller body fizzes with anger. I realize then that Eddie has never liked me. We had the same interests, the same friends, but we were always poles apart. He always wanted to compete, to push. Why have I never stood up to him? He's a bully. I can't believe it's taken this swap to see that for myself.

This weekend was meant to be a celebration of everything. And Amy loves Laura so much she wouldn't want to upstage her. What have I done?

I see the hurt on Amy's face, and it kills me that I've contributed to that. I just needed her to know I am in this forever. I've felt her pulling away and I panicked. I understand now that I need to be braver, to face what

I've never been able to. It seems insurmountable, though: I still need time.

Amy has chased Laura down to the lake. All I can see from this distance is Amy still holding her face—that punch looked bad—as Laura yells at her thinking she's me and that I'm butting in.

Tanya is looking at me nervously, like I might leap on her this time, and Eddie's about to set off after Flynn.

"Just leave him alone," I say to him. "You've already punched him for god's sake."

He scowls at me. "Deserved it."

I take a breath, knowing I need to go to Amy, not make this any worse. My instinct is to rage and throw my weight around, but she needs me. I try to channel what Amy would say and do right now: she would want me to keep the peace. "Look, don't ruin Laura's weekend with whatever this is." I force myself to look over at Tanya. "It's just going to make everyone more upset. And we need to remember this weekend is not about whatever happened between— between Tanya and Flynn."

I try to meet Tanya's eye, but I'm so cross that she is ruining this weekend. If she wasn't here I wouldn't have to be dealing with any of this, lying to Amy, having to think about things I don't want to focus on. "The past is in the past," I say firmly.

Tanya nods miserably. "She's right. Eddie, come on," she says, deflated.

Eddie mumbles something, finally allowing Tanya to draw him away. She'd always been quick to back down, more passive-aggressive than confrontational.

233

It is only then I see Laura racing back up the lawn to the hotel. I crane my neck to see if Amy has followed her as Eddie shoulders past me. "Just tell Flynn to leave Tanya alone. She's with me now. He needs to get over this stuff with Charlie once and for all."

My stomach plunges as Amy appears in the entrance to the bandstand, her tweed jacket askew, one hand still gingerly touching her bruised eye.

She stares at me as Tanya and Eddie walk past her.

"Leave her alone, mate," Eddie hisses.

Amy doesn't acknowledge him, just looks at me, her body still. They step away, swallowed by the darkness.

"What was that about, Flynn? Who is Charlie?"

I lick my lips, straighten my skirt once more. "Let me take a look at that eye," I say.

"Who's Charlie?" Amy asks in a faint voice.

I wave a hand. "It looks nasty."

"Who. Is. Charlie. What happened between you two?"

51

AMY

I can see I'm not going to get anywhere; Flynn has shut down, lips pressed together. Then he's fussing again over my eye, tactics I've started to recognize more clearly in the last few weeks. He is the master of detracting attention away from topics he doesn't want to discuss.

My head is swimming, eye stinging from the punch and miserable with my fight with Laura. She, of course, just thought I was Flynn only making things worse, calling Amy a coward for sending her boyfriend in to fight for her.

I think again of the words she leveled: *Like I haven't worked out what you really think about this wedding.* I know what she's getting at, that I think the whole thing is over-the-top, but that's no longer true. My worry that she is pulling away from me has made me mean-spirited. I should never have made her feel guilty

235

for all the trappings. I *want* her to have an incredible wedding, I want her to have her dream day.

Now Flynn is keeping things from me.

"Fine, don't tell me. Fuck," I say, a hand up to my eye. "This really hurts. Can you get me some ice for it?"

I knew he'd oblige; he always wants to look after me. When I got tendonitis last month he bought ice packs for the house and was constantly checking on the elevation of my leg. I get a pang at that thought: him placing another cushion underneath me, his concerned face as he brought me hot Ribena like I was sick.

He immediately agrees.

"I'll meet you in our room," I say. "I just need to find Laura."

He doesn't question me, and again confusion washes over me. Flynn is a straight shooter. He never holds back things he thinks clients should know, never twists the truth to secure work. A client overpaid him for her daughter's sixteenth and Flynn had immediately returned the money, when she had just wanted to tip him for a great night.

The moment he leaves I set off for the hotel. If Flynn won't tell me anything, then I'm going to use my Flynn disguise to finally find out. And I get lucky, watching Tanya and Eddie in the foyer, Tanya waving her hands around, clearly annoyed. Eddie, his massive frame drooping as he lets her, dolefully taking the stairs two at a time as she continues to lecture to his back.

"You could have let me handle it, Eddie, you didn't need to hit him."

How many times have women thought that very same thing, I muse. Men charging in trying to fix something only to escalate things, when we were happy to sort it out.

I push aside the feeling of female solidarity and step forward as Eddie disappears around the top of the stairs. She yelps as I reach for her, "Can we talk?"

"Flynn, seriously, I'll scream. I'll . . . Eddie'll be back soo—"

"I don't want to hurt you," I say, exasperated, realizing that in my manly frame I'm a threat. That thought stuns me for a second. "I just want to ask you about Charlie."

The mention of the name makes her stop, then she seems to consider something before giving me a quick nod.

She motions to the open door off the foyer. "In here," she says, glancing back up the stairs. "I don't want Eddie to see us."

I follow her into a large, book-lined room full of lamps and hunting pictures and endless shelves, a sliding ladder from floor to ceiling so that you can reach the highest books. It smells of furniture polish and old paper. Fringed lamps on occasional tables give the whole room a soft light and I want to sink into one of the two teal velvet winged armchairs, close my eyes, and forget everything about the last twenty-four hours.

Do I really want to know what she might tell me?

"So," Tanya says, pulling the sleeves of her top down over her hands, "what do you want to know, Flynn?"

"Just . . . how is . . . he doing?" I try.

Tanya's face creases. "Are you pulling my leg right

now, Flynn?" She goes to leave the room. "Tonight's been bad enou—"

How have I already got this wrong? My voice rises, "Sorry, no, I'm not messing with you, I really want to know."

Tanya speaks quickly, words released with a huff, "Charlie is fine, she's doing great."

"She . . ." So Charlie isn't a man. I had assumed that maybe Charlie was someone Tanya had cheated on Flynn with, or a friend, or I'm not sure what. My brain is in a spin with this information, eye throbbing as I try to order my thoughts.

". . . She's just joined playgroup for three mornings a week and she's already made lots of friends."

Charlie wasn't a he. Charlie wasn't an adult. Charlie is a child: a little girl.

"That's, that's good to hear," I say, realizing Tanya is waiting for something. My head is still tangled.

"Look, Flynn, I know you told me you didn't want to hear about her, and I get that, but she's doing well. We're doing well." Tanya's face softens as she speaks, pulling out her cell phone. "Here," she says, thrusting her phone in my direction. "That's her dressed up for World Book Day. She wanted to go as an Alien in Underpants. She loved it."

Why would Flynn want to know about a small girl?

My world tilts as I wordlessly take the phone and stare at the screen, completely baffled. A grinning blonde child wearing space pajamas with tiny pants over them is grinning at the screen. Tanya is a mother to this child.

Charlie. And judging from this photo, Charlie is no more than three years old.

"I never sent you this, but . . ." Tanya takes the phone back and scrolls backward, my brain still not making sense of what I'm seeing and hearing. Tanya has a daughter. But why is that relevant to Flynn? Why does he not want to talk about her?

Then it hits me, and I start to feel the walls of the room close in on me, the shelves of books swimming.

As she hands over the phone I almost don't dare look down. I know this is a moment that is going to change everything.

And yet I can't not look.

I look at the screen in my hand. At the tiny, bundled up newborn, crisp white blanket, a tiny face peeking out of a burrito-shape, and then my eyes are drawn to the person in the hospital chair holding her, the person with the widest smile on his face as he looks at the camera, completely content, cradling the child.

"I didn't know whether you would want the picture, so I never sent it."

I can't help scrolling back a couple of photos, the same child in Tanya's arms, nestled into her hospital gown, her face make-up free, glowing, and then both their faces squeezed together, newborn Charlie pressed up between them.

I hand back the phone feeling nausea swirl inside me. This can't be real. And yet, Flynn's insisted on not dwelling on the past, urging me to live in the present, not to grill him about past relationships . . . What a fool I am.

The entire world blurs.

Flynn has a daughter. A daughter he has never mentioned.

Flynn is a dad.

"Here you are..." Flynn, triumphant, holding up a plastic bag filled with ice cubes, voice faltering on the final word as he takes in who I am talking to, my expression.

"Hi Amy," Tanya says brightly. "I'm really sorry about earlier, with Eddie. Flynn and I were just fixing that..."

I don't say anything, I can't. I just stare at Flynn, who of course looks like a concerned me, his bag of ice dripping on the Persian carpet of the library as, pale-faced, he waits.

"Flynn, shall we go up?" he says in a strained voice.

But I'm too quick for him, pushing quickly past him and out of the room: away from Tanya, Flynn, and the enormous secret that has just blown up my world. Taking the staircase three steps at a time, relishing the fact that my legs are long and I can move quickly. I stumble at the top, grab the banister as my eye throbs, making my vision blur.

I ignore Flynn's call from the foyer as I race along the first-floor corridor toward our bedroom. But of course, that's where he'll look, so I change course at the last moment. I can't believe this.

Flynn is a dad.

52

FLYNN

She isn't in our room, the hotel quiet, the lights dim as I pad down identical soft carpeted corridors searching for her, the bag of ice leaving dots on the spotless cream carpet like a trail of crumbs.

"Amy . . . Amy!" It's a while before I recognize that the voice is calling me.

Trish is marching down the corridor, lilac dressing gown pulled tightly round her, toothpaste on the side of her mouth. "Amy darling, what *were* you thinking?"

"Trish, I . . ."

". . . I've had Laura in with me telling me you proposed to Flynn . . . tonight . . . is that true? I told her she must have been mistaken but she insist—"

"It's true," I say in a weary voice, cutting her off. I don't have time to explain, needing to keep searching for Amy.

"True," Trish says quietly, eyebrows shooting up, "Oh darling, what *were* you thinking?"

"Well," I say, cross with why everyone in Amy's family seems so opposed to my proposal. "Because we love each other, because we're great together, because I want to spend the rest of my life with her . . . with him . . ." I correct quickly, passion making me louder than I mean to be.

"But this weekend, Amy, honestly. To be so thoughtless," Trish says, shaking her head. "Oh dear, and I was rather dismissive of Laura, now I feel guilty."

"Why is this weekend such a terrible time?" I ask, frustration building. "It was meant to be a good thing, a wonderful thing."

"Well yes, of course it is, but a surprise."

"We've been together almost two years," I say, a petulant whine to Amy's voice.

"And I'm glad you're not where you were a few years ago."

Where was Amy a few years ago, I wonder. She seems so sure of things, so certain in herself, it surprises me to hear this might not always be the case.

"But last week you told me you barely knew a real thing about him!"

This other nugget of information is another blow. My toes curl, there is truth in the statement. This was why I needed to propose; I can learn how to open up, I can try.

"Laura says you obviously planned it and hid it from her."

"I didn't mean to . . . I didn't think . . ." In alarm a peculiar sensation comes over me, a thickening in my throat, something pushing behind my eyes. Am I going to cry? I blink rapidly, tilt my head back.

It must be because I'm in Amy's body, I never cry.

"Well, this won't have helped anything, Amy. And you have been very peculiar this weekend. Geoffrey and I have been concerned."

Swallowing, I realize that in my eagerness to show Amy how committed I am, my desire to make her family part of our celebration, I have royally messed up.

"I can sort things, with Laura," I say. "But I really need to go now and find Am— find Flynn," I say quickly, water leaking more rapidly from the bag, concerned water might leak from my eyes.

"Just promise me you'll think about things, marriage-wise," Trish adds. "I mean, I know you get on, he's great fun, and you're right to think he brings out the best in you, but it's a long time, forever, you know."

I've been conditioned to believe all women wanted was a man to get down on one knee, but has Amy ever actually said that? An uncomfortable feeling washes over me. She's been gently trying to put the brakes on—her querying whether we should move in, her probing me about some of the subjects I didn't want to delve into. Instead of sharing more, I'd assumed this dramatic show of love would distract her from all of those worries.

"I need to find Flynn," I repeat, too many thoughts crammed into my head.

"I hear Eddie gave him a black eye over some girl he liked."

"I . . . that is . . . that was a misunderstanding."

243

"Well darling, if you want my advice, I'd fetch Flynn, tuck yourselves up into bed, and start again tomorrow. You've got some work to do to mend things with your sister. And I don't want you fighting, darling, life's too short. And you need each other."

Is it my paranoia or does she suddenly look rather pained saying that?

"Love you, darling," Trish says, pulling me toward her.

"Yes . . . yes . . . er, me too," I mumble into her dressing gown. Better than the thank you I gave her earlier. She pats my face and I feel that strange sensation in my eyes again, unable to stop comparing this motherly concern with my own mother's total apathy.

"I really do," she repeats, her own eyes filling. Trish seems particularly emotional this weekend.

The hotel has quieted now to barely audible sounds: whispers coming from other people's rooms, televisions on, and the hum of the lights that line the hallways. I'm about to admit defeat when I see the door that leads to the roof terrace of the hotel.

The cold air hits me the moment I step onto the enormous flat roof, shivering in Amy's green dress. Along the balustrade large stone pots of lavender fill the space between stone benches in small alcoves. It's in one of them that Amy sits, hunched over herself, in crumpled tennis whites, her head in her hands.

Practically blue with cold, my heart lifts at finding her, her eye now a ripe, blackish blue from Eddie's punch, even in this light.

"Lovely view," I say, still trying to lighten the mood.

When she doesn't respond I realize how often I deflect moments like this with humor. "We really should put ice on that," I say gently, showing her the bag of ice.

"Worried about your face?" she snaps.

She is right to be angry with me. I should have told her about things long before now, not just on seeing Tanya here this weekend. I should have told her months ago. Trish has brought that home even more.

"Amy," I say, clearing my throat, trying to order my thoughts. Where do I begin? Unused to talking about the past, it seems strange to be attempting it now. How far back do I need to go? I blink as I remember Tanya emerging from her bathroom, holding out the white plastic stick that changed my life forever. How I'd felt when she'd shown me, the months that came after, the tiny bundle in the hospital.

"I can't even look at you right now."

"I . . . I'm so sorry," I say, fear for the first time hitting me in the gut. This mustn't derail us, I can't let it. How have I allowed things to get this bad?

"Do you know how humiliating this is? To learn about Charlie now?"

So, Tanya did talk to her. Of course she did, Tanya would assume she'd been talking to me.

My skin feels clammy as she stares up at me, the look making me flinch.

"Two years and I barely know you, Flynn. I can't believe you would keep something so huge from me."

"Charlie doesn't have anything to do with you, with us," I say, thrown by the intensity in her look.

Her mouth gapes open. "It's got everything to do with us, Flynn. For fuck's sake! How can you say that, how can you stand there and be so cold? I literally don't know you at all."

"You do," I say, panic seizing me. "You do know me. I just, I don't know how to talk. I've wanted to, but the longer time went on, the harder it got."

"That isn't an excuse, Flynn."

I rake a hand through my hair, surprised all over again when my fingers catch in her long curls.

"This weekend is practically the first time I've even known Tanya exists. Do you know how messed up that is?"

My head droops.

"What kind of man are you?" Amy says, her tone harsh, judgmental. "She showed me the photo, Flynn. You and Charlie."

I frown. Photo? What photo?

With a punch I think back to the day Charlie was born, my heart twisting. Tanya pulling out her cell phone as I sat, stunned, in the corner of the room looking down at my daughter. I am so blown away by the pain that slices through me that I barely hear Amy's next words. There's a photo of me with Charlie. I am desperate to see it.

Amy gets louder now. "You always talk about having kids in the future, a family. 'We'll live here, Amy, we'll have three, four!' And all this time you *have* a child, Flynn. A child you clearly don't even see . . ."

I come to, as her words sink in, knowing I need to explain, to get her to understand. "Wait! No—"

"Well, you don't need to worry about any more kids. We're done, Flynn. I'm done."

My head is spinning with this. That is the conclusion she has reached? The verdict is in and she hasn't even waited to ask me. She has just assumed the worst about me, despite everything. Is that really who she thinks I am?

"You've made up your mind," I say slowly.

My fists curl as my messy feelings morph into anger. Unsaid things I've swallowed down swim into focus. "Of course you have. Because it suits you when it's my fault. Like everything. Your colleagues are idiots, the world is on fire because of everyone else, your mum is forcing you to stay in Bristol, your sister abandoned you, your dad dying is the reason you don't sing—"

She glares up at me, matching my rage, "Don't you dare talk about Dad."

"So now you don't want to talk," I say, throwing up both hands, letting rip in a way I never allow myself to. The whole sorry weekend coming crashing down. "Just because I don't tell you everything doesn't mean you have to always think the worst. We all have stuff going on, Amy. You don't have a monopoly on the shit stuff."

"I never said I did!"

There's a noise from nearby and a porter appears, surprise on his face as he steps outside, a silver circular tray in one hand.

"Oh, I had no idea anyone was up here, I'm sorry," he stutters, taken aback by the sight of us. "I came to lock up."

Amy is standing mouthing uselessly at me through her one good eye.

"Wait," I call to him; the porter wavers. "I'm not staying," I say, stalking past him, "Please do lock up."

The porter pulls out a jangling keyring. "Yes, ma'am."

I turn back, meet her eye, "We're all done."

53

AMY

I slide the lock across the moment I reach our room, my whole body fizzing with righteous anger, repeating Flynn's words, shocked at the things he said on the roof.

"We're all done."

What did he mean by that? Is it over? Why does that thought make me catch my breath now that I know the truth about him?

It has to be over now that I've learned the kind of man he truly is. Yet a small voice somewhere is confused, tugging at me. This doesn't feel right. Flynn has always seemed so open—telling perfect strangers they look well, telling me he loved me after about three dates, his eyes so earnest that I knew he really believed it even if it was absurdly fast.

The revelation about Charlie has rocked my reality.

I've been frustrated in the last few weeks, wanting to know him better, noticing how often he ducked and swerved questions about the past. But I have never considered my version of him, as an honest and decent person, could be wrong.

Everything is topsy-turvy.

To leave his own child! It makes me shiver.

The rattle of the door handle is entirely predictable, my high, angry voice in the corridor outside when Flynn realizes he can't get in.

"Amy, come on. Open the door."

Will we ever be back in our own bodies? Will this start to become normal? Me listening to my own voice, staring at my own body with someone else's mind.

I move across to the door. "I really don't want to talk to you right now."

"You need to," Flynn says, his fist pounding on the door. Why does he get to be upset?

"Just go away, I'm not interested."

"This is so unfair," he says, his voice traveling through the door. "Of course you've immediately trusted someone you met two seconds ago over me, that is so typical."

Fury fires up within me. "What do you mean?"

"You're always quick to think the worst of me. I don't take life seriously, I don't worry about anything, I can't be trusted . . ."

It is strangely disconcerting hearing my own voice level these things at Flynn. I can even recall times where I've said exactly what he is parroting back at me, the inflections the same.

"It's not like this stuff with Tanya has proved me wrong, is it?" My voice is defensive, sulky.

His voice is louder through the door, "Amy, I'm not the awful person you want to believe."

"Try telling that to your child," I say, spittle landing on the wood.

I wait for his retort, breathing faster. Nothing comes. There's a noise in the corridor and I strain to make out what it is. Staring at the door I hold my breath and press an ear up to the wood.

Quietly I slide the lock across, and inch the door open.

He's not in the corridor. Looking left and right down the empty space, I realize he's left. I don't know why I feel such a twist in my gut that he's disappeared. I'm right about him; I should be relieved. I'd seen the photo.

As I close the door, however, the doubt sneaks in. Do I assume things about him that aren't true? And if I have this time, it's justified, surely?

I'm not wrong about him . . . am I?

54

FLYNN

Five Years Ago

My whole world has shrunk down to this one little face. Tiny, screwed up, supremely angry. I have never seen anyone more incredible. Her existence blows me away. I'm speechless. All I can do is hold her little body, the unfamiliar feeling of soft bones and thin limbs resting on my chest. When she snuffles then yawns, I can't look away. It feels enormous and important, and for a moment the way in which my world has transformed in a few short hours takes my breath away. That I am responsible for this, that I can love and protect this baby and give her all the things I think she should have . . .

We're both completely worn out and the hospital lighting means it is impossible to know what time of day or night it is. She has arrived four weeks earlier than expected but is a healthy seven-pound baby.

Tanya's waters broke in the middle of the night and I tried to stay calm, to swallow down my panic that it was too early, as I picked up the pre-packed bag, following Tanya's instructions to the letter. My organizational skills meant I had been preparing for this like the most important work event, and it helped to focus on the practicalities rather than Tanya's labored breaths, groans of pain.

The baby had to be helped out. Watching Tanya in agony, her cheeks red with effort, forehead sweating, muscles clenched, was the hardest thing. The midwives instructed, soothed. I tried to stay calm, dependable, bring Tanya the things she needed as she went through it all. I tried to stay strong, repeating the words of the professionals, when all I wanted to do was clamp my hands over my ears, hating to see her go through something so raw.

And then the utter shock of being handed this screaming bundle, the strange weight of her as they turned their focus back to Tanya and I was left bewildered in the corner staring, utterly lost, down at the baby.

The last few months have been focused on the impending arrival of our daughter. The things that worried me about our relationship didn't disappear, but I needed things to work. I had to make it work, couldn't not be a father, I'd sacrifice anything. I know what it's like to live without love. I want this baby to have parents who dote on her, her greatest cheerleaders.

When I told my mother she was going to be a grandma she didn't reply for three days, and the pain of that only convinced me more that this time round it would be different. This baby would feel so wrapped in love she'd moan to her friends that her dad embarrassed her by never stopping telling her. Her friends. A teenage daughter. These thoughts are the ones that make me blink.

I'm holding Charlotte—Charlie—and the midwives have left us. It still feels surreal and I'm terrified that I'll do it wrong. Won't support her head, will pull off one of her fingers putting on the onesie or somehow drop her. I sit, tense in the chair, body rigid and uncomfortable as I stare down at this precious thing. I can't move without panicking I will wake or upset her or do it wrong, so I block out the pain in my muscles if it means all is well. It's completely overwhelming and my chest physically aches with the feeling.

I look across at Tanya, now sat up in the hospital bed, pale, toast crumbs on her chest as she holds up her phone and snaps a photograph. Slowly she lowers the cell phone and stares at us, taking us both in. I give her a small smile of encouragement.

"I can't believe what you did, what you went through ..."

She places her phone slowly back on the table and looks back at us. This time her face has changed, the strangest expression stealing over her.

I realize then that her eyes have filled with tears and I want to go to her, but I'm also not confident enough to get up and walk across to her with Charlie, pinned into this chair by my own fear. I sort of straighten, panic, and then sit as still as possible.

"Shall I buzz someone? Are you OK?"

Her eyes have welled up completely and a single tear slips down one cheek.

"Tanya, hold on, let me get someone." I'm worried now. No wonder she's crying, I'd be howling. I am not sure I will ever be able to repay what she has gone through with cups of tea, kind words.

Gently, I cup Charlie's head closer and struggle to stand.

"Don't get up," Tanya says and the ancient armchair sags once more under my weight. "I just have to tell you something."

I smile in relief. "Literally whatever it is, it's a yes."

She doesn't return the smile. A small spark of unease flares inside me. "What is it?" I ask, my voice serious.

"She's not yours."

I don't hear the words at first, not really. They don't make any sense to me.

Then they permeate my brain and my body clenches, my brain fogs.

The next sentences seem to be spoken from a distance.

"She wasn't premature. She was born on time."

I don't, I can't. Charlie snuffles closer to me; I'm aware of the sensation, how our flesh feels together. This can't be true. The things Tanya is saying. That would mean . . . My mind shuts down, the implications starting to rear.

"I lied about the due date. I was going to tell you, I wanted to. I almost did, a couple of times, I was going to go through with it. It's just I can't. Now I see her, I know it's not fair. I . . ."

She stops talking now, her words completely overcome with the tears that are falling freely down her face.

I'm still frozen in the chair, in this absurd scene.

I can't get angry. I can't get upset. I am holding a baby; I am aware I am. My baby. I can't hear her. I can't understand. In alarm, I realize my vision has blurred and I try to focus. This isn't about me. It can't be.

The lies are just completely overwhelming. Small, big, a hundred in the past few months; I'm frozen in the armchair, the room falling away. My mind can't quite compute what I'm being told.

Tanya tries to explain, her chest heaving, "I just couldn't tell you. You seemed so excited, but I have to tell him, I can't keep this in and now . . ."

She glances at her cell phone on the table next to her. She had been staring at it before she snapped the photo.

My head lifts and my heart fills with pity for her. I see the gargantuan effort she has made; she is on her knees with exhaustion. I can't bring myself to feel anything other than an utter desperation.

"He wants to see her. He's coming in. I need you to . . . to leave."

I blink rapidly.

He. Of course. There is a father. It's just, the father isn't me. That's when I unfreeze. When I understand what all this means for me. That this is final, over.

"But. You need, I can't . . ." I start to protest, panic now gripping me. I am holding her, I'm holding my daughter.

This can't be happening. This innocent, precious baby with her sparrow-like limbs and her angry little face is the love of my life. I can't abandon her.

"Please, Flynn. I need you to go."

"No, but . . ." I hold the tiny body closer, as if I can absorb her into me. How can I love something so much that isn't mine? Of course, she's mine.

"Please."

I can't refuse. Tanya breaks down completely. I can't refuse.

I stand robotically, wavering at the foot of the bed, shock making my movements slow. I move across to Tanya who lifts her tear-stained face and slowly holds out her arms in the bed, holding out her arms for her baby.

I stare at them, and then down at the bundle in my arms, the blanket soft and tight around her body. I'd been so proud, a little burrito, I'd practiced at the house with a towel and a rugby ball. I'd been so ready.

The house. I'd have to leave the house too.

"I'm . . . I'm so sorry," she whispers.

Gently I release the little fingers that have circled instinctively around my finger. My whole body hurts as I stare down at the small face, unable to believe this is really happening. For a second I can't do it, her little finger not quite ready to release. But then she does. My finger is free and carefully I lower her into Tanya's waiting arms.

Straightening, I feel empty, my arms wanting a weight, a something, a baby.

I have to get out. I have to get out before I snatch her back, press her to me, break down completely.

Be a man, Flynn.

That icy sheet that had thawed hours before, that felt hopeful, new, fresh. That ice returns, thicker, quicker. No threat of tears, the strange detachment descending as I turn.

She is not mine.

Charlie starts to wail as I push open the door—sensing the atmosphere or just crying because she doesn't know any better? I don't know her well enough to know what her cries mean, and now I never will.

She is not mine.

I move unseeing down the corridor, the antiseptic smell, the busy nurses, wheelchairs, and waiting patients. I step out into the street and catch a cab. The ride back to the house is a blur; the taxi driver, believing I've suffered a bereavement, almost cancels the fare. I pay on a card and step out, thanking him in a strange monotone I don't recognize as my own. I had been a father. I had loved a daughter. Staring up at the house, I can't believe I'm back here on my own.

I'm not a father anymore. I never was.

It's Tanya's house, her parents' base in Fulham that they gifted her. I moved in a few months ago when she told me about the baby. It made sense for us both to live here when Charlie came along. Now I stare at the familiar bottle-green door, the black and white tiles, and reach into my pocket for my key.

The hallway is decorated with a banner, a cheesy one I picked up a couple of weeks back. Something to make Tanya smile when she got back to the house as a family.

I'd run back to sticky tack it to the wall just before we left in the taxi.

The words taunt me now. "Welcome Home!" The banner covered in small babies.

I reread the words, feeling my body turn inside out with pain. There is no baby, no family. Just me. My whole world tilts. I don't know who to phone, who to tell. I know so many people, but I don't have many close friends. I could ring the boys I play cricket with, I could ring Karim at work, but what would I tell them? How would I put this into words?

I move like a ghost through the house putting things into bags and a suitcase. It doesn't take me long and I don't care what I take, what I forget. I just need to get out of this house. My hands are shaking as I zip the last things into a bag. I descend the stairs once more. It was always Tanya's house and I realize how few things I brought.

Something inside me fractures, cracks, the pain so intense I can't breathe as I take a last look at the jaunty banner. I step across to the side table and leave my key. Shouldering my things, I head toward the door. It's started spitting with rain as I step out into Fulham, with no clue at all where to go, or what to do with my life now.

I was a father, and now I'm not. I'm just Flynn. I have no one.

55

FLYNN

The night porter barely blinks as I stalk past him through the doors, hit by a wave of warm air smelling strongly of chlorine. I want distance from our room and Amy and everything about this whole hideous situation. She's clearly made up her mind about me and I'm shocked by how much that hurts, how quickly she has lost faith in me.

The room soars above me, the space echoing as I move around the edge of the pool, the steam and sauna in darkness, the water in the enormous round jacuzzi still. I walk down the side of the pool, past cushioned loungers, towels rolled in preparation for a new day, and slip off the heels that make my feet ache.

Staring across the turquoise water, I want to plunge from the edge and submerge myself, shut off all the thoughts in my head. I make out my reflection, or rather Amy's, in the water, her small frame, her hair loose.

Sighing, I sit on the edge of the pool and lower my feet into the water, sending out ripples that grow bigger as they move away, making her disappear.

Staring dolefully into the bright blue, Amy's painted toenails wiggle back at me.

Seeing Tanya has been hard, and thinking about Charlie makes me feel like someone is squeezing my chest tighter and tighter, making it impossible to breathe. My anger that Amy hasn't stopped to question things is mixed up with anger about everything that has happened. Normally kept under wraps, I feel closer to exploding with it all than ever.

I'd not expected the bombshell that Tanya was pregnant but quickly tried to be supportive. She'd been distant at times, struggling with the pregnancy, anxious, googling all sorts of medical things, nervous about the impending birth.

I was out of my depth in so many ways, but I tried to think of things I could do to help, always pushing the problems in our relationship to the back of my mind. The baby was bigger than anything else.

I was finally going to be part of a family. My lonely years as a child, the pain I carried with me like a constant stone in my chest, started to splinter and break up. My mother's eyes drifting over me, never resting despite my efforts to please, to joke, to be happy, a good boy. People's well-meaning comments, that I looked so like my father, made her flinch.

Had I? Was that why she was so quick to agree to send me away?

She removed all the photos, never spoke of him, and Patrick swept in and obliterated the last traces he'd existed. In my mind Dad was a blur, a collection of memories that soon jumbled into photos I'd seen, and blanks so big I started to confuse them with real things. Now there is simply a blurred nothing where his face once was and all the memories I tell people are fabricated. They distract people and mean no one probes. Until Amy, Amy asking for more details, Amy who has known loss and wants to share. How can I tell her I've made up a collection of memories? It will only confirm in her mind that I'm a liar.

As I lean over the pool, the tears drip from my nose, splashing into the water beneath me. Grief for that time, for that tiny baby, for the person I had been, making me finally succumb. Is it being in Amy's body that means the tears are closer to the surface? Amy who weeps over an *X Factor* back story, a charity ad, a slow song. Or is it that I am finally giving myself permission to feel these things?

I'm drained and exhausted, unsure how much time has passed as I drag myself across to a lounger, pulling one of the immaculate, fluffy towels over me and shutting my eyes, spent from thinking about a past I'd been determined not to return to. I never meant to lie to Amy; I just have no idea where to begin to unpick the truth. I'm not sure who I really am beneath the fabricated past and the faux-cheery present. I think of her upstairs somewhere, sad and angry, and know something is broken between us that might never be repaired.

56

AMY

The hotel has provided Molten Brown toiletries and a bottle of lavender-scented bath oil which, after I lower myself in the water to calm down, I wish had been bubble bath. Staring down at the unfamiliar flesh, the hairy chest, my new lower half, I cringe. Closing my eyes, I attempt to clear my mind but keep running through every part of this evening.

I can't see beyond it: I'd seen the photos; Flynn hadn't denied anything. He had never mentioned Charlie before: not a word. This thing is real and big and he'd completely failed to tell me any of it.

My dad was trustworthy, dependable. When he died I promised myself I wouldn't settle for anyone less than him. In the last two years there have been so many moments when I've wondered whether Flynn was that guy. Yet there was something behind it all niggling at me, a voice asking why he wouldn't let me delve too deep. I never imagined he'd be hiding something like this.

My heart aches when Flynn says or does things Dad would have liked. Encouraging me when I doubt myself, defending me even before he's heard my side. In the last couple of weeks I kept fretting that Dad wouldn't have liked him, with his posh education and his privileged upbringing, but I know that's wrong. Dad would have loved the core of him. They are both kind men, they both loved me so much.

I shake my head at that last thought. All of this is irrelevant if I can't trust him. And yet . . .

Skin wrinkling, I finally leave the bath, wrapping myself in towels and the dressing gown, putting my feet with Flynn's horrible hairy big toes into the mono-grammed hotel slippers.

Propping myself up in bed, I wait, looking around the room at the sumptuous suite we should have been enjoying as a couple. Snuggled up on the two-seater sofa, lounging in the bed, stepping out of the double glass doors to the balcony that looks out over the lake. Gazing across the bed now, at his empty side, I feel completely alone.

Worry presses down on my chest as my eyes start to droop, still wrapped in the towels and waiting for Flynn to return. He isn't coming back. My weary eyes take in the time on the winking clock. I don't know what to do, I don't know where to get help.

Before I fall into an uneasy sleep, I know where I need to go when I wake up. There's one thing I can try, at least.

57

FLYNN

Face pressed into the pillow, dribble in a little puddle, I jerk awake, totally confused as to where I am, curled up in a shivering ball, feet cold and poking out from under a towel that has half slipped off.

From my spot I can make out the still surface of a curved swimming pool, and then I remember where I fell asleep and why I'm not tucked up in bed with Amy. My body feels instantly heavier as I recall the events of the night before, the angry words exchanged. Hurt, she'd jumped to assume the worst about me, as she so often does. This is not a work call she claims is a sports website or scrolling TikTok viral videos: this is real.

The dawn makes me blink in surprise. Through the glass roof overhead is a hazy, pale blue sky, the sun already forming stripes on the surface of the water, spilling through the floor-to-ceiling glass windows. As I crane my neck up, body screeching in protest, pink streaks the horizon, a layer of mist settling over the hotel lawn and lake beyond.

I slowly sit up, my long hair dangling down, reminding me all over again that I'm trapped inside Amy's body. Will I wake one morning and find us miraculously switched back? Thinking of Amy forces me awake.

I readjust her dress. Will she let me in to talk? If not, I'll have to wait in the corridor for her to leave our room—she can't stay in there all day; it's Laura's wedding and she can't miss that.

That thought brings a fresh wave of panic when I think of the timetable ahead. Amy was going to play a central part in the day, but if the last thirty-six hours has taught us anything, it's that we absolutely cannot go ahead like this. I can't do it; there is no way I won't mess things up for her and Laura and I don't want to be the cause of more angst.

"Oh," the male voice reverberates around the cavernous room, making me start.

"What the . . ." Hand to my chest, I look around and see Jay standing on the other side of the pool in swimming trunks, goggles in hand, one of the hotel towels around his neck.

"Oh . . . hey," I say, trying to act casual.

"Hey," Jay says, frowning and moving around the edge of the pool. "Thought I'd sneak an early swim," he says, "before the big day begins."

"Good idea," I say brightly, standing up.

Jay chucks his towel down and frowns as he takes in

my appearance, yesterday's crumpled outfit and the lounger with the towel draped over it like a duvet.

"Did you . . . sleep here?"

I smooth my hair down, feeling the tangled knots as I do. "Um . . . no, of course not, I just . . ." I lower my head, "Um . . . yeah, yeah, I did."

Jay lowers himself onto the edge of the sun lounger, "Argument with Flynn? Bit of an asshole move by him to lock you out."

"Oh, he didn't," I say quickly. "I chose to sleep here."

"OK," Jay says, snapping on a pair of goggles. Then he sighs, removes them again, "What's up, Amy?"

"How do you mean?" I try to keep my tone neutral. Where to begin? I wish I could tell Jay what's up.

"With you, this weekend? What's your problem? You've been weird the whole time. I mean, you're always drama but this has been next level."

"I haven't been, well, OK, I haven't been completely myself."

"Laura's pretty pissed off with you," he warns.

My stomach drops. I know how miserable that news will make Amy.

"She thinks you're being selfish, not putting her first on this one special weekend."

"Amy's not selfish. I mean," I say, fiddling with my dress, "I'm not being selfish, I just have a few things going on . . ."

Jay frowns, glancing over his shoulder like he's worried someone else's in the room. "It's not anything to do with me and Laura, is it?"

I frown. "Why would it be to do with you guys?"

"Well," Jay says, not quite meeting my eye, "I was worried you thought maybe I wasn't good enough for her. You've never been a massive fan of mine, have you?"

"That's not true," I say, thinking back to the way Amy talks about Jay. She likes him, doesn't she? Sometimes she might roll her eyes a bit. But she's always had a hang-up about anyone she deems posh. She thinks I am, despite the fact all the money is Patrick's. I don't want any of it.

"I assume it's because of that night. But I told you that was a mistake!"

This shuts me up. What night?

"Well, I love her, Amy, despite what you might think of me . . . and, look, whatever is going on with you, I need you to pull yourself together, OK, for Laura?"

I nod, staring at him. Now I see it, him in his swimming trunks. He's pretty well built, a good-looking guy. What would Amy have not shared? What night?

I've never seen Jay in a competitive light. New confusion seizes me, my head swimming in the too-warm air that is already steaming up the bottom of the windows.

"Amy?" Jay says, waving a hand in front of my face.

"Need to get dressed and get moving," I mumble, scooping up my heels.

"Are you OK?" Jay asks.

"Just need to get back," I say, knowing I need to talk to Amy and straighten out whatever the hell all this is.

It seems swapping bodies might be the least of my problems.

58

AMY

Five Years Ago

Mum's left me a vegetarian lasagna. It's on the kitchen counter when I get back from work. I slip out of my rank purple polyester shirt with the garish gold estate agent emblem on the pocket and pad across in just my bra. Mum's left me food almost every week since I moved out last month. The accompanying note tells me to cook it at 350 for 25 minutes and then has lots of kisses. I think she feels guilty about Geoffrey moving in.

Maybe she should—I don't really get why he had to—he had his own terraced house a few streets away. Laura told me I should be more supportive, that they'd been dating for more than a year.

Mum is giddy. I just don't get the appeal; she is energetic and fun and has incredible legs—Geoffrey's a part-time geography teacher who has a hobby that involves owning over 1,000 different types of rocks. Seeing him sitting in the armchair Dad used to sit in still makes me catch my breath. Dad had dynamism, charisma, big opinions. Geoffrey has a soft voice and eczema. Laura says I need to give him a chance, but Laura isn't here watching him steal Mum away, is she?

I pick up a spoon and pick at the lasagna; some of the sheets stick to the roof of my mouth. My phone pings and I glance at it: "Ralf."

"Going to head to the city center for more signatures—wanna come?"

Do I feel like standing in the cold asking people to sign a petition? This one is something Ralf and I both believe in—to create an animal registry so that people who abuse animals can't own another one. I know I should go, I need to put the hours in. Dad was always fighting the system, trying to give people without a voice a platform. The hard ball of hurt inside me feels less hideous when I'm fighting something.

Sometimes, though, the causes blur into one another and I despair we'll never change anything. Ralf is so much more determined than me, it's one of the reasons I like him, that focus. And he is always fighting something. He gives me books about Marxism and human rights abuses in other countries too. I try to read them. I do. A flash of guilt runs through me. It should be enough to be with someone who cares about the world, but sometimes I see Mum giggling at something Geoffrey does and feel a flash of jealousy.

I set the phone aside. I don't think I have the energy
tonight. I know people should care about things like he
does, but sometimes I just want to curl into a ball on
the sofa, drape a rug over my legs, and binge-watch
something. That thought makes my toes curl with guilt.
I know I need to fight on. Dad isn't here to do it, and
I want to spend my life making up for how I let him
down at the end.

A video call starts and I smile in relief as I see the
name. Laura's face is very close up and she seems to
have drawn-on whiskers, which immediately makes me
snort.

"What's with the beard, babe?"

She widens the shot and I take in some ears.

"Why are you dressed as a cat?"

"I lost a bet with my housemate. Why are you in your
bra?"

"No good reason."

"It's very sexy!" She waggles her eyebrows and I laugh.

"M&S finest! Why are you phoning me?"

"Because I love you, weirdo."

"Oh!"

"When are you coming to see me? It's been ages."

"Soon," I promise.

"No, you won't," she says, but she's still smiling.

She's right, I've visited her new Clapham flat once and
refused to stay the night. I told her I had to get back to
Bristol, that work only agreed to one day off. It wasn't
that at all, but I was too ashamed to tell her the real
reason. Something about seeing her up there in London,

a wardrobe of trouser suits, friends I didn't recognize, made me feel smaller.

"I'm down next month but Mum's not going to be there—apparently, she's going to some rock convention or something to do with the Cheddar man, or, I forget. She showed me her new Birkenstocks. I'm worried, Ames—will she be wearing them with white socks like he does?"

"Very possibly," I say, nodding earnestly.

"I like him, though," Laura adds, "Geoffrey."

"He's OK," I say, that strange feeling like I'm betraying Dad rising again. Laura sees right through me.

"He would have liked him," she says gently, and yet again Laura is spot on.

I miss her. For a second I can't speak, I miss her so much. No one knows me like Laura, no one calls out my shit like my sister. It had always been me and her in corners, inventing games, staring at the sky together, making plans. I want to be dressed like a cat with her, making her laugh.

"Still with Ralf? How's it going with him?"

"He just messaged," I say, avoiding the question. How is it going? Sometimes I think we're colleagues raving against the world, rather than a couple. None of my relationships have lasted a year as yet. I'm not absolutely sure what I'm looking for and get teased for dumping them before it gets going. I just know I want a love like Mum and Dad had.

I'm about to say that, wanting to talk more about Dad, about the past, sift through memories like picking at a painful scab. I know Laura will indulge me. But I notice she isn't concentrating, she is glancing over her shoulder.

"I've got to go, Ames, we're going out."

"As a cat."

"As a cat," she laughs.

"Oh yeah, well, I'm . . . I'm off too," I say, not wanting her to feel she has to stay, but most of me wanting to kick back on the sofa and talk to her all night. I'm alarmed to feel tears push their way up my throat. I blow her a quick kiss and hang up with a "Miaoww" that makes her laugh.

The sound makes me smile sadly as I flop down onto a chair in the kitchen.

Mum on a rock convention with Geoffrey, Laura with her life in London. Sadness sweeps over me and I sit on my sofa, look around the barely furnished flat. I wanted adventures, I wanted a bigger life. Where did that Amy go? I crave more but have no idea how to go about it. What it even looks like.

A ping and it is Ralf sending another message—this one with a time and place. I stare at the words, like a little life preserver. I'll go and meet him. At least he seems to know what he wants and I can just put off thinking about any of this stuff for another day. We can rage against the world together, I can direct my anger at other things, other people and put off focusing on what I need to do, what I need to fix. I pick up the phone and tap out a reply.

"See you in ten!"

Taking a slow breath, I stand, push my shoulders back, ready to go into battle.

59

AMY

Through the open curtains the sky is a hazy pinkish blue, the island on the lake obscured by mist; two deer joyfully leap and spring across the lawn. I place a large hand on the glass, trying not to be distracted by the hand that isn't mine, and focus on the serene scene.

It's only then I notice Flynn's cell phone charging on the bedside table. I glance at the screen and see notifications from Karim and Bex with updates and comments. I pick it up and stare down at them, imagining Flynn as the boss of this company. The detail makes my eyebrows shoot up. Even on a weekend away he is getting messages like this; it makes me feel ashamed that perhaps I haven't truly understood how never-ending his job is. I place the phone back, even more desperate to share all of this with someone who might care.

Wrapping a dressing gown around myself, I creep out

of our room, the hotel deadly quiet so early. I half hope to step over Flynn curled up asleep in the hallway, but no one is there. For a moment I panic he's actually left. Would he do that?

The smell of beeswax and fresh flowers is stronger on the top floor as I make my way up the stairs toward the honeymoon suite. Knocking quietly, I rehearse my opening line, still drowsy from broken sleep and Eddie's punch to the head. She needs to believe me.

"Laura," I whisper through the door and knock again. "Laurs."

I'm desperate to get in, plead for her help.

She opens the door in her new green silk crepe-de-chine pajamas, black cats stalking across the fabric. I'd sent her the link to them from the Net-a-Porter website.

"Oh my god, that print looks so good on you."

"Flynn? What the—"

She steps back from the door and I step inside, immediately flummoxed by the sumptuous setting.

"Holy shit," I laugh, eyes rounded, the opulence obliterating everything else in my head.

I have never seen a room like it. It's not a room, it's about four rooms that all flow into each other. The walls shimmer; different shades shift in the light like the inside of an oyster. Mahogany tables, polished to perfection, line the entranceway, vases atop filled with pink roses and white orchid sprays, the scent making my head swim.

In the main bedroom there is a copper bath positioned in front of one of the floor-to-ceiling windows to take advantage of the view. From this height you can see out for miles, rolling Devonshire fields of browns and greens currently emerging from a layer of mist.

"This is insane," I say, jaw dropping as I take in the rest of the place, bigger surely than our childhood home in Bedminster. The pale pink velvet chaise longue in the corner, the elegant, curved silver floor lamp, the raised platform with a soaring cream four-poster bed, intricate carvings around the headboard, thick gold curtains pulled back theatrically.

I lift a hand to my neck and rub at it. "Shit, you've made it, Laura."

I know now I should have been less judgmental about this venue. Who wouldn't want to wake up here on the morning of their wedding? And if Patty, who can afford it, has offered to foot the bill, why shouldn't Laura accept and simply relish the whole experience? Why hadn't I realized this before now? Do I always assume the worst? Is Flynn right about that?

I'm met with a defensive press of the lips, hands moving to her hips. "What's that supposed to mean, Flynn? Like, I'm not good enough for the room?"

Flynn. Christ. Of course, I'm Flynn.

"No, of course you are," I say, flapping my hands in panic. "I just, I came to talk to you and this place just blew me away a bit."

"So," she says, still glowering at me, "spit it out, why are you here? Where's Amy?" For a second a look of worry crosses her face. "Nothing's happened?"

It makes my heart melt a little that she does care, gives me hope that this is going to go well.

"Amy's fine," I say.

"Well, she shouldn't be after last night, she should be feeling like shit."

"Laura, Laura . . ." I hold out both my hands and clamp her flailing arms to her side.

Startled, her mouth snaps closed and her body goes rigid as I try to get her attention. Horribly, she looks momentarily frightened and I immediately let her go. I think of the times when I've felt nervous, a man a little too close, an unwanted hand on my arm or shoulder. "Sorry, I didn't mean to scare you, I just need you to listen to me. Laura," I say slowly, licking my lips, mind racing, head pounding as I stare at her through my bad eye.

I take a breath. "Laura, it's me, I'm Amy. As in I am Amy, in Flynn's body."

There's a moment's pause as Laura, hands still hanging at her side, stares at me.

I wait, trying to gauge her reaction, but it doesn't come.

"I know it is unbelievable but it really is true. Seriously. I'm your sister. It's me."

She doesn't react, still just staring at me, muscles still, everything suspended.

Then she lets out a sort of strangled laugh. "Why are you doing this, Flynn? Is it a wedding day joke? Because I don't get it." Her face turns steely, "And it's not funny."

"It's not a joke, Laura, I'm Amy. I'm your sister. I was born in Frenchay Hospital, Bristol on July the twenty-fourth. I'm a Leo," I say loudly, "which you were always

277

a bit jealous of because you are a Virgo and Louis Jones told you Virgos are nerds. Our parents Trish and Robert always wanted two little girls and got them . . ."

"Flynn, seriously, stop it," she says, her forehead creasing.

"No," I say firmly, breath quickening. I must convince her. "We used to stand on that little table in the front room and put on shows for them. You used to be Posh Spice and you made me Mel C because I liked wearing Kappa tracksuits, but I *always* hated it and wanted to be Baby and I wore my hair in bunches for like a year to convince you. And then we cried for about a week when Geri left the band and we burned the tickets we got for Christmas in the trash can under the hall table because they'd sung 'Friendship Never Ends' but it had ended and we were devastated. And Mum told us off because we scorched her new carpet in the hall and nearly burned the house down. And Dad took us for McDonald's and told us Mum would come round and we chose her a new can which every time she used she'd sigh thinking of the other can."

Laura was frowning as the information spilled out of me.

"You had a boyfriend called Callum who had a skateboard which he'd bought from Argos but he'd bought special new wheels and always carried tools round in a fanny pack so he could tighten them and he called kissing 'French kissing' because he thought that was more grown up and Dad called him an idiot because his dad had put a Tory poster up in his window—and you didn't talk to Dad for like a week. But then Callum dumped you anyway because he booked to go to Majorca and didn't want a girlfriend to 'tie him down.' "

My chest is heaving as I finish, rooting around for more to say.

"She could have told you this stuff," Laura says quietly, confusion crossing over her face. "This is just stuff you could have learned."

"I haven't learned it," I insist.

"I don't get why you guys are doing this to me."

Now there are tears in her eyes and I'm frightened and desperate. I put my hands on her shoulders and I feel her body turn rigid once more. "Laura, please, I'm not doing this to upset you. I *wish* it was a joke. Believe me."

"Flynn," Laura says, holding two fingers up to the side of her head like she does when she's stressed. "It's my wedding morning and I don't know why you've been sent along to play this trick on me—"

"It's not a trick, Laura, you *have* to believe me. It was on the way here, we were hit by lightning and when we stood up we had literally turned into each other . . ."

"Stop it, OK, stop it, this is the worst bullshit to get Amy out of behaving badly this weekend. She's always been weird about me and Jay."

I think of what I could tell her, about why I'm funny around Jay, but I bite down the words. She doesn't deserve that. It's fair enough that she's really confused—why did I think anyone would believe me, even Laura? It's absurd.

She pushes me backward, my dressing gown coming loose, her hands on my bare chest. "Get out, get out." Marching past me, she flings open the hotel door. "I won't let you both ruin the whole weekend."

"But I can't go. I don't have anywhere else to go. I don't know what I'll do if I go." I'm suddenly petrified. If Laura doesn't believe me, no one will.

"Shut up."

"Laura, please," I say, my eyes now filling as I turn in the doorway. "We have to talk . . . please, Laurs."

But Laura isn't looking at me; she's looking beyond me to a man three doors down, hair wet and sticking up, towel wrapped around his waist, hotel key card in his hand.

"Jay," Laura whispers.

He is frowning as he looks at her, disheveled in her silk pajamas in the doorway, chest heaving, cheeks red. Then he looks at me, bare-chested, my dressing gown flapping, shoved out of the honeymoon suite by his flustered fiancée.

He steps forward. "Flynn?" His forehead puckers. "Laura? What the . . ."

"Flynn was leaving," Laura says in a desperate shout.

"Why is Flynn leaving? Why was Flynn *there*?" Jay says, voice raised, his hotel key card slipping from his grasp.

"I'm not Flynn," I shout to nobody, "I'm not fucking FLYNN."

Another door opens and Patty, complete with large

hair rollers and an eye mask pushed up her forehead, peers out. Then she steps into the corridor.

"Jay? Laura? What *is* going on?"

I suddenly see what they are all seeing. And although I'm frustrated and scared, I can also see how terrible this looks for Laura.

"Did he spend the night?" Jay asks, his voice a husk.

"Of course I didn't," I interrupt.

"Laura?"

Patty is moving down the corridor toward us. "Laura, I think you owe Jay an explanation."

"Mum, stay out of this."

"He didn't stay the night, he just turned up," Laura says, about to burst into tears.

"Why?" Jay asks.

Laura throws up her arms, "Because he's an imbecile, because he's trying to ruin our wedding. I don't know."

She is crying now. Guilt pierces my own devastation. I have done this to her. I must fix it.

Then I hear a voice that makes my heart sink. It's about to get a whole lot worse.

60

FLYNN

"He's not trying to ruin your wedding and he's *not* an imbecile."

I'm not completely sure what's going on, but I'm immediately upset by the sight of Amy looking so lost and bewildered, her eye still battered, as Jay and Laura direct their fury at her.

"Seriously, Laura, I'm going to need a proper answer to this," Jay says, water dripping from his hair and down his neck.

"It's honestly not Laura's fault," Amy says, stepping forward, palms raised as she approaches Jay, her one good eye pleading with him.

"Shut up, Flynn," Jay growls.

"Hey!" I say, blood starting to simmer again, wanting to rescue Amy from this situation.

"I can deal with this," Amy warns, one hand up in my direction like a stop signal.

"Amy, stay out of this." Laura shoots me a look of pure loathing.

"This is ridiculous. Clearly Am— clearly Flynn hasn't done anything wrong . . ." I say.

Jay spins round to look at me. "Well, I saw Flynn just leave her room, Amy. And I know he wasn't with you last night because you slept on a bloody sun lounger so . . . I want to ask Laura, my future WIFE, one more time, what the hell is going on . . ."

"Nothing," Laura insists, her face collapsing.

"Stop lying," Jay roars.

"She's NOT," Amy shouts back.

Jay advances on Amy, pushing her back into the wall of the corridor. It is strange seeing it so clearly now, how as men we resort to a physical response when we're stressed. I've known men punch tables, kick walls, pin other men to walls. I see these appalled faces around it and wonder why I don't say more to stop it.

Frightened she's going to get another black eye, I move quickly across and pull Jay back. "Stop it."

Patty is still asking questions as Laura shouts, "Stop it, both of you!"

My own rage builds as I push between them. "It's not like Jay is white as snow," I spit, chest heaving, anger clouding my vision. I need Jay to step back from Amy, so I spin and face Laura. "He's kept stuff from you, Laura. So don't act all holier than thou," I hurl at my friend Jay, allow the betrayal to fuel my righteous anger.

Laura is quiet. "What's that supposed to mean?"

Amy has gone completely pale. "Don't," she whispers to me, body still pressed into the wall, her one open eye wide with panic.

I'm too far gone to stop. "Why don't you tell Laura about 'that night,'" I say, parroting Jay's own words back at him, doing the quotation marks. That should stop him beating up Amy, and I feel a momentary pleasure at hurting my friend.

His mouth drops open. Laura frowns and Amy's face, my face, drains.

Patty is still staring at our small group. And now a man five doors down has peered round his door, his mouth an angry line as he glares at us.

"Jay, what is Amy talking about?" Laura asks, a line between her eyebrows.

"Not Amy," Amy says, expression morose.

"Shut UP, Flynn," Laura and Jay chime together.

Amy's eyes film over.

Shame fills me up. I wanted to rescue her but I've managed to hurt her instead. I have completely screwed up this weekend. Amy's right—I don't listen to her. She told me not to hurtle in and I did and I've made things even bleaker.

"Jay?" Laura is looking at him, misery etched on her own face.

"Don't deflect," Jay says, clearly deflecting.

Then everyone starts shouting at once and I lose track, simply staring at Amy and feeling utterly awful for making her look so miserable.

A flustered porter appears from the stairwell, dabbing

at his forehead. "We've had a number of complaints about a disturbance," he says. "Please can I remind you that it is not yet seven o'clock on a Sunday."

Patty is the first to leave. "I'll be in my room if you need me, Jay," she says pointedly at her firstborn. "It's never too late, remember," she says ominously, a glance back at Laura.

"Laura, please," Amy says, almost in tears.

Jay is looking stony-faced, ready to leap on Amy once more.

"I want to see Jay," Laura says to everyone, "alone," she stresses, glaring at me and Amy.

Bereft, Amy slumps against the wall, all fight gone from her. I approach, touch her arm, but she shakes me off.

"I'm so sorry, Amy," I say, realizing how badly I've messed up. Tears in her eyes, she ignores me as she pushes off the wall and walks down the corridor.

"Amy," I shout, chasing after her.

Before I take the stairs, I look back and see Laura has opened the honeymoon suite door once more and is staring after us, a strange expression on her face as she watches us leave.

61

AMY

"Amy . . . Amy!"

Flynn is hurrying after me in my rumpled maxi dress as I push past a couple emerging for the first breakfast sitting.

"Come on, Amy!"

As we reach our hotel door I swipe angrily at the key card, just wanting to get inside so I can be alone and wail.

"Hold on," Flynn says, shooting a hand out and squeezing in through the door as well. "Amy, come on. I was trying to stop you getting punched again!"

I can't reply, I can't even look at him. I'm so angry. I *told* him to let me handle it with Laura, but of course he flew in, sword at the ready to save the day, and he made everything a million times worse.

I shrug off the dressing gown and head straight to the corner of the room, grabbing my suitcase. Then of course

I realize there's no point grabbing my case because I can't wear any of my stupid clothes because I'm not me.

This makes me collapse onto the cream armchair in the corner of the room.

I know I'm not just angry about Flynn, although it is a fairly substantial portion of my fury. I'm angry that Laura didn't believe me, I'm angry that despite assuming she would understand, I couldn't persuade her. I'm angry about the things she accused me of. And I'm angry because I am still stuck in this body I don't want to be stuck in, and I don't know how the hell I'm ever going to get out of it. I close my eyes, only just noticing I'm shivering with cold as Flynn drapes the cashmere throw from the foot of the bed over my shoulders.

"Amy," he says quietly, "I am really, really sorry. About everything."

The energy leaks out of me; the gaping loneliness of a night without him, the bereft feeling I had when my sister wouldn't listen to me, melts away. "I know you are," I say, and I'm so sad that we are here on this morning. A morning I'd imagined for months.

About now I was expecting to be waking in the super king size bed, rolling to my side to smile at Flynn who would stroke my face and tell me I'm beautiful, before stroking other places too. After sex that would leave us in a sweaty, happy tangle of limbs we'd order room service and eat breakfast on our balcony, Flynn making my sides hurt laughing, before kissing each other good-bye for me to disappear to that luxurious honeymoon suite to drink from champagne flutes and toast my gorgeous older sister the bride as someone flits around the room doing our hair and make-up and making us look fantastic.

I lost sight of all of that in the last few weeks but now it's all I want; this foreign body I'm in aches with it.

"I can't believe this," I say, wearily standing up from the chair and grabbing one of Flynn's T-shirts without bothering to ask.

"I know," Flynn says, "it's mad."

As I pull the T-shirt down over my head I say it out loud, "So, I'm leaving."

Flynn's jaw drops open. "You can't." He looks a state. Hair greasy and knotted, green dress torn at the hem, he's managed to chip one of my perfect nails, my make-up entirely smudged or worn away. He really isn't taking care of my body; I look like I've had about two hours' sleep.

"I can. I need to . . . look," I say, motioning between us. "She thinks I'm you so she'll be pissed off with you, and I can't be here like this," I say, looking down at Flynn's body. "I can't, I can't, I can't . . ."

"Hey, it's OK," he says, crossing the room and trying to hug me.

"Don't, Flynn. I don't want to keep screwing up Laura's wedding but mostly," I swallow and look him in the eye as I admit, "I don't want to be here with you."

He looks as if I've struck him, his eyes wide and filled with pain.

"You don't get to make me feel bad, Flynn," I say, angrily wiping my own tear away. "Don't give me that look when you've been lying to me forever."

"You lied too," Flynn points out, a weak attempt to get back at me. "With Jay, what's 'that night' about?"

"A tiny lie," I say, throwing up my hands. "Just something I didn't want to share. That night you invited him to meet us in the pub. Well you were late and he didn't know who I was, and he asked for my number."

"He was there to see me. To meet you!" Flynn says, aghast.

"And he realized the moment he asked my name, so I didn't say anything. And I knew if Laura found out she might feel funny about it. But he was totally smitten with Laura the moment we introduced them, anyone could see it. So I told him to forget it happened, because I *knew* telling Laura might hurt her. But now you've swept in and told her anyway. On her wedding day. I didn't lie about, hmm, let me see . . ." I put a finger to my lips, "HAVING AN ACTUAL CHILD."

Heat rises again as I feel the injustice of him leveling accusations at me.

"I'm not sure anymore that we can work, Flynn. I know you love me, but it's made me realize I don't know you, and I need to know and trust the person I'm meant to be with forever."

Flynn takes a breath, meets my eye. "Look, normally, as you know, I'd dive in and tell you you're wrong but," he takes a breath and straightens, "I get it. I know I have to change."

This admission surprises me, it's so unlike Flynn to reflect on things.

He looks utterly broken. "Are you really leaving?" he

asks in a small voice. "What if I told you everything about Charlie?"

Pain twists my gut. I'm not sure I'm ready to have this relationship end, but I don't say anything like that. I don't dare. "Would it make a difference?" I ask.

Flynn looks at me with an expression I rarely see on his face: absolute sincerity. "I think so," he says.

An age passes as I take in his bedraggled, sad appearance.

"OK," I agree.

He breathes out quickly, reaching over and adjusting the cashmere throw around my shoulders.

"Hey," he says, "this throw really brings out the colors of your bruise."

In spite of myself, I laugh.

62

FLYNN

Exhausted, angry, tearful, I think we both feel like we've lived a million years in one night. I make us both coffees, unlock the doors out to the balcony and lead Amy outside. The mist is clearing, the lake now silvery blue, the air streaked with a wash of colors above the patchwork of fields that stretch for an age. The gentle chittering of birds is the only noise we can hear as we settle on the white wrought-iron chairs outside and sip at our drinks.

I know I need to make this right.

Setting my cup down, I lean forward in my chair, grateful for the knitted pink sweater that Amy forced me into. "Ames," I say, "for starters, I am so sorry that you found out about Tanya and Charlie this weekend. I stupidly assumed that the past is just my past and doesn't affect you, but that was selfish."

Amy simply nods. I can't believe how difficult I'm

finding this. Good with words at work when it comes to being truthful, sharing things I find painful I'm screaming to be silent.

I take a breath and press my palms together. "The thing is, thinking about Tanya, well, not Tanya as such, thinking about Charlie hurts," I say carefully, airing things I have not said aloud, have not dared mull on for years. Another huge thing to add to the other hurts.

"Tanya got pregnant when things were not going well with us," I explain, "and after the initial shock, I was pretty blown away that I'd be a parent. I thought I would be a good dad, you know." I look up then, meeting Amy's eye.

She doesn't agree with me, her knuckles white where she is holding the cup, so I soldier on.

"Charlie was born, and she was perfect. Well, actually she was pretty beaten up and covered in rank goo, but to me she was this wonderful little person. She had the biggest yawn, you could see her tonsils when she opened that mouth and," I can feel my throat thicken as I recall the details, "and the tiniest fingers. I remember clumsily dressing her in one of those little white onesies and I thought I'd pull off her fingers—I was terrified!"

I swallow, take a sip of my coffee. Is this too much? Is Amy going to hate me? Get up and leave? I take a breath. If I've learned anything in the last twenty-four hours, it's that I can't ever be truly close to her if I don't share this stuff.

"I knew when I looked at her that whatever I felt about Tanya—and I'm not going to lie," I say, voice hardening, "we were not doing well. Well, whatever happened, I would be there for this girl, this baby. I felt completely overwhelmed. I can't explain it, Amy . . ."

"You loved her," Amy whispers.

I nod, not able to respond. Sipping my coffee and licking my lips. "I felt this overwhelming peace that I could stop searching for something."

As I say this out loud I blink, aware now that my feelings toward Charlie are linked to the other person in my life. Struggling to look at Amy, I go on.

"Ever since my dad died there has always been this gap inside me." I shift; a lifetime of never speaking about this robs me of breath. My vision narrows, the blackness closing in.

"You never talk about him," she says.

My chest is heavy as I finally admit what I've never been able to tell her before. "I . . . I can't remember him."

She frowns then.

The silence goes on. My breathing gets shorter. This is too hard; I can't do this.

I see my own hand rest on my arm as Amy says, "But . . . the Ferris wheel, the—"

I force myself to meet her eye. "I made things up. I have one or two stories about him. I . . . I make them up. I've never been able to remember anything, not for years."

Amy's hands cover her mouth.

I force myself to go on; I need to say everything now because I'm not strong enough to do this again.

"I just see blanks and I wish I could, I wish I could remember his face . . ." I clear my throat, try to feel the seat beneath me, focus on Amy opposite me. "But, for the first time, as I stared at Charlie, I felt that weight lift. I loved her, immediately," I admit now, my voice soft.

I try not to break down. "Tanya showed you the photograph, but it all changed after she took it. She'd been so quiet. I thought she was allowed to be quiet; I mean, I'd watched what she'd gone through and it was pretty bloody heroic—the woman was allowed not to be sitting up in bed, cracking jokes—but something was weighing on her. I thought she was overwhelmed too. I mean, it felt scary to be suddenly entirely responsible for this new human being. The hundred different ways we could mess it up, you know?"

Amy nods quickly, her coffee slopping in her saucer.

"But then she told me."

My voice cracks as I return to that room, can almost feel the weight of Charlie in my arms. Amy reaches for me, squeezing my fingers. I shut my eyes.

"She told me Charlie wasn't mine."

Amy's fingers clamp deeper on my hand and I hear her breath catch.

I don't want to let the tears leak out but so much is building inside me I could burst. It's as if my smaller frame can't contain the swell of emotions.

"Sorry," I say, huddling into myself as I become aware that tears are escaping. "Must be the hormones," I sob-laugh, and that finally makes Amy scoot forward on her chair, her arms, or rather my arms, around me, shushing me as I cry.

"So, she wasn't mine," I stutter. "She was never my daughter. Tanya meant to tell me, but time just went on and it got harder." I can't stop the bitterness making my words brittle, but a smaller voice reminds me that is what I've done too, put off the truth for another day, week, month until it feels impossible to ever admit things.

Amy's hand is still warm on my back.

"I didn't want to go. I felt so guilty, like I was abandoning them. Even though she told me to go."

"So you had to," Amy said gently.

"Did I?" I shudder in my chair, still hating that memory, the feeling that I had done the very worst thing. I'd left her, tear-stained, exhausted, bewildered, and holding her tiny baby to her chest.

"Fuck, Flynn, this is . . . a lot," Amy says, sitting back. "Why did you never tell me?"

My head is still bowed as I try to get into words what I'd felt.

"I felt ashamed that I'd left her, confused because I loved Charlie. I used to go on Facebook and look at photos of her, I wanted to send her a card every birthday but couldn't. I didn't know what to do with those feelings. I wasn't her dad. I was literally nothing to her, and yet I felt like I'd walked away from my first child."

This was too much. "Fuck," I say, pressing my fists to my eyes, "this is like therapy Ames, are you going to charge me fifty pounds?"

"Fifty pounds?" she says. "Sixty-five at least," her voice wobbling too.

I look up at her then, my head woolly, my mouth dry. "I am sorry, I genuinely just wanted to forget it, try to move on, force myself to not think about it, to plan ahead. Thinking about Charlie still hurts. I'm not good at things hurting—never have been. I guess that was what got me baby obsessed. Even the business became about the kids' parties. It was my way of honoring her, making other children happy."

Amy is quiet for a long time.

"Thank you for telling me now," she says, then she looks up at me, her expression serious. "I'm so sorry."

And I don't know whether that is a final goodbye or whether it has changed anything.

63

AMY

This feels surreal seeing him grapple with this stuff. My heart breaks for him. It's so unfamiliar, and it's not just that he's telling me through tears, or even saying it in my body; it's the raw emotion I never get from him. I want to bundle him into my arms, which I can right now because they can easily fit around him. His admission that he made up memories about his dad almost broke me.

Whenever I'd talked about Dad, I'd insisted on him sharing something. He always paused but then offered up a brief anecdote: a happy memory. A Ferris wheel where he dropped his toffee apple, a ruffle of his hair after a rugby match, a roast dinner when he dropped the turkey. I see now these were all fabricated, rosy glimpses of a man he had made up to fill the gaps in his memory. It explains his reticence to introduce me to his mum, the sure knowledge I'd discover it all. I know what grief feels like but at least I can remember my dad, have a treasure trove of gorgeous memories.

It's obvious as he shares this stuff that he's also admitting these feelings to himself for the first time and that brings a lump to my own throat.

I understand why he lied. I really understand it. I can see from the pain etched on his features how much it's costing him to relive that day, admit these things about himself. I can hear it in the way his words are catching, see it in the way he is hunched over, fiddling with his saucer, the table leg, his hands, pushing them together in a prayer.

I hardly trust myself to speak. I'd assumed this was the end, that whatever I learned would send me running from him. Now I'm a jumble of emotions. The primary one is shame. How come I missed all of this? How did I make everything about me? Laura is right, I am selfish.

It's a beautiful morning. The misty lake, early workers humming around the pier as they set up the chairs and flower arch where Laura and Jay will marry. It's the day that Laura had dreamed of for her wedding, warm already and the sun is barely up, a light breeze ruffling the long grass and wildflowers along the fringes of the lawn.

I was going to leave. I was going to get in the car and head back to Bristol and miss all of it. But as I look down at the scene, across at Flynn, broken in the chair next to me, I know I can't do it. Today is bigger than anything else, and Flynn needs me. I feel closer to him than I ever have.

A knock on our bedroom door stops me telling him that, and I get up and make my way back into our bedroom, sunshine forming golden stripes on the carpet and walls.

Laura stands in the doorway, a gray sweater over her pajamas, the hotel slippers on her perfectly manicured feet.

"Laurs!" I can't help the wide smile that splits my face open.

She pauses a beat, tips her head back slightly, searching my face.

"Come in, come in," I say, gesturing her inside.

She follows slowly and I call out, "Flynn, Flynn, look who's here."

The scrape of a chair and Flynn is in the room, discreetly wiping his face.

"Sorry, he's just a bit emotional," I laugh, because this is funny and ridiculous and, "Oh god, you are here because you believe us, aren't you? Or the wedding is off. God, please be the former, please," I gabble. Mildly hysterical, all the emotions of the last twenty-four hours, the reveals, the relief, the exhaustion tip me into this crazed mood. "It's like the most lush day to get married."

Laura's eyes are round as she stares. "Is it really, really true?"

She moves closer, not breaking eye contact, reaching both hands up and cupping my cheeks so they squidge together, my mouth a pout, searching my face. "Amy, are you really in there?"

The unbelievable relief of being believed makes my whole body relax. I can't talk because she is still pressing my cheeks together so I just nod furiously.

"It's true, Laura," Flynn says, stepping forward, red-eyed in my pink sweater. "We have no idea how, but it happened on the way here . . ."

Laura releases my face and then steps across the room, circling Flynn like she's inspecting an animal in a zoo. "So, you are actually each other. For real? I kept thinking about this weekend, all the things that didn't make sense, how weird you've been. It's real?"

"Real," I confirm.

"OK, tell me something only Amy would know," Laura says. "Please," she says, staring at me.

I look at Flynn, almost expecting him to speak, but I can see him watching me, knowing I need to do this. That he needs to let me. And I'm so grateful to him.

I pause, not wanting to screw this up again.

Shutting my eyes, I think back; I push past the pain of that last night and think about the weekend before he died. Laura, Mum, me, and him all overlapping conversations, screeching, teasing, laughing. The four of us had always been enough.

"That last weekend with Dad," I say quietly, "we had no clue we'd never have another weekend like that. We wanted to go out drinking, but Dad forced us to sit in front of the TV and watch an old episode of *The Chase*. Neither of us wanted to but he insisted, so we huffed a bit and then we gave in, because we always did with Dad. And he paused it on one of the answers—"

300

"Bristol Rovers," Laura whispers.

I nod, my throat closing. "Bristol Rovers! He was so pleased. He turned and beamed at us."

Laura's own face wobbles as I continue.

"He said, 'Rovers! My loves!' and then the moment was over, and we kissed him goodbye, and we went out for our drink. And that was the last time we kissed him goodbye. And the last time he told us he loved us."

I don't need to ask if she believes me now. I feel her arms around me, feel her own body heave. I cling to her, like I had that day, and feel Dad in the room with us. "He loved us so bloody much," I sniff into her hair. "So bloody much."

"I know," she mumbles into my chest.

Laura pulls back, a few seconds before she can speak. "I can't believe this," she says, touching my face tentatively. "It's impossible."

"I know."

"Now," she says, briskly wiping her face, the efficient City ball-breaker in full force, "what the hell are we going to do about it?"

"But . . . is there going to be a wedding?" I ask tentatively.

Laura frowns at the question. "What on earth makes you think there wouldn't be?"

"What Flynn told you, about me and Jay."

Laura purses her lips together, almost looking like she is suppressing a smile. But surely not when what I am mentioning is deadly serious.

"You mean about the night he first met you?"

301

I nod miserably.

"You mean how he hit on you at the bar?"

I nod again, wanting to weep. So maybe there won't be a wedding.

"You mean how he hit on you but then met your much fitter and cooler older sister and fell completely head over heels in love with her and proposed to her a year later?"

I peek up tentatively.

"Amy, he told me ages ago—we do, you know, talk. I didn't know him that night. And you're hot!"

"But—"

"I just wanted to talk to him before we went down the aisle. Not everything's all about you, Amy Norman."

"I'm starting to realize that," I say, as she pulls me close and laughs into my chest.

I'm so relieved and so happy I haven't harmed anything, I tear up all over again as I squeeze her close.

Her muffled voice emerges, "Don't get a boner, OK?"

64

FLYNN

I'm feeling lighter inside, overwhelmed with the relief of letting some of this out. I know it's just the beginning, but I feel like it's the start of something. I think back to the day I last tried to talk to Mum, really talk to her. How she had simply walked out. I'd believed her response was about me, but was it more than that? Could she not dare either? Had her grief robbed her too? I vow to reach out after this weekend.

Conversation among the men I hung out with was shallow: sports and small talk. I was adept at swerving anything real, made friends easily but failed to truly get to know anyone. A couple of friends probed me, wondered why Tanya and I had split, but none of them pushed me on it. I wonder now what they thought. Had they judged me? Assumed I'd left my own child? Why hadn't they said more? Why do some men not dream to ask?

"So, you're not cross?" Amy checks for the sixteenth time.

Laura sounds exasperated, "How can I be cross? You didn't deliberately switch into your boyfriend's body to mess up my wedding, Ames."

"Well, I know, but," Amy fiddles with the hem of my T-shirt, "I do this kind of thing. I make things about me . . ."

Laura opens her mouth and then closes it again, a small sigh as it's her turn to look awkward. "I'm sorry I've made you think that," she says. "It's not your fault you're someone who lives life out loud. And . . ." She picks her next words carefully. "I was always jealous of what you and Dad had, jealous of how he loved everything you did."

"I think being the second child was easier," Amy admits. "I wasn't expected to do things; you were forced to trail-blaze, so if I seemed to be doing it too I think they gushed a little more over me . . ."

"I could be jealous," Laura admits, her head drooping. "You and Dad had all these things in common, with the marches and petitions, the music and the song-writing, and no matter how hard I tried I didn't share them."

"Well, I should have realized how much pressure it was to always be the first, be the one who has to pretend she's all grown-up and capable. And you were so amazing, moving to London at eighteen—I would have been petrified!" Amy said.

Laura couldn't keep the surprise from her voice, "I always thought you thought I was too good to stay in Bristol, stay at home." Her head dips low, "Dad thought that too . . ."

Amy scoots nearer Laura, her voice reassuring, "Laurs, he thought you were brilliant. He couldn't stop boasting to the pub when you got into university, the first one in our family, his chest puffed out with pride that you'd be going to London."

"I always thought it was you he talked about," she admits. "I was envious that you could sing a song and he'd be putty. . . . It wasn't fair of me to make you think that was your fault. I love your songs, I miss them, they're beautiful. . . ."

I leave them both to talk as I scan my cell phone for news from work. Two days ago I might have made light of something or steered the conversation away, but I know now that the best thing I can do is let them talk and listen to each other. I'm starting to think I might have inherited some of Amy's emotional maturity when we switched bodies.

Karim has forwarded me an email from one of our clients gushing about the company. All three events went without a hitch and a small, guilty voice reminds me I hadn't had faith. I need to trust my team more to shoulder some of the stress.

This gives me an idea and, when Amy and Laura have finished talking and hugging, I spin around.

"Go on," Amy says, over Laura's shoulder. "You have something to say."

She's smiling as I burst with it. "So," I announce, brain whirring like this is a day in the office, "I have a plan, Laura."

65

AMY

"Spaghetti arms!"

"What?"

"Spagh . . . how have you never watched *Dirty Dancing*?"

"Because I'm a virile man—haven't you noticed?" Flynn says, indicating his tiered maxi skirt covered in tiny flowers and the frilly peasant blouse I dressed him in for the morning. Hair shiny once more with make-up that looks good, a light dusting of powder, and the tiniest flick of eyeliner.

"Yep, that's you. Says the man who makes me watch *Stardust* every time I ask what movie."

Flynn laughs, tongue out as he attempts to copy the last few steps of the routine. As I watch him really try, I'm struck by the fact that for the first time this weekend I'm not panicking or miserable, I'm starting to enjoy myself. That is largely due to Flynn. He seems a hundred times happier since sharing his history over Charlie. Then he swung into action detailing all our movements so that Laura could have the best day and share it with me.

I truly can't believe he was carrying all that stuff around with him. I should have guessed that a lot of his "live in the present" chat was masking a refusal to face up to hurt in the past. I'm ashamed that I'd been so quick to assume that he didn't have things in his own life that were complicated or upsetting because he seemed so upbeat. Worse, that I had started to believe he was simply not serious.

He's not even rich, or posh. He told me he just paid Patrick his stepdad back for years of boarding school. It's why he practically lives at work, desperately paying what he owes. I need to stop assuming things about people. And even if he did go, I need to trust the person he is: I've been biased and judgmental and I don't want to be like that anymore. I think sometimes I'm always wondering what Dad might have thought, rather than what I really think.

Flynn's desire to look on the bright side is a trait I want to emulate more. Some of the things I've fretted about in the past seem silly now in comparison to what can happen. We have both experienced big losses; it reminds you what truly matters. He has been right in the past to try and bring some perspective to my life.

The music goes again, bouncing around the glass walls of the Orangery. It's such a striking room, ivy crawling up the windows outside, lemon trees in large pots inside the room filling the air with their scent. Bunches of grapes dangle, their vines twisted around the rafters above us, making me feel that nature is inside the room. Many of the panes of the glass roof are rolled back to reveal wispy clouds and white airplane trails in a clear blue sky.

My Converse trainers squeak on the polished cream tiles as Flynn tries twisting to the floor once more. Then he collapses, panting on one of the large cream sofas that we pushed back against the wall.

"Mercy, mercy. How do you get your hips to move like that?"

"Um . . . loosen them?"

I drop into the seat next to him, pretty pleased with his progress. "You're getting there, you shouldn't embarrass yourself too much . . ."

"Too much . . ." he says, jumping to his feet again, playing the music one more time. The steps are more fluid as, pink-cheeked, he goes again.

I rest my head back against the sofa and watch him, his earnest expression, a clear determination to get this right. He'd listened to all my instructions, copying me as best he could, and now I can see he'll fit right into the group. I know he'll hate it; for a confident person he is hilariously frightened of being on any kind of stage or dance floor—he's a two-step kind of guy.

Closing my eyes, listening to the beats, I think of the day ahead, relieved Laura and I are back on track with her in on the secret. In fact, I'm starting to suspect she's almost enjoying the madness. She has suggested electrocuting us in various different ways after the wedding, so that's something to look forward to. I forget how well she can take things in her stride in her work in corporate finance, and perhaps Flynn and I are like another project to be tackled.

"What are you two doing?" a voice calls out. Mum is standing in the entrance to the Orangery, a different pair of spectacles in lime-green on today. She has croissant crumbs on her top and I want to run over and give her a hug. Geoffrey waits a little way behind her.

"Just going over the dance, Amy was just . . . showing me her moves," I say, smiling as Flynn grinds to a halt.

"Geoffrey darling, I'll meet you back in the room," Mum says, waving him off. Then she steps inside, stands next to Flynn, nods to me to start the music and joins in.

It's a joy, watching her shake her hips, attempt to twist, surprisingly flexible, but then that's Mum, constantly surprising, constantly exceeding people's expectations. It was often Dad that got the accolades in our house, Mum kept in the background, letting him have his moments. When she would clean and cook and organize, he would play. He would swing us around, take us to the corner shop for a quarter of strawberry BonBons and get all the credit for being the fun parent. Watching her collapse now in laughter, one arm thrown casually over Flynn's shoulders as they finish, reminds me Mum has always been fun. And Geoffrey lets her shine, perhaps I'll admit, a little more than Dad had. That disloyal thought gives me a twinge but I don't dismiss it—I need to accept that I'd assumed things about Dad and Mum too, and that had to change.

Another stab of pain runs through my chest as I remember Mum is carrying around her own secret. I must set my own situation aside and find out what that is—Mum isn't one to keep secrets.

Then into this mix whirls Reggie, Eddie giving up on the leash and watching as he flies into the room, making an excited beeline straight into Flynn's crotch, his nose sniffing at the flowers on the maxi skirt.

"That dog really loves you, Amy," he calls, making Mum and me grimace.

Flynn is too busy on his knees, getting his powder licked off by the craziest Golden Retriever this side of the M5, to hear him. "I'll leave him with you. Jay says he'll need a walk." Eddie pointedly ignores me, a quick glance at my black eye.

"Amy, why don't we take him," Mum says. "It's a gorgeous day and Laura won't need us up there for another hour or so . . ."

Flynn looks across at me, and I'm grateful he wants to check.

"Let me just go and put some better shoes on," Mum says, and I realize she just had breakfast in the hotel monogrammed slippers. "Honestly," she says, "it's like walking on a cloud. I assume we can nab them. I mean, take them at the end of the weekend . . ."

"You can," I laugh and watch her leave, glad we all came to this sumptuous place, that my lovely, hard-working mum is getting a proper treat too. Laura deserves all of this—everyone deserves to be spoiled if it's possible.

"And the robes?" she asks brightly, glad to hear I have the answers.

"Er, that would just be stealing."

"Shame," she says, then pats Reggie and goes to leave. "Won't be long, Amy darling."

"Are we done here?" Flynn asks, pulling his long, curly hair back behind his shoulders.

"You nailed it," I say, wanting to kiss him, but still not wanting to kiss my own mouth. I opt to reach up for a quick peck on the cheek, making Flynn start too. It's clearly too weird being kissed by yourself.

He straightens with a strained laugh, one hand up to his face.

"So, you'll let the dog kiss you," I joke, but for a second we both seem to panic about the same thing. That this swap is permanent. What that means for us.

Not ready to tarnish the morning, I change the subject.

"Flynn," I say in a low voice, "when you walk with Mum, if she says anything, important will you tell me . . ."

He frowns. "What's happened?" He can tell something is up, alarm on his face. "I think you should go," he protests, one hand stroking the top of Reggie's head.

I shake my head. "You'll know what to say," I assure him, aware I really mean those words. "And judge if you want to share it. Also, we need to think of Laura," I say, "she shouldn't need more to worry about today."

"No, Ames, I can't do that. I don't want to keep anything else from you."

"I trust you."

It's true, I do. Him opening up has altered things between us in a way I'd been desperate for. Now I realize this intimacy, this trust was what I had been lacking; it was why I've been convincing myself he's all wrong for me.

"But . . ."

Mum returns in her sneakers, cheeks flushed, interrupting us both. I search her face as she steps toward us. What is going on that she won't share? She looks content, happy. But haven't I learned that people can mask big feelings, that some people carry their secrets and pain quietly, which doesn't make them any less real? Particularly Mum, who has always protected us from her pain.

I think of the months after Dad died, her smile plastered on the moment I got home, the fun events she planned on weekends Laura came back from London. Those quiet moments when I saw her reflection in the kitchen windows, her quick swipe at her face before she turned to us. Not wanting to face the fact her grief was equal to my own, dare I say it, even more devastating. My chest hurts as I realize I have often put my own feelings first, never the same after that night with Dad.

"Have a great walk," I say, trying to keep my voice steady.

I'm scared.

Reggie springs about, delighted to hear the word.

Flynn gives me a last look back as Mum links his arm.

"Love you," I mouth to him.

It's only after they've left I crumple back onto the sofa.

Mum has to be OK: she has to be.

66

FLYNN

"Where to?" My mouth snaps shut as Trish looks at me.

Be casual, Flynn, you're being Amy, not a West Country farmhand. The trouble is, my insides are leaping around since Amy hinted that her mum is about to reveal something to me. I shouldn't be the one here.

"Are you alright, Amy darling?"

I nod, not trusting myself to say more.

Fortunately, she's distracted by the setting as we leave the lawn and make our way into the long grass and on to a pathway through the woods. "Oh, isn't it bliss."

Reggie races ahead of us, tongue out, every now and again twisting back with a delighted bark as if to tell us, "Look, guys! Summer is here! Isn't it marvelous? Isn't the world a magical place!" No dog could look happier.

The woods are full of bright green leaves making

dappled marks on the twisting path. I look about and choose something Amy might comment on, "Nice ... bark," I say, stroking a nearby tree trunk.

Trish gives me a sideways glance and moves on.

"So," I cough, feeling the weight of what Amy asked of me heavy on my shoulders, "how are you?" Great start, Flynn. Small talk. Trying to break a lifetime of avoiding conversation is not going to be straightforward.

"I'm well," Trish says, reaching to link arms with me once more. I feel instantly more connected to her. I wonder what Karim would think if I started asking to link arms with him? Why don't men do this? Why are we not allowed?

Moving together makes the strip we're walking narrower; my calf brushes up against the long grass that lines the pathway. The long skirt snags on a bramble bush.

"Balls," I say, hearing a slight tear, "Amy's going to be pissed."

"Have you started referring to yourself in the third person, love? Very regal."

"Hahaha." The laugh doesn't sound genuine.

I think I just need to dive in, get this over with. I take a breath, "Look, Trish, I mean, Mum, the thing is I'm a bit worried. About you. I know you're keeping something from Laura and me and, well, I was hoping you might share what that is?"

"Oh," Trish says, clearly taken aback. "That is ... well, that is getting to the point."

Normally I might ruin the moment with an ill-timed joke or a remark that would let her off the hook, but I need to do this for Amy. She deserves to know what's going on with her mum, so I press my lips together and wait.

"Let's sit down, shall we?" Trish suggests.

There's a clearing a little way along and she leaves the path and walks across to a large fallen tree trunk, its moss-covered bark making the ideal spot to sit and talk. Around us insects chitter and the sunshine breaks through, lighting up an array of bright yellow and greens. Trish closes her eyes and breathes it all in, her face peaceful as I wait.

"I wasn't going to tell you this weekend. I know there's no way you'll be able to keep anything from Laura and I didn't want to upset either of you when this is about love and celebration. It's her big wedding and I don't want anything to spoil it."

My breath is caught in my chest as she reaches for my hand on the tree trunk beside her.

"Geoffrey told me to, of course. He thinks you're both very strong, independent women, and of course I think that too, but to me you're also my baby girls. The girls I held in my arms, the girls who wrapped themselves around my legs when they didn't want to go to preschool, the girls who came running to me in tears if they needed a Band-Aid, the girls who lost their father when they'd barely stepped into adulthood." Her own eyes film over and she pauses.

I steel myself.

"I don't want to hurt you any more than you already have been."

What would Amy say right now? I think. "You couldn't hurt us. Whatever you say, we'll always know how much you love us."

Mum smiles and gives my hand a pat. "You see, Geoffrey is right. And maybe you won't miss me."

Miss her? Reggie seems to sense my unease as I reach for the comfort of his fur.

"What do you mean by that?" I say, my voice steady, grateful for Reggie settling at my feet, shuffling up to me with a contented sigh in the long grass.

"The thing is, Amy," Trish says, tucking a strand of my long hair behind my ear, "I had a scare last year. I found a lump and got tests done . . ."

My vision blurs.

"I didn't tell either of you. I couldn't bear the thought of causing you additional pain when everything was fine. You'd already lost so much; I know how close you were to your father and how much losing him cost you. I'm sorry," she says, head dipping.

My brain is scrambling. This is it, then. This is big. Bigger than I think Amy realized. How will I tell her? How will I explain to her that she might have to prepare to lose another parent? Also, shouldn't Laura hear this? This feels too colossal and suddenly I want to back-pedal. This feels wrong. I should not be the person she shares this news with. "Mum," I say, placing one hand on her arm, her expression still utterly

318

morose. "Wait. If this is something that's going to upset us then maybe you're right—maybe we should wait and talk to Laura too?"

Trish picks at another bit of bark and nods miserably.

I scoot closer to her and put an arm around her shoulder. "Is that OK?"

She presses her hands to her eyes and lets out a little half-laugh. "Absolutely," then, sitting up and straightening her shoulders, she gives me a watery smile. "How about we both make sure it's a really wonderful wedding for our girl?"

"Good plan," I say, dread pooling inside me.

She reaches across and gives me a hug, her hair smelling of vanilla as Reggie leaps up at our movement.

She stands and I go to follow. "Hey," I add, catching her hand and linking her arm through mine like I've seen Amy do a hundred times with her mum. "You know whatever it is we'll be OK? You've raised us to be pretty awesome humans, you know . . . like you . . ."

And I'm heartened that she laughs at that, despite my churning fear as we move out of the clearing, the sun lost above us in a canopy of leaves, the path back in shade. I hadn't thought Amy really believed her mum was keeping something big from her daughters, that her secret would be a devastating one.

Just before she returns inside, I turn to her, take a breath. "And Tr— and Mum," I correct, thinking how easily these words should come to someone. I close my eyes briefly, "I love you, Mum."

She presses her lips together and nods, eyes filling.

How am I going to prepare Amy for this?

All I do know is I must say something; I don't want to keep any more secrets from her anymore.

Reggie licks my hand and I'm grateful for his knowing look and the quiet way he is simply there for me.

67

AMY

There are shrieks when I appear in Flynn's tuxedo, a white bath towel folded over my arm like a waiter. Flynn helps me with the tie and I catch myself in the full-length mirror.

"Leave it," I tell him as he fiddles with the strap on his blush-pink bridesmaid's dress for the millionth time. "You look great," I promise. How often have I grumbled about how I look? Yet now I'm out of my body I can treat myself how I treat other women.

Laura is on the dusty pink velvet stool, her hair in rollers, a girl fussing over her as she delicately applies enough make-up to make it look like Laura isn't wearing any make-up at all. The soft light in here makes her look dewy and gorgeous. I step over and offer to fill her flute and she gives me the widest smile.

"Looking foxy, Flynn," she says, patting my bottom and ensuring this is met with more shrieking.

I can see Flynn's surprised face as he sits uncertainly at the foot of the bed, smoothing the dress before placing his hands piously in his lap as he gazes round at all the women staring in mirrors, blowing on fingernails and sipping drinks. A giggle rises up and I move across and hand him a Buck's Fizz which is almost entirely orange juice.

"Alright, Amy?" I ask, nudging him with a foot.

He just stares up at me in bewilderment.

Being in the middle of this energy, Taylor Swift playing on someone's Bluetooth speakers, makes me want to break into dance. I'm so much lighter now than a few hours ago. Flynn returned from the walk, an arm around me as we watched Mum disappear inside to find Geoffrey and pack up their room. He told me I should talk to her, then pulled me close and whispered that he loved me.

When I look across at Mum, carefree on a seat next to Laura, anxiety flutters. What did he learn? What should she tell me? We will have to ask her, I know that. Mum isn't someone who keeps secrets from us. I'm sure it's simply that she doesn't want to overshadow Laura's weekend with something worrying her. We'll sort it after this weekend.

I am extra attentive, making sure she is waited on too. I realize I often don't put Mum first, don't fuss over her, have always let her look after me, the baby of the family. I was always Daddy's girl and proud of it, then since he died I've been so wrapped up in losing him, I've neglected Mum.

I want this to be the best day, and Flynn laid out the ways we can practically help. Also being in this body, channeling Flynn's energy, I reflect on what he would do right now if he was me. He is a magnet for fun. I have realized since Dad I'm so quick to be a killjoy, a mix of guilt and self-importance stopping me from cutting loose.

I suggest a ridiculous photoshoot, getting each hen posing with Laura, getting Mum in the mix, forcing selfies with Flynn and bouncing around the room, ensuring everyone's glasses are topped up and they're having a good time. It feels good to simply be sharing this moment, watching Mum crease with laughter and pride as she rests a hand on Laura's shoulder. Laura was right on the call the other day—I do need to loosen up and allow myself some fun. I can't rail against every injustice all the time. I can take a day off.

I'm just lining up another shot when Patty strides into the room. She's like a Dementor, everyone quaking as she swoops around the room, threatening to descend on her victim. In this case it is, of course, the bride.

"The wedding planner isn't up to muster," she announces, her wide-brimmed lilac hat like a spaceship we might all be forced to board. "The band seem to be wandering around the grounds with no clue where they're to be playing. I've lost the flamingos, I think they're hiding. The chef's outraged because I dared to ask him a question about the duck—the French can be so sniffy about their food—and don't even get me started on the napkin placements . . ."

Throughout her speech I can see lines appear on Laura's glowing face, her mouth turning down, the light dimming in her eyes.

I want to throw my hand towel over Patty's head and bundle her outside, but I know I need to behave impeccably and not upset Laura. Flynn, however, has stood up, smoothing his blush-pink bridesmaid dress as if he's about to go into battle.

Stepping forward he grips Patty's forearm and in a loud voice starts sympathizing with her predicament. "This is frankly dreadful," he says, making me sound posher than I have ever sounded before. "But I am certain that together we can get these things sorted and it will all be just lovely."

Patty starts mouthing underneath the hat, but Flynn steamrolls on.

"I mean, with both of us on the case, we can make all those problems go away. I insist that we get going immediately. Shall we?" he suggests and Patty, clearly determined to have Laura leaping up, seems to wither in the face of such confidence and meekly allows Flynn to steer her out of the room.

"Now where is the band, then?" he says loudly in my Bristol accent, clearly for my benefit.

Laura's jaw unclenches, her whole body relaxing as she watches Flynn steer Patty away.

He gives me a wink as he leaves, one hand fiddling

with the strap on his dress as he waves goodbye. My eyes meet a grateful Laura's in the mirror.

"Buck's Fizz, anyone?" I suggest, and I bustle around the room once more, delighted to see her laughing again.

68

FLYNN

My disguise made me the perfect trouble-shooter for Patty's largely made-up problems. Disasters they are not. Who knew the linen napkins did not match the theme? Or that the lighting in the ballroom just "would not do." Still, I spent my time reassuring, cajoling, and sometimes fixing too. My experience as a party planner came to the fore. She marveled as I turned a napkin into a swan. Every time I wanted to make a bolt for it, I pictured Amy and Laura up in the honeymoon suite having a brilliant time and knew this was the best place for me.

"I think we've earned a break," I say, clapping my hands together before Patty can finish telling me her story about the time she went to the petty claims court over a parking charge notice and won.

"You want to go back to your sister," she says, her mouth puckering.

"If it's alright by you, I'd love to talk more—maybe we could get a cappuccino?"

Patty's eyebrows lift and then she gives me a curt nod. We step outside to the balustraded terrace, the lawn beneath us striped to perfection, two men in the distance laying out the last of the chairs for the service as the waiter brings us two cappuccinos on a round silver tray, chocolate dusting in the perfect shape of a rose on both.

"It's looking good," I say, settling in a chair and looking toward the lake. The flowered arch is a riot of purples, pinks, and creams, the water glittering behind it. The four flamingos are preening in the shallows like wedding guests.

"Oh look, there they are," I say, pointing down to the flamingos. "They've come out of hiding."

"Flamingos are monogamous you know," she sniffs. "And they co-parent, they both take turns incubating the egg. The man stays."

Patty glances down and for a second I can see her wrestling with something. The realization strikes me suddenly. Perhaps the bonkers requests are a way of concealing something more? I recall the moments between her and Jay at school: the warm hugs and smiles. Her stoicism when Jay's dad left them, Jay's phone calls home to check on her. Then I think of my own way of handling the pain of losing Charlie and find myself reaching for her hand.

She draws back as I touch her. "You love Jay," I say simply, realizing ultimately that this is what it is all about.

A flash of pain crosses her face and she adjusts her spaceship hat with a cough, "Of course."

"It must be a bitter-sweet moment, watching him get married? Realizing he's no longer quite yours."

She doesn't answer, reaching for her coffee which leaves a milk moustache I do not comment on. I bite my tongue, remembering the many times Amy has told me I like to fly in, try to resolve people's problems rather than simply listen.

"I always imagined doing this for my own daughter," Patty says, staring down at the worker bees now stapling clumps of greenery along the bottom of the musicians' platform. "We lost a girl," she says carefully, wiping at her mouth. "Rather late."

"I'm so sorry," I say, shocked by the admission.

"Jay has been very good," Patty says, her eyes filmed with tears as she forces a smile. "And I know I've asked a lot and Laura's been very accommodating." She clears her throat and adjusts her cup and saucer.

"It's going to be a wonderful wedding," I say, trying to choose my words as carefully as Amy might.

"Laura is a pleasant young woman," Patty sniffs, the words clearly not coming easily.

"She is. She loves Jay, and family is very important to her," I say, knowing that is the absolute truth. I think too of Trish, of what she has hinted at, "And I think she'll need you to be around," I add.

"I hope so," Patty says, not meeting my eye as she twists a napkin in her lap. "Some of my friends tell me you lose your boys to women. And Laura swept in so quickly. I've always been close to my son, so I very much hope not."

I swallow. After the last forty-eight hours I can see Mum through a different filter now. A woman who lost her husband shockingly, suddenly a widow and single parent to a seven-year-old. A stepdad with money, offering solutions. Agreeing to send me away to prep school to be surrounded by other boys, camaraderie, a network of support. Building up a wall that neither of us knew how to dismantle.

I need to introduce her to Amy too. Amy thought I was embarrassed by her, that my mum would judge her, and, shamefully, I hadn't disagreed, not wanting to put Amy onto me by letting her meet Mum. I can see now that Amy and Mum meeting is vital: families are flawed and messy and I need to accept mine is too and try to build something good.

Below us Eddie passes, Reggie yapping at his feet as they crunch over the gravel. Looking up he calls out, "Amy, have you seen Flynn? I was told he was meant to be looking after this bloody dog."

The weight of the last few moments lifts as I step across the terrace and peer down. "Bring him up." I cast a look at Patty over my shoulder, "Fancy walking him with me so he doesn't embarrass them during the service?"

Patty looks down at her expensive cream heels and then shrugs as if making a decision. "Why not," she says and by the time we leave the terrace I think we might be friends.

It's warmed up when we return, puffing a little, back at the hotel, and Reggie flops down happily on the terrace. "I'll wait with him," Patty says, cheeks flushed. "You should get up to Laura."

Guests have begun to find their seats; Jay is waiting down by the lake with the other groomsmen. We were a while on our walk, a rather inspired idea hitting me halfway round.

I find myself reaching down, searching for her cheek under the massive hat and kissing her, "Thanks for a lovely morning."

She nods again, lips pressed tightly together. "Get on, get on, I'm fine."

I turn to leave and just as I reach the glass doors back inside I hear, "Oh, and Amy," as she calls over her shoulder.

I look back at her.

"As you said—what happened in the woods, stays in the woods, yes?"

I laugh and nod and give her a wave goodbye, gratified to see a wide smile beneath the hat.

69

AMY

The band is in place, the guests assembled, and the air smells of freshly mown grass.

We stand behind the congregation waiting to emerge behind a wall of flowers, guests peering between foliage for their first glimpse of the wedding party. Reggie is resplendent in his little bow tie but keeps ruining things looking around for Flynn and growling up at me.

We hear a hush descend and the first bars of music fill the air. I step out with Reggie on a lead, but after every two steps he sits down in protest. Flynn and Laura, linking arms behind us, keep having to come to a grinding halt.

"This could take a while," I say as the band continues, heads craning to wonder at the delay.

The back row of seats are peering round, taking in Laura, ethereal in her ivory silk Chantilly lace fishtail wedding dress, with its sweetheart neckline and beaded lace bodice. The scalloped-edge tulle train flares out from behind her and I've warned Flynn not to tread on it.

"Oh no," Flynn says, clutching his leg under his bridesmaid dress. "Cramp," he says dramatically, looking around him with wide eyes.

I stuff a hand to my mouth and try to look alarmed. Reggie, sensing melodrama, starts barking. We cluster together as a foursome, loud enough for some of the guests to hear us as we deliver Flynn's script.

"Ow," Flynn adds, looking at me pointedly. He might as well have shouted "LINE."

"Do you want me to help you up the aisle, Laura?" I ask, my delivery a little wooden.

"That would be excellent, thank you for offering, Flynn," Laura says. The back of the congregation swap glances.

"Poor me," Flynn adds loudly, limping exaggeratedly forward in his chiffon dress. He takes Reggie's lead as I move between him and Laura to prop him up and link arms with her. Reggie immediately leaps up and skips off.

"Sorted," Laura whispers with a giggly hiccup. I can feel her joyful jittery nerves and am glad I'm here with her in this moment.

I stare at her as we stand together, Pachelbel's Canon in D swelling to fill the still air around us. Dad had a surprising love of classical music, our childhood spent begging him to change the radio from Classic FM. "Philistines," he'd shout and turn it up louder. This was one of his favorites; he could play it on the clunky upright piano in our front room and bring the whole thing to life.

Laura blinks at me and I know she is feeling the same. "Dad would be so bloody proud of you, Laura. You are thoughtful, kind, insanely efficient, and you've been an amazing sister to me. And you look incredible FYI."

"Shut up," she says, nudging me. "My mascara isn't waterproof."

"This is it," I whisper. "You sure? If not, I'll get Flynn to distract them with some kind of broken leg while we make for the hills? Everyone will believe it—you know I bring the drama."

Laura can't stop a laugh at my admission and then swats my arm. "I'm sure. Let's do this."

"Alright then. Love you."

"Love you too."

From the front of the aisle Jay peers round, no doubt wondering at the delay.

Flynn has straightened up, pain obviously completely forgotten now that our plan has been put into place. He starts the procession with Reggie, the congregation smiling as they pass.

Jay's face changes as he sees me, or rather Flynn, arm in arm with his beloved future wife. He watches as Laura leans into me, completely relaxed and happy.

Ah.

We move down the aisle, whispers on either side, admiring glances at Laura's dress, and Mum dabs at her eyes as she watches her daughter move past her. Jay, however, looks less than thrilled.

"What's up with Jay?" I whisper out of the side of my mouth. "Oh, shit," Laura whispers. "One of us should probably have said something to him."

I look at Jay's stony face, as he meets my eyes. "Yup. Yup, that's a thought."

Both of us can't stop shaking with giggles as we step forward once more.

70

FLYNN

"... and maybe once in a lifetime you find someone who not only touches your heart but also your soul, someone who loves you for who you are and not what you could be. Maybe the art of true love is not about finding the perfect person, but about seeing an imperfect person perfectly."

I say the words slowly and carefully, being sure to look at Laura and Jay as I do. I need Amy to feel I am doing her proud as I stand in front of everyone and complete the second reading. I resist the urge to add a "really lush" in there for kicks and can't help sneaking a glance at Amy, a blubbering mess next to her mum who is staring at her, all six foot two inches of her, as she offers up her last tissue.

I step past a watery-eyed Patty, Jay's dad in his wheel-chair, his second wife beside him, and join the front row next to Amy who offers me a watery smile. "Well read," she whispers.

Trish reaches over and pats me on the arm. Then she whispers under her breath as she stares at Amy dabbing her face, "Weddings are Flynn's kryptonite, I see."

Giving her a shrug, I simply smile and reach to take Amy's hand in mine.

In that moment it doesn't feel strange, it simply feels right.

71

AMY

As I listen to the words, the emotions choke me. I thought it would hurt more, but it's better this way. This means I get to listen to the words Jay and Laura selected, watch their expressions as Flynn reads them out, stand next to Mum as she passes me another tissue ("I like to see a man in touch with his feelings.")

The reading is perfect. Actually, it's about a million times posher than I'd make it sound. It seems to have taken about forty-eight hours for Flynn to almost completely lose my Bristolian twang. As he licks his lips and looks around, I realize how nervous he was to get it right and my heart expands for him.

The words resonate in me, shame me a little too. I'm all too often pointing out Flynn's flaws, holding up a mirror to the things that bug me most. I overlook all the many brilliant things about him: his ability to shoulder stress, to allow me to moan about my day and vent, without mentioning his own worries. His ability to look on the bright side, seek solutions, and not just mope.

When he joins me in the row, the reading folded carefully in his hand, he reaches for me and I take his hand, not finding it peculiar, simply glad to be holding onto him, so grateful to have him by my side, my body instinctively wanting to be close to him. I miss our touches, the frisson I get when our skin meets, how he makes me breathless with a kiss that flutters and teases, my stomach dipping with desire.

The service is perfect, the setting filling everyone with a blissful calm; even Reggie behaves in his squiffy bow tie, happily nestled at Flynn's feet.

Mum reads a piece from *Winnie the Pooh* which sets me off again. Geoffrey envelops her in a hug when she gets back to our row. As she shuts her eyes and lets him hold her, I am so glad she found him after Dad. I've taken him for granted up to now. He's been there for Mum, bending to what she wants, fitting in around her family. I'm glad she has him.

It's the signing of the register and I shift as the band looks in my direction. Frowning, I watch in amazement as Flynn nods beside me and stands up. I almost stop him, ask him where he's going. Then Laura brings her hands together and smiles happily as he sweeps past her, chiffon skirt blowing in the breeze.

What is he doing?

Flynn stands beneath the arch, glances at the band and then tilts his chin up in that determined way I recognize.

Is he seriously doing what I think he's about to do?

"Laurs," I hiss.

"Hush," she says, twisting round and holding a hand up. I realize this is what they had been whispering about; Laura is in on it.

The familiar notes start, the keyboard plays the opening bars. And I can't help my eyes widening as Flynn opens his mouth and begins to sing. The first line soars, the music floating across the lake, amazingly confident and in tune. I stuff a hand in my mouth as a delighted gasp escapes my lips.

"When the rain is blowing in your face..."

Oh my god.

Laura grins at me as she takes Jay's hand and moves across to the table to sign the registry, Patty clutching her hat in two hands as a gust of wind threatens to carry it over the lake.

I can't keep my eyes from Flynn, my hair braided, my make-up neat, my posture assured.

It's perfect. I think back to all those evenings in the flat, Flynn standing in the doorway of the kitchen, head resting against the frame. Every time I realized he was listening I'd stop, swatting away any compliments. It was Flynn being nice, he's my boyfriend. And he's tone deaf, he doesn't really know.

He's singing it now, steady, simple, and I am crying again, really crying, because I can hear that I do have a voice, I've just been too frightened to use it. Dad loved Adele, first took me to watch her when she played in Bristol's Colston Hall and told me I could do it too. This incredible artist, sat on a stool in a simple spotlight, sharing her pain and loss with the audience. She'd inspired the single I'd written and recorded. The songs I'd wanted to make into an album. I'd let my music die with Dad too. And he would never have wanted that.

"She's got such a beautiful voice," Mum whispers, wiping her own eyes underneath the lime-green glasses with her sleeve because I'd used the last of the tissues. "Her dad always said so."

As Flynn comes to the end of the song I glance around at the congregation, so many people dabbing at their faces, mascara long gone, heads tipped onto shoulders, mesmerized as they watch him, silhouetted by the silvery lake behind. Even when Reggie escapes his lead and starts howling along to the last verse people can't stop weeping. Although that causes Flynn to dissolve into a heap of laughter, bending down to nuzzle his fur.

"I thought Amy was scared of dogs?" Jay says to Laura.

"Amy's made some changes," Laura whispers back and I am almost able to laugh again.

I will make changes. I will. Flynn's given me back my voice.

72

FLYNN

Well, that was absolutely terrifying.

Why would anyone in their right mind want to put themselves through that? I can't believe Amy wants to do this. It's madness. I thought I might pass out. Everyone was watching me; it was like that dream when you're naked on a stage. I'm trembling as I rejoin her. Then I worry I've done the wrong thing, that I've messed up. I just wanted her to listen to herself, to hear what we all hear.

The relief as I realize she can't speak because she's about to cry is overwhelming.

"I never had Flynn pegged as a crier," Trish whispers as we side-step out of the aisle and across the lawn where people stand waiting with trays full of the most delectable canapés. "But you never really know a person, do you," she murmurs.

There is happy chatter and laughing as we are instructed to head inside for the wedding breakfast. The tables are laid out in the dining room, glasses twinkling, the room filled with sunshine that pours through the enormous glass windows. Everything looks perfect, pink and cream flowers in the center of each table, crisp linen napkins and polished silver, pots of sugared almonds and Polaroid photos in clip frames of Jay and Laura in various places.

The smells coming from the kitchen are otherworldly. The starter is already laid out, delicate morsels of salmon, miniature croutons, green flecks of something herby. It has a jus in a tiny jug because of course it has a jus. Patty told me one of the chefs was on *MasterChef*.

Just when I think I might be able to finally relax, I notice the place name two seats from mine, the man between us—one Martin—not yet in his chair.

"Oh, hey, that song was amazing," Tanya says as she takes her seat, and her slightly too-bright smile is so familiar I want to laugh. "And your dress is lovely," she adds, pointing at me.

I plump for a polite, "Thanks" and pull out her chair for her.

Puzzled, she sinks into it as I push her in.

"You're really talented. Did you get lessons?"

"Self-taught," I say, putting my napkin over my legs with a theatrical flourish.

"Well, you're really good."

"Yeah, I know."

Fortunately, Martin appears between us, mustard

on the side of his mouth, as he introduces himself as Kia's partner.

He embarks on a monologue about his job running a printing firm which I have to say is so boring he wants to make me grab my own fork and plunge it into my eye for something to do. Did I know that they can do letterpress, hot foil, calligraphy, even wax seals on the same site? Jay and Laura's invites were handcrafted with a traditional hot foil press; the rose-gold was debated over a while, with "one party" (a million pounds on Patty) not sure "it lent the right note."

He is yet to ask me a question, laughing rather like a seal when I tell him I run an events company, as if that idea is amusing. I frown, not sure what is so funny about my reasonably stressful job juggling two full-time employees, a load of freelancers and over sixty events a year. No one has ever laughed at it before. I recall Amy once telling me how some men dismiss anything serious she says as if she's being cute. I feel this now.

The waiter appears and pours wine, allowing me time to check for Amy at the other end of the long top table. She's removed her jacket and rolled her sleeves up, laughing with the woman next to her, face relaxed as she listens. It makes me smile.

"Nice salmon," I say loudly, desperate for a change of subject.

Martin looks up mid-bite, a little fleck of fish on his lips.

"Fishy," I add.

Then Martin turns to talk to Tanya and I sit drinking too much wine staring around the room and reaching for a sugared almond. From the other end of the table I can hear my low laugh as Amy is apparently in full throttle. This time I scowl in her direction. I'm not used to being ignored or deemed irrelevant.

Martin leaves the table after the main course and I notice Tanya slumped in her chair, the saddest expression on her face as she stares at something on her phone. She's either been bored to tears by talk of a soft silk finish invitation versus a pearlescent shimmer, or she really is sad.

Before I remember that I do not like her because she lied to me about sleeping with another man behind my back and tried to pass his child off as mine, I have scooted across to sit next to her.

She quickly turns the phone face down and I gesture to it. "Are you OK?"

This close up I can see her lower lip is wobbling, a sure sign she is about to start crying, and I look around for Eddie or someone to help, but everyone's heads are bent in conversation. Eddie is dropping wax onto another man's hand from a candle as another guy pisses himself next to him. I vow to stand up to Eddie in the future, no more pretending it's banter or harmless. I see him for who he is: a bully.

"Tanya?"

"I'm sorry," Tanya says, voice choked. "I'm suddenly a bit lost," she admits. "Martin was telling me about his niece. Apparently she was a flower girl at a wedding last weekend and refused to wear the bridesmaid dress so she took it off and walked up the aisle in her knickers."

344

I snort, wondering why that might make Tanya sad.

"It made me miss Charlie. This was a kid-free wedding. And also Eddie and I are pretty new and, well, I'm not sure . . . I haven't actually introduced them yet . . ."

"Oh," I say, taken back by this admission.

Tanya speaks softly, "I don't want to mess with her, you know, not until I'm sure about someone."

A familiar anger flares as I hear the words. Mess with her? That seems pretty rich from someone who could not have messed me around more. "Right," I say, reaching for my wine glass, pity fading fast. I'm even starting to miss Martin telling me about how if you select foil printing you need to factor in an extra week for delivery.

"Amy," Tanya says, looking at me, turning in her chair.

It still takes me a few seconds to register she's referring to me.

"I'm sorry about this weekend, if it's been awkward. I was quite nervous about coming, wasn't sure how Flynn would react."

"Oh," I say, one finger circling the top of my wine glass, emitting a high whine. I take a mouthful, "No problem."

"I do feel terrible about what I did, you know. I don't know whether he'll ever forgive me for it, I'm not sure I could if I were him . . ."

This time I can't speak, my ears ringing as I think back to all the times I'd cursed what she'd done. The shame I'd felt at pining for a child who had no connection with me at all. How I'd wanted to pick up the phone so many times, beg Tanya to see her so I could hold Charlie again, and then hating myself for thinking like that.

I shift in my chair, swallowing as I meet her eye.

"He can," I say.

She nods sadly. "The thing is, he was such a decent guy, the best boyfriend. My mum was appalled, barely spoke to me for months when I told her what I'd done. He would have been the most amazing father, and maybe it was that that kept stopping me. I was so scared of losing him that I just sort of hoped that maybe I'd never have to face up to it." She hangs her head. "Even in the hospital I almost didn't tell him. I just saw him looking so besotted, and I just couldn't rob her of a man like that in her life. It didn't help that Charlie's dad was the opposite. He only stuck around a couple of months and then left us. Flynn wouldn't have left us." A tear rolls down her cheek and plops onto the white tablecloth. "That makes me the most selfish human ever, doesn't it?"

I can't bear seeing her like this, hearing the pity. "Hey," I say, placing my hand over Tanya's, "you're not selfish, OK, you just . . ." I search about for the right thing to say, understanding dawning, "You just thought you were doing the best for your daughter."

The grateful look she gives me as I say the words does something to me. Inside I'm clear-headed, years of bitterness toward her finally dissolving, that last thorn removed.

"Hey, can I see her?" I ask, glancing at the phone face down on the table.

She bites her lip. "Do you really want to?"

"I really do."

She can't help the eager way she snatches up her phone, clearly longing to show her off. My chest twists a little at that and my skin prickles in nervous anticipation as I watch her unlock her phone, move to the Photos app, and click. I could still change my mind, I could still move back to my own seat, wait for Martin to come and tell me more about how calligraphy is a dying art form, but I feel pinned to my chair as she presses on a tiny thumbnail, a flash of purple and green.

Then there she is: Charlie.

She's grinning at the camera, holding up an enormous green leaf, practically as big as her head. I can't help the loud laugh that escapes me, cut short as my breath leaves me. She is adorable: mud on one cheek, hair in uneven bunches, completely delighted with her find.

"She's really cute," I say, my voice distorted.

Tanya is so busy looking at the screen she doesn't seem to notice the fact my eyes have filled. I've spent years wondering what she might look like. A child in the street with a certain shade of blonde hair, another with dimples in her cheeks: I could never help wondering how they'd compare to her. Here she is: beautiful, happy, perfect.

"She looks really happy."

"She is," Tanya says, her own face mirroring Charlie's, eyes sparkling with love, "she's joyful—she's reminded me what's really important. I'm better because of her," she admits.

"No wonder you miss her," I say and as Martin barrels back between us, barking that someone's sitting in his chair, and the waiters start bringing round the dessert, I slide back across to my own.

Amy glances up from her own chair and gives me a wink.

I swallow and return it, grateful that I've seen Charlie and I can truly close that chapter on my life now with no feelings of anger or remorse.

"Now have I told you about digital printing? It doesn't always have the same finish as the handcrafted invitations, but it can work out a lot cheaper . . ."

73

AMY

The speeches go smoothly, the meal is delicious, and I'm sitting next to two great women, one a graphic designer missing her kitten, one a screenwriter who just got her first show green-lit. They were both so fun and kept exclaiming at how brilliant at listening I was and how no man normally ever asks them questions. Their enthusiasm made me marvel at how low the bar is for a good man. We just want one to show an interest, to listen, react, take us seriously.

Then the wedding party traipses through the grounds, past sparking braziers on the lawn, the smell of woodsmoke in the air, and toward the bandstand, lit up with fairy lights and lanterns for the dancing.

Laura looks stunning as she and Jay stand in the middle of the floor waiting to start their first dance together, hair swept up into a chignon, her back smooth above the low V-neck of her dress. I watch as she laughs up into his face. Jay can be serious, sometimes missing a joke by seconds, but they've always fit together. She brings out his more playful side, but he can also be the good sense she needs, someone steady who listens and supports her. They move cautiously over the floor, Jay wooden, dancing lessons in evidence, as he attempts to show his new bride off to the world.

He looks relaxed and relieved as they meet for a kiss at the end, the audience in a ring around them, cheering the touching moment. Then suddenly the music shifts and his face contorts with alarm as Laura drags him to a chair that Kia has placed just behind him. The opening bars of "Don't Stop Believin'" ring out, so familiar after months of watching and practicing it from a private link on YouTube. Delighted, he watches wide-eyed as Laura and her bridesmaids, Flynn included, begin their routine.

It is brilliant, chaotic, vaguely in time, over-the-top, and has the room screeching and clapping, hollering names and watching as more people from the crowd pop up at different times to join in. Mum is one of the last in, joining the chorus with a confident shake of her hips. Skin glowing rainbow colors in the disco lights, she looks utterly electric, grinning and sending thumbs-up to a proud-looking Geoffrey puffed up on the side. I can't help it: feet tapping, I catch Laura's eye and join in with a loud whoop just as Patty, uncertain but earnest, descends onto the space.

Stopping to stare, I can't believe how perfectly in time she is, hips waggling, getting the lasso action absolutely spot on. Laura and Jay's jaws drop to see her spinning past them, her timing exceptional, her enthusiasm knowing no bounds. Time to flash the briefest thumbs-up at her son and his new bride. When it finishes and everyone is shouting congratulations and gripping their sides with laughter and stitches, she looks round, momentarily lost. Then Jay leaps up from his chair and folds her into the most enormous hug.

"That was amazing. How did she know?" Laura yells at me, her face glowing, hair and dress still immaculate as she bowls her way over.

"I have no idea," I gasp. Then I see Flynn grabbing Patty's hand, his chiffon skirt bunched in his hands as he jives with her, and realize with a jolt it must have been his doing. Heart swelling, I wave as he passes and gives me a round thumb and finger before hitching up his blush-pink bridesmaid dress once more and heading back into the fray.

"He's pretty brilliant, you know, Amy." Laura voices what I'm thinking. "If he does ask again, you totally have my blessing."

I nudge her in the ribs. "Stop trying to marry me off because you are."

"Breather?" she suggests, and I nod.

She disappears down the steps of the pavilion and I go to follow her. Just then someone pulls on my arm.

"Hey," Jay says.

"Oh hey!" I try to disguise my surprise with an added, "Hey, mate!"

Jay runs a hand over his shaved head. "Flynn, I'm

351

sorry about this morning. I've been on edge with this wedding stuff, I know you'd never do anything like that. You've always been a straight shooter since school."

"Oh, well, thanks."

"And Mum told me Amy taught her the dance. That was so nice of her."

"I'll tell her," I say, touched by the comment.

"Yeah, probably better coming from you. Amy's never liked me much."

My face falls. "Oh, oh well, I suppose she might give that impression," I admit. I straighten. "It's just she's always been a bit intimidated by you, well, the idea of you and your family." I watch surprise cross Jay's face.

"She's intimidated by me! Oh my god, I'm terrified of her!"

"What?"

"Are you kidding? Laura adores her, she is so forthright and to the point and well, she's great. I want to know her better."

My heart swells. I had no idea. "Thank you. Thank you, Jay," and I can't stop myself reaching forward and hugging him. "You will."

Jay freezes in my arms, before placing a hand on my back. "This is new," he mumbles.

"Men should hug more!" I say.

"I guess so." He smiles as he gets pulled back onto the dance floor.

I turn and leave, feeling a weight shift.

Laura is still waiting for me at the bottom of the steps. The breeze is a relief as I pull off my jacket and fling it over the newel post on the stairs. The day is darkening, the sky ribboned with oranges and pinks as the sun sets over the hills beyond, turning them a ghostly blue. The hotel is up-lit, its façade majestic from this angle.

"Wow, Laura, this is something else," I say.

"It's not the Goat and Boots function room, our original choice, is it?"

"Less spit and sawdust on the floor, but poorer for it, of course," I add, making her laugh.

She's quieter then, both of us looking across the lake as the sun makes its last gasp.

"If we'd done it with our own money, we would have crisps in a pub, and I know Dad and Mum did that and good for them but . . . I don't mind being treated like this. Patty has money and wanted to spend it on her son . . . and I'm grateful to her."

I take her hand. "I know, and you don't need to justify yourself to me. I know I've been chippy about money and privilege, but I need to let that stuff go. You have."

Shame fills me as I realize I'd always assumed Laura was too successful, too glossy to feel pain like me. That she had moved on.

"You're a lovely human being, Laura Smithington-Waller."

Laura looks aghast as I use her new full name. "OK—Dad might have pissed himself at that."

At that moment the four flamingos waddle past and this seems to make it even funnier.

We both start giggling and my heart swells, feeling closer to her than I have done since Dad died, grateful for this whole weekend and everything it has high-lighted for me.

We fall into a peaceful silence. I know this is the moment I have to tell her the secret I have kept for the last five years. She has the right to know.

"Laurs. That night. The night that he died. I . . . we fought . . . before he went on and . . ."

She looks aghast and for a panicked second I regret ever opening my mouth. This obsession with sharing truths and I choose now?

"Mum told me he was on stage, Amy. He died in his favorite place."

"But he wouldn't have died if I had sung with him, if I hadn't shouted at him seconds before he went on . . ."

Laura pulls me round to face her, her face etched with concern, "Amy," she says firmly, "Dad would have died that night whatever happened. Have you really thought that all this time? That's horrific."

I swallow, throat closing with grief. "I really thought I'd caused it."

"Amy," Laura says, "seriously. You need to stop imagining everything pins on what you do. That's too much."

I nod dumbly.

"He loved you. He loved both of us."

"He did."

"I miss him," she says, and I feel a lump in my throat as she says the words I'm thinking too, the gap in the day, the gap in our lives that will always be there.

I reach and take her hand, giving it a squeeze.

She looks around at the pavilion, the lake, back to the

hotel, a strange expression clouding her face. "I worried, you know, that this place . . . that he'd hate it. Think it was over-indulgent: a place for the rich."

"He'd be wrong," I say, always struggling to not view my dad as anything other than perfect. Dad had loved us, but he had wanted us to stay with him, even if that meant having a smaller life. When he teased Laura about getting into her London university there had been an edge: that she dared to leave, to do more.

"All I know about Dad for sure is he loved us both whole-heartedly," I say firmly. "And it's got actual flamingos!"

"It's so extra, isn't it? I thought Patty was nuts, but you know what? Who doesn't love a flamingo?"

I rest my head on her shoulder for a moment. "They mate for life, you know? It feels apt."

Laura gives a small smile. "You don't think he'd take the piss? Think this was all just a bit much?"

I don't wave the question away. "I think he would say you deserved this, all of it, the very best. If he teased, it was his misguided way of telling you he'd miss you, but also admitting that maybe he too had wanted to fly . . ." I think back to him appearing in that pub, the flash of pain on his face as he realized I wasn't joining him on stage.

"Thanks, Amy," Laura whispers, leaning her head onto my shoulder as I wrap an arm around her.

At that moment Flynn appears, practically falling down the stairs in his kitten heels, his braid half-falling out, hair grips flying, sweat beading at his hairline. Laura and I break apart.

"Could you at least try to make me look vaguely ladylike, please," I say, unable to really sound cross as he joins us. I grab his hand, righting him. "And that was kind of you, to think of that," I say, gesturing to Patty, seen sweeping past with Geoffrey who gives a terrified glance down at us.

"Oh, it was fun," he says with a shy smile. "I struggled to explain body popping to her, but she'd clearly put some practice in."

"Clearly," Laura says, and grabs his other hand so we're all standing in a small circle. "Thank you. I think she's really worried about losing him. The wedding has meant we've seen and heard SO much of her, but I should have realized she's scared of the silence afterward. I should have thought of including her—it was a very good thing."

It's Flynn's turn to look embarrassed, his cheeks getting pink as he stands there staring at us both.

"Am I breaking up a happy scene?" Mum asks, sipping a glass of water and moving down toward us, one hand on Flynn's shoulder.

"Never," Laura says, letting go of Flynn's hand and leaning in to give her a hug.

"My gorgeous girl," Mum says. "My gorgeous girls," she corrects, pulling Flynn toward her too. He yelps and then relaxes into it with a grin. "I'm so pleased and relieved you're both looking so happy, together too."

I have the strange sensation of watching the trio that is me, Laura, and Mum—our closeness, the pride and adoration she has in her eyes as she gazes at us. Mum, the central cog in our trio, who held us all together after Dad was gone, insisting we still live our lives. She'd done everything for us, uncomplaining even when Laura and I were at our most testing.

"Are you alright, Mu— Trish? Need a breather? A rest?"

Laura gives me a puzzled look.

And I know I can't put this off anymore, I know Laura wouldn't want to either. I need to know if we now need to be there for her. "And is everything OK? Anything you want to tell us, I mean, the girls?"

Flynn's hand slips into mine and I am grateful that he's with me.

"Mum?" Laura says. "What's going on? Are you OK?"

Trish wrings her hands and stares at Flynn, who gives an encouraging nod.

"You were telling me earlier," he whispers. "About a lump."

Mine and Laura's heads snap up.

Flynn swallows as he continues, "Have they found cancer?"

"Cancer." Laura's face drains at the word.

Cancer. My insides lurch.

Mum looks at me, Laura, and Flynn, an appalled expression on her face, "Oh no, no." Her voice is so loud it makes the couple nearby glance over. "No . . . I'm healthy. I'm well. Oh, my loves, no."

My rapid heart slows as I hear those words. She's healthy, she's all right. I can't stop the wide smile splitting my face, the small laugh that hiccups out of me. "Oh, thank god . . ."

My relief is short-lived, however, as I remember what got us to this point, a secret she was carrying around. I'd heard her talking to Geoffrey.

"So . . . what's going on?" Flynn says, clearly surprised. "Why would Am— why did you say earlier that I would miss you?"

Mum pleats her skirt, her eyes looking anywhere but at us. "The thing is, darlings, that I did have a health scare last year, and those tests changed things for me. They were an urgent wake-up call, forcing me to look at my life and really take stock." She looks up, her eyes trained on Laura. "Since your father died, I hadn't dared leave the house, forcing Geoffrey to move in when I knew he wanted us to start again somewhere fresh. But I wasn't ready and he respected that. And I wanted to be there for you both, be two parents for you." She reaches across and touches Flynn's cheek.

"You've been the best mum," I say, then, remembering what I look like, "to them, that is . . . the girls . . . I know Amy thinks it all the time."

"Thank you, love."

"So . . ." Laura says, knowing there's more.

Mum tilts her chin upward, the lights from the band-stand illuminating her face and reflecting on her lime-green glasses, as vibrant as her personality. "Those tests made me want more from my life. I want to feel that I've had a great adventure, I want to explore and see different places and experience new opportunities." She looks around at this grand setting, her voice growing in confidence. "Geoffrey and I leave for Canada in just over a month—we've seen a house in a wonderful community in the mountains. It's stunning. I know you're both going to love it. And if we love it, I want to sell the house, we want to move there, to live . . ."

My eyebrows shoot upward.

"Canada!"

She nods. "Geoffrey has always wanted to go, and he's traveled all over—every school holiday he was always off to a new country for weeks on end!"

A Canadian adventure. I'd always thought of Geoffrey as someone who might not own a passport. He didn't seem the intrepid sort. How wrong I'd got him, too. Shame creeps over me; had I ever really asked him? He often stepped into the background at home, but I realize now that maybe that was to give Mum time with her girls, a generous act, not a sign he had nothing to say.

Mum's waiting for our responses, the silence stretching on.

Before this weekend, maybe I would have instantly seen the negatives: Canada is a long way away, I wouldn't see her all the time, FaceTime isn't the same. Inhabiting Flynn's body, thinking how he might react to news like this, allows me a momentary pause. My mum looks absurdly excited. She is clearly nervous about telling us, but I can see that frisson in the way she is standing. Maybe she'd felt life was small too, maybe she wanted to stretch her own wings.

"Don't hate me, darlings."

"I don't hate you," Flynn says, watching my face,

trying to gauge my reaction. I meet his eyes with the slightest nod and smile.

"That's amazing," I add.

I had convinced myself Mum was a homebody, that Geoffrey wasn't adventurous, assuming things I didn't know at all. I'd got people wrong, and this weekend had shown me I need to probe more, ask, really listen. I am always so quick to come to my own conclusions.

"I'm so relieved it's that," Laura exhales, grabbing Mum in a hug. "I mean, it's nuts, obviously, and we can talk about the bear risks in Canada, but oh my god, Mum, you scared us."

Mum looks stunned and then her shoulders drop about an inch and she smiles, putting her head in her hands, "Oh my goodness, I have been fretting about how you'd both react. I didn't want you to think I was abandoning you, but with Laura marrying Jay and you and Flynn so happy, darling, I'd started to feel perhaps I could do this, that perhaps I don't need to worry so much about you both."

"You don't have to worry about us!" Laura bursts out.

"You don't," I whisper, feeling my chest tighten.

"You don't," Flynn adds, wanting to join in.

Reggie sits up and howls and I can't help reaching to stroke his fur, feeling comfort as he nuzzles into me.

74

FLYNN

The dancing has ended, Patty the last to be dragged
away, giggling with Laura as she attempts the Macarena.
That woman has energy. The hotel staff have laid out
striped wooden deckchairs on the lawn, blankets folded
on top of them, and the braziers are still crackling as
Amy and I collapse into two of them, tucking ourselves
in like an old couple on a rainy Brighton beach.

Amy leans back with a contented sigh and shuts her
eyes, her shirt rumpled, my suit jacket lost in the melee.
"What a bloody brilliant wedding," she grins to nobody.

My calf muscles ache, or rather Amy's legs ache from
dancing and my head is a woozy mix of booze and
contentment. Across the lake on the island the first of
the fireworks are let off with a whine and the wedding
party all turn as one, heads craned back to stare into
the sky at the riot of pops and flashes and color.

Silvers, pinks, reds, greens burst above us, making us jump, the air smelling of spent smoke. Amy reaches across and puts a hand on my knee, both of us snuggled underneath the blankets and staring up at the spectacle. Laura and Jay stand on the very edge of the lake, pressed together, ready to start their lives together.

The final burst of fireworks is beyond anything I've ever seen in my life. The sounds and sights are so extraordinary that both Amy and I have struggled back up on our feet, unable to stop gasping and clapping every time more appear.

"This is incredible," I shout.

Amy turns to me and I suddenly get an overwhelming urge to kiss her.

I think of previous kisses, the feeling I get when our lips meet, my stomach plunging, my skin tingling with anticipation. I've never fancied anyone more, never loved anyone more.

"Can I kiss you?" I ask, feeling strangely shy all of a sudden.

Amy grins, bow tie loose, top button undone. "That's exactly what I was thinking," she says.

She takes another step closer, moving both her arms onto my shoulders. "Shall we?"

"Let's do it," I say.

Swallowing my nerves, staring up at Amy, I exhale slowly. And as I reach up on my toes to find her mouth, trying not to think too hard about what I'm going to feel next, our lips touch. Then there's a horrified, confused shout in our direction, a strange and terrible whining noise: so very close.

"Look out!"

"Shit!"

A scream.

And suddenly the space between us is bright white and burning hot. Squeezing my eyes closed, I pull Amy into me, trying to shield her from whatever is happening. She gasps, I can feel the breath on the top of my hair. Then another flash and I keep on gripping her.

There's a strange silence as we pull apart seconds later. My brain is in overdrive, adrenaline coursing through me.

"Are you OK, are you OK?" I repeat, panic gripping me. And then I stop.

Because this is my voice, and I'm looking down at Amy. Amy in a pink bridesmaid dress, her hair half up, half down, her expression as bewildered as mine.

"Flynn," she says, staring up at me, her hand reaching to touch my face. Reaching up. Because I'm taller than her.

"Flynn," she repeats and then her face breaks into the most enormous smile. "FLYNN!" she shouts and with zero warning leaps from the spot, wraps her legs around me and sends both of us crashing to the floor.

"Holy shit!" she says. "Holy shit!" We're in a bundle on the grass, people peering round as she kneels up, her legs still round me. "Holy shit!" She frantically pats herself with both hands: her body, her hair, her face, breaking into delighted wonderment.

I'm shaking with laughter on the ground beneath her, feeling the grass tickle my face as I relish the fact that I'm back in my body, although my left eye fucking stings.

We struggle to our feet, both unable to stop reaching for the other, in amazed silence just taking in the fact we are back in our own skin.

"I can't believe it," she whispers. And her voice cracks a little. "I had really started to . . ."

"Shh!" I say, not wanting her to say it.

And instead of fighting me, wanting to see the worst, she simply pulls my finger away and nods.

"Thank god," she says, throwing herself into my arms. "Thank god, thank god." She draws back and gazes up at me. "It is *so good* to see you."

Electricity sparks in my stomach.

I clear my throat, my expression serious for a moment.

"Now we're back," I say, and I take both of her hands in mine, enjoying their soft feel. The electricity leaps and flashes inside me.

"Oh my god, Flynn. You're not going to propose, are you?" she says, worry clouding her expression.

"Amy Norman," I begin firmly, knowing exactly what I need to say, and what she needs to hear.

She looks up at me, her brown eyes round. I can't believe it's her. I can't believe we're back.

"Amy Norman, I love you. Will you please do the honor of *not* marrying me. Will you promise to love me, get to know me better, and then maybe reconsider in a couple of years' time, or when we *both* feel ready?"

She can't help the quick snort of laughter, one of her hands flying up to her face trying to stifle it.

Then her face breaks into a wide smile and she throws her arms over my shoulders. Leaning in, her face inches from mine, she whispers, "I do. Absolutely. I do."

Acknowledgments

A lot has happened since I wrote the first draft of *If I Were You* and I have some people to thank. I also didn't keep a running list so inevitably I will leave someone out. Please, if this is you, don't hate me and know that it is very much not you, it's me.

First to the teams at William Morrow and Harper-Fiction—thank you. To editors Tessa, Martha, and Belinda—we got there in the end! Thank you for helping me shape an actual body swap in book form. In the UK thank you to Meg, Emilie in publicity, Vicky in marketing, Lynne for her cheerleading, and Ellie for the fantastic flamingo cover. In the US thank you to Kerry for the best body swap image I could think up! It's so wonderful to love both book covers equally. And to have an excuse to buy so much flamingo merch.

This book is in development as a feature film with the excellent production company 42 and I want to thank

Acknowledgments

Erica, Kari, Ben Pugh, and Ben Cavey. I feel very lucky to be working with such a brilliant company.

Thanks to Luke for first introducing the book to Erica, and to Camilla in the film dept. at Curtis Brown. Thanks also to both Alice at Curtis Brown and Kristyn at CAA for their excellent insights, honesty, and support. I feel lucky to have such strong women on my side. Thanks also to their assistants Olivia and Lauren. The foreign rights department at Curtis Brown have also been excellent champions and I'm so grateful to Emma and Sam for being the best team talking up *If I Were You*.

A particularly big thanks to Katy, Joanna, Hilary, and Holly for being so generous with their time reading earlier drafts and making absurdly helpful suggestions for edits. And so sorry to Katy for missing her in my last Acks! Thanks also to Flynn Durrant for letting me steal his (very excellent) first name.

It's been a tough time for creatives so I have never felt more amazed at the kindness and cheerleading of my fellow writers. I have met so many really amazing, generous, wonderful people over the last few years. The fun and excitement that surrounded *Maybe Next Time* both being selected as a Reese Book Club pick, and being optioned for film with Hello Sunshine and Apple Original Films (thanks Michelle Weiner at CAA!) was made all the nicer by the many generous comments I was sent by friends, and writers I've never met IRL. A particular squish to Kirsty and Izzy for always being at the end of a (sometimes hysterical, sometimes panicked) phone.

Acknowledgments

Thank you so much to Reese Witherspoon and her fabulous Hello Sunshine team—Lauren, Gretchen, Olga, Jane, Corinna, Melissa, and everyone else who works tirelessly to lift up stories about women by women. I'm so proud to be working with you all, and to be selected as a Reese Book Club pick.

Love as ever to my parents—David and Basia—to my sister Naomi aka My Number One Fan and early reader.

The best and biggest thank you to Ben, Barnaby, Lexi, and Inessa for being brilliant. It's been such a busy few years but I'm so lucky to have you all. I love you so much.

And my last thank you is a huge one—and that is to you for reading this book. There are so many books out there and I want to thank you for choosing to pick this one up and take a chance. And if you now want to go and tell twenty friends to buy it, or you want to leave positive reviews all over the internet—I certainly won't stand in your way!

Thank you, thank you though. There is literally nothing nicer in the world than receiving messages or photos or comments from strangers who have read and loved your book. You make it the best job in the world.

About the Author

Cesca Major is a novelist and a screenwriter. She has shows in development with companies including the BBC, 42, and Monumental Pictures. The film adaptation of her debut novel, *Maybe Next Time*, has been bought by Hello Sunshine and Apple Films.

Cesca has written other books under pseudonyms in a range of genres. She has been nominated for the RNA Romantic Comedy Award and the CWA Gold Dagger Award. She loves talking writing tips on her social channels.

She lives in Berkshire with her husband, son, and twin girls.

𝕏 @CescaMajor
▣ @cescamajorauthor
f /Cesca Major—Author
www.cescamajor.com